I0824628

HOUSE OF MARGINS

Also by Tlotlo Tsamaase

Womb City
The Silence of the Wilting Skin

HOUSE OF MARGINS

TLOTLO TSAMAASE

an imprint of Kensington Publishing Corp.
erewhonbooks.com

EREWHON BOOKS are published by:

Kensington Publishing Corp.
900 Third Avenue
New York, NY 10022

erewhonbooks.com

ISBN 978-1-64566-104-7 (hardcover)

First Erewhon hardcover printing: June 2026

10 9 8 7 6 5 4 3 2 1

Printed in the United States of America

Library of Congress Control Number: 2026931877

Electronic edition: ISBN 978-1-64566-105-4 (ebook)

Edited by Sarah T. Guan and Viengsamai Fetters
Interior design by Leah Marsh
Interior images courtesy of Jacob Lund/Adobe Stock (Langa); Michael Kyule/Unsplash, Jay Soundo/Unsplash, leaf/iStock (Anaya, composite); Christian Agbede/Unsplash, Kamil Kalbarczyk/Unsplash (Ogone, composite). Icons by Google, licensed under the Apache License, Version 2.0. Architectural drawing by Tlotlo Tsamaase.
Quote from *Go Tell the Sun* by Wame Molefhe courtesy of Modjaji Books.

The authorized representative in the EU for product safety and compliance
is eucomply OU, Parnu mnt 139b-14, Apt 123
Tallinn, Berlin 11317, hello@eucompliancepartner.com

HOUSE OF MARGINS

RANEWA

My sister, Anaya Sebeya, disappeared eighteen months ago.

I thought by the time my birthday came around again, she'd be here. But I am twenty-five now, and she's still gone. If Anaya was here, she'd be bickering with the DJ for his selection of music, or we'd be on the dance floor singing our lungs out to a Sho Madjozi tune. There was no party today.

I'd spent the morning watching old videos of Anaya pranking our parents in the garden, and Mama throwing a shoe at her for her foolish behavior and the other at me for taking the video, and all of us breaking down into laughter. But I needed more than a video. I missed Anaya's voice and her scent. I entered my sister's bedroom to cull the anger and the grief.

We still kept Anaya's bedroom windows open, as if she'd come floating in during the night, rippled like her windblown beige curtains waving through the moon-stained night, the air thick with heat.

Something new on her bed caught my eye: a black smartphone nestled in a woman's scarf. The headphones snaked out of the cloth when I picked it up. I thought it might belong to our cousin, who'd come over during the blessing of the house meant to clean the spirit from my sister's bedroom. I reached for the phone, turning it over, and gasped. It had

a faded sticker of a typewriter blooming flowers and words plastered to the back.

The investigators had never found Anaya's phone. How did it get here? My heart drummed faster. The phone lit up, warm in my hands.

The lock screen was of a poem:

Huis.
Our little Dutch House.
Such Dutch style.
Such thatch hair.
She's a glutton for pretty girls
with sad hearts.

Huis? I wondered. The only thing coming to mind was Günter Huis, the last place my sister lived. I pressed the phone. It had just one app: a white question mark imprisoned in a black circle. When I opened it, the app displayed a single audio file. My finger skimmed the play button; as I listened, my heart drove hard into my chest, caged.

It was my sister, the bare hints of Setswana notes intermixed with her soft voice. The voice of a ghost, some would say. I pressed pause, my knees weak as I sat at the edge of my sister's bed.

A pop-up message appeared: *Listen to me, please.*

"Anaya, is this you?" My voice trembled in a whisper to the phone.

How was this message being sent? I didn't see any way to access texting, Wi-Fi, or Bluetooth. No signal, no network connection. So how could it be transmitting

communication—from where? Or had my grief suddenly relegated me to hallucinating the impossible?

You're not hallucinating, the pop-up message said.

My heartbeat drummed faster. Relax. There was no one in my mind. I was not going crazy. But why were these messages responding to my thoughts? I hugged myself to feel myself contained in this reality, that I was real.

If you want to know the truth of what happened to your sister, press play, the pop-up message said. *The real truth.*

I moved closer to the windows, for cold, for wind, for breath. I saw the sun, the clouds, the neighborhood houses. Yes, I was still here. On earth.

For a moment, someone was breathing heavily against my nape where my braids hung loose. A moist and stale breath. I turned. No one stood behind me. I was alone. The dense air slunk into my lungs.

The smartphone display flickered. When I looked down, the play button had turned into a  symbol. I pressed it, and when I removed my thumb, it was bloody, pricked by the surface of the device's screen. Fear gripped my heart as if I'd just signed myself away through a blood subscription.

The track lingered in my ears. The sound invaded my mind, and I became paralyzed by the voice I hadn't heard since Anaya, oh, Anaya, disappeared.

▶

Tap, tap.

Welcome, Crimies.

I'm your host, Michele Visser, award-winning author, interdisciplinary artist, and Günter fellow. And you're listening to *What Happened to Ana?* Episode 1 is sponsored by Writer's Studio, a book packaging company bringing you middle-grade, teen, and adult literature.

Today, I bring you to the beginning of Anaya Sebeya's unsolved missing person case. We listen in as Anaya, then 25 years old, travels to the coastal city of Cape Town, where she stays in the award-winning architectural residence Günter Huis. It is in this beautiful home that I lived with Anaya and had a front-row seat to her life as well as the other suspects of the case. This story is close to my heart as an avid true-crime podcast listener with a long list of favorite shows.

Listener discretion is advised. Please note that this show contains violence, suicidal ideation, religious discrimination, racism, and other content that may be uncomfortable (subscribe to receive your ally starter pack).

If you have any information surrounding this case, please visit our website:

TIP JAR

Will you be my alibi? Join our membership tiers, a small contribution of support that grants you early access to podcast episodes.

I AM YOUR ALIBI

Will you be my partner-in-crime? Join our premium private membership tiers and be part of a community investigating and sharing tips and intel regarding Anaya Sebeya's case.

I AM YOUR CRIMINAL

WHAT

HAPPENED

TO

ANA?

WHAT HAPPENED TO ANA?

135:07:16:36

BEFORE I DIE

Episode 1

Call Me Huis • Anaya

Hello, Crimies, welcome to the first episode of What Happened to Ana? *I'm Michele Visser. Let's get into it.*

This season's case is one close to my heart. The victim, Anaya Sebeya, was a dear friend and a literary fellow, who I spent a lot of time with during the last summer season; living with her at the Günter Prize's writers' residency, I had a front row seat of her life leading up to the day she disappeared.

Ana was a talented, voracious writer, and we had our own private writing sessions together in my bedroom, talking about our writing and struggles. She would often seek advice from me. For the first time in a while, it felt like all her dreams were coming true: She was a runner-up for a huge literary prize, which would not only resolve her financial woes, but would clear the issues she had with her parents. Four months later, Anaya mysteriously disappeared. Join me as we follow the victims and suspects.

To tell her story, I spent painstaking eighty-hour workweeks compiling this podcast from both Anaya's and my recordings, diary entries, and writings (click the links in the show notes to

see screenshots). I've known her personally and studied her literary and personal voice. I hold myself accountable as more of an expert of Anaya's story than any other true crime podcasts' failed attempt at depicting an authentic representation.

I'm Michele Visser, and this is Anaya Sebeya's story . . .

[upbeat music]

The August night is a deep grave. I've arrived at Fisq, an exclusive restaurant in Cape Town, for the welcome dinner with the founders of the Günter Prize. The Günter handpicks five to six African women writers every year for their residency, and they've chosen me out of the whole continent—little me!

The maître d' stands poised at an extravagant granite trapezoid of a reception desk. "Welcome! You're Ana?" she asks me, cross-checking a reference picture with furrowed brows.

"Anaya," I correct her sheepishly.

Standing opposite the maître d' is another woman: wispy, thin, white, elegant, soft voice and delicate features complemented by her short pastel pink hair and bangs. This must be Michele Visser, another of this year's Günter fellows. She beams, closing in for a hug. "Oh, my gosh, you must be here for the Günter dinner. Me too! Congratulations! You can call me Miche."

I squirm out from her hug, uncomfortable at the sudden imposition into my personal space but at ease that she's at least kind. Miche gushes, "I loved your story, by the way. I don't often read speculative work like that, but it made me a huge fan."

"I loved yours too," I say, reflexively twisting a loose loc of my hair around my finger. We each had a short story

publicized by the Günter Prize on the unveiling of this cycle's selected writers. Miche's piece was exquisite prose, a raw depiction of a young white woman trying to find her voice in the elitist art world.

My nerves are in a twist as the maître d' sweeps us across glassy granite floors, through rooms delicately traced in floral lines of gold, installations in the ceilings a mimic of stars. I feel like grime on the surface of this elite restaurant.

We come to a majestic arched door opening into a private dining room. Three glowing heads are bowed closely together like the bulbs of flowers arched into a bouquet of prestige: Grace Miller, co-founder of Writer's Studio, an American book packaging company that has sold countless books to the Big 5 publishers; Anouk Rijks, co-founder of Rijks & Busz Literary Agency in the Netherlands; and Katja Günter, head of one of the top international publishing companies, Günter Books, family inheritance et al., in Germany—fiction and nonfiction, literary leaning. So tenderly thin the stems of their bodies. Their hair either tied into a neat bun or poised in curls short to their chins. Eyes of blue and green and hazel, skins flushed like rose petals. They rise in waves as we enter, smiling, beaming, hugging, kissing us with perfumed words.

Once I'm relieved of their greetings, I'm left with the pollen of them, as if a powdery substance of their being has left itself on my skin, sunk through my pores, and changed something within my being that I can't quite pin.

I am nervous to meet the other fellows, and soon Ogone and Bessie flow in, in satin and chiffon and elegantly styled hair, perfect makeup, and expensive-smelling perfume. Then Ruvimbo arrives, wearing a long-sleeved gold-sequined dress and an amber hijab. Nilza is behind her in a floral shirt and

white tailored pants, a gold cross earring dangling from one earlobe.

Anouk calls for our attention. "It is a pleasure to have you all here."

Katja stands. "As you know, the prize prides itself on supporting African women's voices on the continent and the diaspora through mentorship and fellowship. Your portfolios captured and dazzled the judges. We know your novels will as well."

"Brilliant, very brilliant," Grace adds. "Come on, raise your glasses."

We clink our champagne glasses in heartfelt words and squeals, then settle into our seats still chattering. Three waiters, primly dressed in black, enter carrying a tray of food, laying it before us. The dish is laid fancily with specimens of food unknown to me.

I notice Grace quietly engages Bessie in a private conversation. Curious about my competition, I do my best to listen without drawing their attention.

"Bessie dear, how are you doing?" Grace asks her.

"I'm so sorry for being emotional over the phone," Bessie says apologetically. "I was just in a lot of pain."

"No, no, please do not worry about it, my skat," Grace says, stroking Bessie's shoulder. "This is the first time we have hosted a fellow with a disability, so if you ever need anything, please, we are here to help."

"Thank you for saying that," Bessie says. "I would like to believe that. I will ask, then—it's just, it would take me longer than the rest to complete a manuscript, which may conflict with our deadlines for submissions."

Although we're well aware we need to produce a manuscript, we don't know the deadlines yet. From across the

table, I catch Nilza's ear almost perk up at the mention of inside news.

"I see; don't worry, I will find a workaround for that," Grace says warmly.

How come Bessie's aware of submission deadlines that I'm not clued into? The intimacy between the two frightens me. For a second, I wish I was also sick.

I know what wins the Günter Prize. The stories themselves are always pandering in their portrayals of an African country. The winning writers usually have a tragic background story—violence, poverty, oppression. That's what's expected of African writers, as if the continent's a monolith. The only thing I could use is that I'm bisexual. How can I get a leg up on Bessie? I almost believe that if I embellish my life story, that could sway destiny in my favor. I wonder if I should feel guilty for thinking it. Without this award, my career will be nothing.

Miche turns to me. "Your name is so beautiful. Can I call you Ana for short?"

"No," I say, which comes out colder than I intended. I used to go by Ana as a pen name. On paper, in virtual spaces, I could be anyone; I thought maybe then my writing career would take off. But being "Ana" felt like chemically relaxing my entire identity.

Miche is waiting expectantly. Maybe she wants me to apologize. Instead, I turn to Ogone. As we continue chatting, Ogone and I overhear Miche telling Ruvimbo how the Dutch language traveled to South Africa and evolved into Afrikaans, which makes me choke on my drink.

Ogone just rolls her eyes, whispers, "Traveled, fam. Is that what they call colonization now?" We grin at each other, and suddenly I feel less alone.

As we eat, Anouk begins to explain what we should expect from the residency. "As you know, you will be attending seminars and workshops, but we also have one fun new thing cooking up: a little mix-and-match event." She rubs her hands together. "In mid-September, we'll throw a private function for you to perform your novel pitches to us. Then, we will determine who becomes your mentor, which is a vital process for the judges to determine the ultimate winner."

"Perform?" I ask, swallowing panic.

"You may not be accustomed to this in Africa," says Katja, sipping her drink, "but in places like the US and UK, authors need to be able to speak in front of an audience. You may need to attend pitch events, conferences, trade shows, author talks; this is not a skill you can succeed without."

Bessie stabs her fork into a mound of something red and pea-sized, which jiggles.

Anouk chirps, "Yes, we intend to polish you all to our standards. While the winner of the Günter Prize will receive a publishing deal and a €100,000 book advance, we want to emphasize that there is no losing here."

Grace leans in earnestly. "Being a finalist for this award will garner you interest from publishers. You have an advantage."

This is why I came. I can do a lot with that advance—one and a half million Pula can go a long way in Botswana, it would be a relief if they just divided the money amongst the six fellows—but the prize is not just about money; it's about having literary leverage toward financial comfort and a secured future.

After all, I am unemployed, unmarried, broke, a stay-at-home, dropout aspiring writer. There are only so many ways

to fail as a daughter of Batswana parents, and I'd ticked all the boxes. I'm only twenty-five, but by their standards, I am far behind schedule. They didn't want me to come to Günter, but it's my best chance for the future I want.

Cutlery scrapes against porcelain plates. In four months, our lives could change.

"Writing a book is difficult, we know," Katja continues, waving her fork with her long fingers. "We picked you because of your sheer talent and capability. The Günter Fellowship prides itself on providing you with dedicated time and space to work on your writing so that you can establish yourself as a prominent African author."

Something about her intonation makes my guts squirm.

"That being said, each of you will be scored throughout the process. Your manuscript, your platform and social media presence, your comportment, your engagement with the literary community—everything counts. Make the best of this time to work on meeting these goals. It's for your future," Grace adds with finality. Bessie stares at her warily.

I rest back against my seat and gulp my third glass of champagne. Are they scoring us now?

It's just about sunset, and behind us, Table Mountain monopolizes the entire sky, a chunky fist of a mountain.

Glamorous cars sweep by us on the drive to Camps Bay, reminding me that all this is above my station. I marvel at the culture in the architectural landscape, unapparent in the buildings back in Gaborone. I'm the only one—the other fellows stare dully into their phones, scroll social media, and type messages to people who probably support their writing.

Another chauffeured car trots behind us with Grace, Anouk and Katja.

The road twists and turns. I am traveling outside of myself, outside of who I used to be, and onto who I am becoming, a world of such richness that my stomach turns. *I belong, I belong, I belong.* I practice the mantra hoping it manifests confidence within me.

Soon, we pull up to a sheltered driveway with a five-car garage. A pedestrian wooden gate that passes into the back garden and a cove of trees obscure the house's form, except for the thumb of a white chimney. The driver unloads our luggage and wishes us a good night.

As we approach, I eye the residence, its stone walls covered with crawling ivy. Günter Huis, a coastal home, has characteristic tropes of the Cape Dutch design: whitewashed, stuccoed, bristled with a tinge of foliage. Its vernacular tongue of the stoep and central gable, a glimpse of history.

Whitewashed, whitewashed, whitewashed, bleeding Black—I crave a pen, a notepad—*This house is haunted with poetry.* The thoughts sprout in me, unnatural to my way of creating words.

The founders arrive in laughter and in chatter, gathering us in an embrace, guiding us to the front door.

"This is Huis," Katja says, sliding the wooden front door open across the terracotta floor, bringing us from the balmy night air into the tight hug of a foyer, a swirling sky of stars peeping in through its skylight. We stand on the threshold, not yet settled in, like ghosts pondering which rooms to haunt.

A nudge against my back pushes me forward, although when I turn, there's no one behind me.

Katja guides us into an open-plan communal area: a dining area wedged between the kitchen and living room. Heavy concrete ceiling for the kitchen's side, scrapes and scratching textured into it, a dazzling contrast to the terracotta tiles.

The maid is in the kitchen, an old Xhosa woman dressed in a uniform of pale green like grass depleted. She's wiping down surfaces, hair sealed back with a tukwi. An old kettle on the stove begins to whistle steam, and she pours it out into porcelain cups arranged with butter scones. Anouk pops one into her mouth, saying, "Thank you, aunty," snapping me out of the trance of Huis's rules.

"Yebo, madam," the maid says, her name a suffocating absence in the room. It makes me uncomfortable, this arrangement. It's not like my family doesn't hire help to clean the house. Maybe it's because we all look alike in that familial arrangement. Anouk stands back, nibbling her scone. We wade through the dining area to the spacious living room backed up with a floor-to-ceiling bookshelf, healthily stocked with books; adjacent to it, a hearth, soot smudged up to the ceiling in an artisanal aesthetic.

I trace my finger against the spine of books by their roster of bestselling authors. Literary fiction, of course. No Afrosurrealism, which is my specialty; a shame, but fixable. One full panel of a shelf is a door to a private sunroom, like a diamond of glass overlooking the garden. It feels strange that I'm going to live like a rich person when I'm not one, a Motswana focusing on writing as if that can cure poverty, ailments, cancer, or politically rife regions; that's the fight Mama started with me. I pray I become something out of this journey. I tread back into the living room.

The ribbed underside of the concrete ceiling undulates, like crests of wave caught in form, framed in pieces of warm wood. Running the living room's full length is a bay of windows, and the arresting view of the Atlantic Ocean takes the breath from me as I drop my bags. We are living in a poem.

The indigenous garden, as they call it, runs the length of the yard, creating pockets of privacy where our bedrooms intersect with it. Movable louvers help the house breathe, inhaling cool air and exhaling hot air. Brick floors lead to internal courtyards; something about the house feels in harmony with nature. The sliding glass doors open onto a balcony, expanding the space outdoors, an illusion such that it seems the living room hangs between sky and ocean. A deep, fathomless silence. Salty sea breeze, the air so pure.

Katja pats the upper portion of the wall near the stairs, the living room beside it.

Engraved in a gold plaque near the staircase, a poem of rules:

Call me Huis.
No smoking, *the rules say.*
No pets, *the rules say.*
No parties, *the rules say.*
Maid comes once a month.
Keep Huis clean.

I remember my strange thoughts of the poem I came up with as I entered the house, and I feel the sensation of being watched, prickling at me, slipping into my pores.

Katja, Grace, and Anouk proffer snippets of information and advice as they lead us through Huis:

"Two bedrooms below, three bedrooms up with their en-suites, and a studio where you can render your artwork in oils, sketches, and canvasses." Miche beams at this, which doesn't surprise me—she seems like the artsy type.

Stairs run the length of the living room dressed in yellowwood, warm hues of deep citrus orange and browns. The three founders observe us with silent gazes.

I go up the stairs that seem to float up the wall.

My bedroom is squarely fit, with different hues of white on the wall, bedcovers, and pillows, and a glass wall glimpsing the ocean.

The left wall has a large stained-oak shelf, a writer's desk furnished with an ergonomic chair, notepads, and an antique lamp—I fantasize about sitting by the nook window writing stories—then a side red door leading to a private garden walled in foliage, little spots of outdoor lighting dripping from the roof of treetops. There's a concrete bench and stoep; I feel as if I've stepped deeper into myself where I can reside quietly with my thoughts, like I'm a word on a page scented in the sea breeze.

I'm afraid that if I close my eyes for too long, I will wake up in my claustrophobic bedroom of my parent's home to Papa telling me to grow up, take up responsibility, go back to school, and stop being a failure. I move silently, not a wisp of my breath to disturb this scene and dispel its dreamy quality.

I am here to stay, a ghost wishing never to leave.

I sit on the bed facing the mirror. In the reflection, the space above my bed has a hole in the wall, a wide, dark mouth of a recess, its borders like a knife's edge. For a moment, I think I see a black chiskop scalp poking out of the hole, like the curvature of a crescent moon. I blink, spin, gasping.

It is a solid wall, not the frame of a window protruding. I stand on my bed, patting the wall for a hidden enclosure. There's no sealed door, just the whitewashed wall, so white it's glaring, leaving traces of dust that smudge deeper into my fingerprints.

One panel of the wall slides to reveal a surprisingly spacious en suite bathroom, complete with the thick fluff of white towels, the soft notes of jasmine and eucalyptus. I run hot water over my hands, uncertain why I'm panicking. Even after washing them, my fingertips are white as paper.

I return to the room and climb my bed, tracing my fingers against the wall like there's braille I'm reading, but it feels like the wall is reading me.

"What are you doing?" Katja pokes her head into my room.

"My fingers were turning white."

"White like this?" Katja raises her hand, a smirk cast across her face. "That's Huis, she likes to leave a little bit of herself on guests."

"Why do you personify this house?" I ask.

"One must honor the place they live in. Huis was my childhood summer home, you know." Imagine.

"Are there any enclosed alcoves behind this wall?"

She knocks thrice on the wall, like a secret code. "None that I know of."

Someone calls her, and she heads out. When I stare down at my hands, *my* skin tone has returned.

I walk down the stairs to the living room, where someone's slid the glass walls open, and the night and sky fill the room. The founders lounge on the couch as we trickle back in. Before wishing us a good night, Anouk pulls out a folder from her handbag. She dispatches shimmery cardstock embossed with the residency timelines and instructions.

I gape at the submission deadline dates. My drafts are usually messy and not linear. I'm also a pantser; sometimes I write the endings before I even know the beginnings or middle of my story. And I've only written a novel once. The other fellows' silence confirms my concerns that I'm not the only one anxious. Ruvimbo stares up, says nothing, takes in a deep inhale and is unable to release it.

When I head to my bedroom, I step into the private garden, one last sweep of my eyes. A Cape Dutch roof, two of them, thatched in grey black, with gables set in a Holbol style with a baroque flair to it. Once, to persuade me into a serious career like interior design, Mama bought me all these South African home and design magazines. The architectural language stayed with me, but not the passion to pursue a life as an interior designer.

I stare at the skies and the mountains, eager for my new life here. I will be me, the real me, in this glorious Mother City: Cape Town, South Africa, my new home, my new embryo, a bare canvas.

As night falls, I slide open the door to the en suite bathroom. A thick-rimmed bathtub, freestanding, onyx black clawfoot; it overlooks a porthole window, the misty grey of an ocean. Vintage sinks. Foliage. Jars of bath salts, shower gels, a beautiful perfume. Behind the bathtub stands a tall mirror, reflecting the space back into me, as if extending reality into another sphere. I fill the bath with boiling hot water until steam mists up the space, step inside, and wash the dirt of my old life. I run my hands through my dreadlocks as they hang over the edge of the bathtub. Sleep enfolds me in this cocoon of warm waters.

In a wispy dream, Grace and Anouk appear in my bedroom, following Katja's directives, their skins a white glow like that of a luminescent ghost. The tips of my fingers are smudged ivory. They lean down, whispering into my ear:

"a pigment for my paint,

your pain for my paint,"

they chant, paintbrushes at their fingertips, tracing the arch of my cheekbones. I can't move, I can't blink, I can't scream. At the edge of my bed stands a canvas staring at me like a mirror. The rest of the house's walls fade away. Slowly I gain control of my limbs. Panicking, I hurry from my bedroom, escape through the front door, but the outside is different: a field of yellow stalks, swaying back and forth. I cast a hand over my eyes. The sun shines alone in the sky. I survey the never-ending fields. The horizon, sand and veld only.

And on the other side stands a majestic Cape Dutch house different from the Huis I entered tonight. On the stoep stands a woman with a bald chiskop cut, her clean-shaven head shining in the sun.

I make way to step forward, to go to her. My feet, my body refuse. A force holds me tightly, and I can only watch.

Men of bone appear from the distant veld, from the river. The woman can't run. She has no more to give. The men of bone climb her back, consume the flesh of her body. There is no sound in this plane. Her death grows from the earth, a seedling forming into a baby. The men of bone feed off the baby's brown, the flesh, the Afro, discard the baby's bones into the earth, into the veld. Little seeds of bone shards become blooms with thorns.

The same woman sprouts from the earth, whole and alive again, walks forth and weeps into the bloom of thorns. Her

tears are blood. She points to the house, tries to speak, but something about the Cape Dutch house holds her still despite its distance; she seems to be fighting herself as she uproots the thorn from its bloom, digs it into the bulb of her lips, sews them shut with blood and sinew of her dead child.

The woman points to the house. The wind of her voice withers through the gaps in her mouth. "Huis," she says, pointing at the Cape Dutch house behind me. "Ntlo e sule." The house is dead. A few metres from me, the men of bone turn, shear through the veld toward me. Their fingers reach out to me, but before they can touch me, I open my eyes, waking up in the cold bathwater, the sleep having lasted over an hour.

Huis moans through the pipes.

I am Michele Visser, signing off. Thank you for listening to What Happened to Ana? *If you enjoyed this episode, please share, subscribe, and leave a review. We are a small two-person team, my assistant and I, and every like and subscription goes a long way. Thank you!*

[theme music]

RANEWA

THE TRACK CAME TO AN END, MY SISTER'S VOICE FALLING INTO A vacuum, an abyss. I spun the phone around in my hands as if I'd find answers glued to its body.

I'd first met Michele Visser during the initial investigation of my sister's case. Miche was very sympathetic to my family's loss during our time in Cape Town. She grieved with us, delivering baked delicacies and sharing with us her beautiful memories with Anaya before she disappeared. She was kind and soft-spoken. But this was my sister's *voice.* How many people would only know a version of Anaya that Miche wrote?

I picked up my own phone and performed an internet search for the podcast. There was no mention of this particular podcast about my sister anywhere. So what the hell was going on?

I dialed Miche's phone, but my calls went straight to voicemail and my messages weren't tagged with delivery confirmation: She'd blocked me. Alarm bells went off, and I clenched my hands. A confused and unquenchable anger began to brew inside me.

My parents and I, we don't keep secrets between us no matter how grave the news might be, and they'd been desperate for new updates. I didn't bother knocking. Mama was by the bedside, prostrate, arms in prayer. I nearly called for her

from the doorway, but I stepped back. I couldn't tell her about this. She'd break.

Mama, the former chain smoker and heavy drinker, stopped the unhealthy habits when her daughter disappeared. God existed all of a sudden. She talked to Him a lot at night. She was at His mercy. Knees nailed to the ground, lips holy. The air in our home was always hung with incense and mothballs and T. D. Jakes preaching. Papa was gone for his usual therapeutic golf sessions with old friends, a respite from his grief. As usual. Probably locked the wine away, as usual, afraid I'd start drinking again, which could trigger my cutting myself again. We needed agency, action—for someone to get off their ass and look for Anaya. Mama, a doctor, had no body to mend, no bones to blend, no skin to sew. The house was a broken spirit. I was a broken spirit.

Many tactics had been used to help me process my mourning for my sister. As if the pain of Anaya's absence could be removed by churchgoings, group therapies, counseling—as if I could be healed. The loss was still a keen slice through my body. Sometimes it came in huge waves and panic attacks; I often worried that maybe we were finding new ways to be useless instead of being instrumental to the case. I felt like my chance to get her back was slipping away—that maybe I could find her, help her, be with her.

It didn't make sense for a human, a whole entirety of wonder and complexity, to just disappear. I wished she'd be like the moon and sun, waning and dissolving into the pale blue and darkening sky, then returning once again to illuminate what we couldn't ourselves. She had always been like that for me.

What if Anaya lay buried somewhere under the blanket of earth, worms knotting through her bones, her dreads wiry and stiff? My knees gave way beneath me. My throat hurt. I didn't know why until Papa stormed into my stuffy bedroom. The wail coming out of me was a creature scraping every surface. It left my voice scratchy and dry.

Before he left me, tears filled his eyes, and I watched the grief overwhelm him, stooping his gait as if he were about to collapse. I knew that powerlessness triggered him, for he couldn't save one daughter, and now he might lose another. In times like these, he steps away to recollect himself. I was itching for a drink and a joint, but I'd become sober since Anaya disappeared, hoping we'd rejoice together over wine. Instead, I lay in bed that night, awash with shock, into inaction, trying to make a sense of everything, when Anaya's phone pinged.

A new track had been loaded onto the app, and as I pressed play, I wondered if it would reveal the truth of where Anaya was, if by playing it on repeat I could catch any clues. I fell asleep to the sound of my sister's voice.

Loxion Kulcha

NEWS FICTION NONFICTION POETRY ESSAYS ABOUT

The Günter Prize for African Women's Literature Announces New Fellows

By Moremi Gadifele
19 Aug

The Günter Prize for African Women's Literature (GPAWL), well-known by its moniker the Günter, has announced its six fellows.

Although the Günter family sponsors the high-profile writing residency for unpublished African women, the founders—Grace Miller, Anouk Rijks, and Katja Günter, all notable women in the international publishing scene—provide the vision for the prize and decide on the winners as a committee.

Despite its prestige, the Günter Prize has its critics. Award-winning author Langa Mangezi reports that "The Günter is exclusionary of other African countries by focusing its lens only on Southern Africa. I highly question their selectivity agenda and wonder if there were no other prospective writers from other African countries."

The Günter has two selection processes: Their committee's main goal is to talent-scout the entire industry—the African continent and its diaspora—finding aspiring and emerging authors. From this

pool, a private judging panel selects, according to their criteria, six of the best writers to be fellows at a semester-long residency that runs from late August to early December. From there, one fellow will receive the grand prize.

Here are this year's Günter fellows:

Ogone Uetuu Molefhi (Botswana, 23) is a poet and writer from Botswana. She is a math genius and a literary/lifestyle content creator. She co-founded the slam poetry series Diboko tsa Rona in Gaborone, runs a book charity foundation, FreeWord, and received a Botswana Presidential Award for her BGCSE examinations and is currently pursuing a BA in quantity surveying as a research fellow. She's a finalist for the Taolo Writing Award and Africa Future Short Story Award. She is working on her first novel.

Bessie Kgositsile (South Africa, 25) is a writer, a cultural organizer, chronically ill, and chronically fated for a happily ever after.

Ruvimbo Nkosi (Zimbabwe/London, 24) is a queer London-raised Zimbabwean author, a wannabe sugar baby, a coffee aficionado, a parent to a moody cat, and a lover of rain. She has been a guest speaker and teacher at several events in Kenya, Nigeria, London, Chicago, and Italy. She holds no degree/s, thank you very much, and is a content school dropout.

Michele Visser (South Africa, 21) is an artist, author, and content creator currently living in Cape Town. She is the creator of the Grace of Life series on YouTube. She's been an artist-in-residence in Florence, Italy.

Nilza (Mozambique, 22) is professionally known by her mononym as an international singer. She's also a poet, writer and holds an MFA in screenwriting from New York University. Her poetry and short fiction have appeared in *Loxion Kulcha, Elegant, Blackaficionado* and other places.

Anaya Sebeya (Botswana, 25) is a writer from Botswana. Several of her stories have appeared in *Gaborone Review* and *Tswana Post*. She won the Afrika Short Story Prize.

The prize is €100,000. The winner will be announced on 20 December.

WHAT
HAPPENED
TO
ANA?

WHAT
HAPPENED
TO
ANA?

114:08:42:03 **BEFORE I DIE**

Episode 2

Identity Crash Course • Anaya

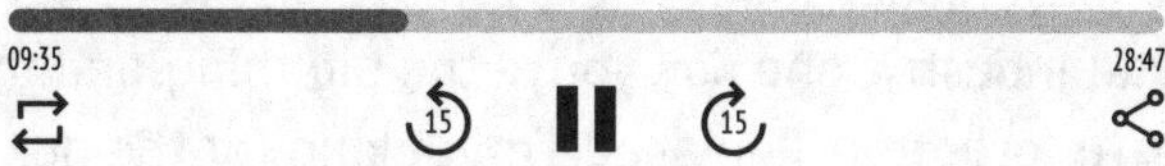

Welcome back, Crimies. I am Michele Visser, host of What Happened to Ana? *Last we left off, Anaya had learned about the Günter program requirements and arrived at Günter Huis.*

Günter Huis is beautiful, but the weeks that followed became very challenging, even more than we expected. It was like getting homework on the first day of school and it being due that very same day. We were scrambling to prepare ourselves for what that day would bring. Join us three weeks later, as the competition changes without warning.

This is Anaya Sebeya's story . . .

[upbeat music]

We slog, half yawning, downstairs for coffees and teas and smokes, like we have every day for the last three weeks, but this morning we stop short in our tracks. Dressed in a chic linen vest, paired with a flowy silk skirt—all white—and ballet flats that dangle loosely from her feet, Katja Günter is

perched on our living room couch, fingers teasing through a slim novel—one of Katja's authors', a Black British woman whose debut made waves internationally.

"I've been here for the last two hours, and there's been not a peep from any of you. You are sleeping on a lifetime opportunity." Her voice is languid as she peers up at us on the stairs.

Damn. I chew at my lip, realizing that she's been here since 6 a.m.

"You must realize that you are *competitors*," Katja says. "This is a brutal industry; one day, you're the big thing, and the next day, you're forgotten. Replaced. I'm looking for the next great African writer, someone who's hungry and willing to do everything for their career. So far, none of you impress me."

Bessie steps down, moving to speak, but Katja raises her hand. "A wise person once told me that death is indiscriminate—it doesn't care what your circumstances are: rich, poor, important or"—her eyes lazily draw up to Bessie—"'*chronically ill*.' Death, it will devour you. Think of publishing the same way. It wants a book from you. And many more books. In your case, Bessie, you would fare better with strategy. One well-placed punch can do what many reckless ones cannot. You understand my *gist*?"

By now I can tell when Bessie's feeling sick. When she's not enduring a flare-up, her laugh, her confidence, her thick body fill the room with joy. But when something's not right, her light and form dim, take up less space. Bessie feels like this to me now, and I'm starting to feel the same, as if Katja's presence is siphoning our auras.

"That's ableist," Ruvimbo says stepping down the stairs. "If we're receiving different instructions from the judges, it creates confusion for us."

Katja waves her hand. "Oh, these trendy, politicized terms don't faze me. You have free will. Sleep or labor; it is up to you."

"Understood." Miche glides down the stairs with a bounce in her step. She's wearing yoga pants and a sports bra; I don't think I've seen her repeat an outfit yet, even for bed. "Thank you so much for clarifying things for us. This will not happen again."

Ogone and I glance at each other with raised eyebrows.

"I'm making known to you girls the kind of mentee I'm looking for. As I mentioned during our welcome dinner, we have curated a soirée where you'll meet with potential mentors. I won't mince words: Tonight will play a pivotal role in determining who champions you to literary success."

Tonight? That's hardly any time to prepare.

"Your social currency matters, girls. We are investing money in you, and we want to see it count," Katja says with finality. "Ogone and Miche have a head start with their personal brands; I suggest the rest of you catch up." She stands. "I will provide you each one fifteen-minute PR session on how best to market yourselves. Nilza, you're up first."

Katja and Nilza disappear into the sunroom, leaving the rest of us in a mist of dread. Ogone determinedly ties her hair up and moves to the garden with her notebook, while Miche quickly bounds back up the stairs to her room. I also head to my bedroom, writhing with anxiety. Katja had a point; Miche and Ogone are influencers, and I have nothing going on with me. I had purchased a tripod in hopes of elevating my social media accounts—to make me *more* interesting, *more*

seen—but there's always something off about my angle, the lighting, the quality. I can't finesse the editing. I can't curate a vlog with unique aesthetics. I can't be a personality that will get thousands or millions of views like Miche and Ogone. They've racked up a loyal following that could translate to a good business deal. All I do is record every day and fail to post anything.

Everyone has the smarts about them to gun for Katja as a mentor. The award is named after Katja Günter, not Grace Miller or Anouk Rijks—*that* says a lot. I try to calm myself down—being a Günter finalist will still be advantageous to my career; agents and editors will still be interested in me whether I win or not. That's why I'm here.

Katja's visit reminded me that we're being scored on everything. Why am I hiding in my room? I must remain visible.

I hurry downstairs, bumping into Nilza, as the book-lined door to the sunroom closes snugly in line with the rest of the floor-to-ceiling bookshelf.

"What'd she say?" I ask.

Nilza walks past me without so much as a glance. "You've got ears. Find out for yourself."

And that's exactly what I do, plant my ears against the wall of books, catching chinks of words:

"Lose the sexual slash gender identity through a Christian lens"—I can't hear all of Katja's words, as if Huis muffles my ears—"elevate your work while bringing commercial appeal for the mainstream market."

"My faith is to God, not a capitalist market," Ogone responds.

"We already have fiction about Western African spirituality, but Southern African spirituality? That could be you. A

new voice. Your work is very literary and intellectual; having awards legitimizes our BIPOC writers, but we need a book that sells. You could do both."

"I'm not sure about promoting the worship and idolization of African deities and committing syncretism. Sure, it's marketable, trendy, and considered 'pro-Black' but it's not within my interests."

Idolization, what the hell is she on about?

"Mmm, well it's a good premise—and *tension*—but do not say that in public. I strongly advise you consider your decision, but reframe your ideas in a more positive light. A controversial author is a considerable trait for us, but be strategic about it; we don't want to alienate nor insult our audience."

The door carries my weight as it slides open to an unsurprised Ogone. "I thought I was being called," I say, embarrassment warming my cheeks.

"You may enter," Katja says, glancing dully at her watch.

I sit across from her; the glass door behind her overlooks the greenery of the garden, which serves as her backdrop.

"You've got exceptional talent, Anaya, with what I see as a promising career as an African writer who has something important to say." She launches in immediately. "The experimental nature of your writing makes it distinct, but that makes it niche and hard to market. You want to be an easy-to-consume product—" Katja waves her cigarette around, its smoke a wispy rope around us. "Pick your brand instead of jumping around topics so much. Your writing, although exemplary, is not going to work on a global stage. Translate for us; don't use so much Setswana. There are ways to reference your culture whilst being inclusive to your English audience."

I open my mouth to speak, but Katja raises her hand, and the light winks across the gold rings on her fingers. "That's it. You may go."

That wasn't even five minutes. Mentally, I cross Katja off my list of mentors.

◆

Streaks of purple, reds, and rose paint the sky, the sun a sinking orb into the horizon as we prepare for Huis's Midnight Mix and Match event with the Günter founders. Taking Katja's threat to heart and afraid I may fall short, I go to Ogone for guidance.

Ogone is a makeup enthusiast, and she does makeup appliqué in a way that complements her complexion and beauty. Ruvimbo too. Every time those two huns step out of their bedrooms, they look like goddesses.

When I approach Ogone's room, I overhear her on the phone with a former Günter fellow who's giving her tips on preparing her pitch. It catches me off guard. That gives her a leg up. I don't know any famous authors. I knock when she hangs up and play clueless.

"Ready for the makeup tutorial?" she asks. She's wearing a mauve slim-fit track suit that exposes her midsection. I feel shabby in comparison.

She glances at her phone as it rings. "Eish, this guy won't let me breathe, bathong ba Modimo. I'm down for a good time and grooving, but I'm not up for sex until I'm married." She nudges her phone to me. "Block the nigga for me, asseblief. He busy telling me he can buy me an iPhone and weaves and give me monthly allowance. Just because you can afford me doesn't mean you can have me."

I sit on her closed toilet and laugh when I see his caller ID: Ugly Rich Nigga. I block his number. Ogone starts arranging her camera onto a tripod and another on a shelf near the mirror so she's able to record different angles.

"Don't worry, I'll make sure you're out of the frame," she says as Mpho Sebina's voice flows from Ogone's Bluetooth speaker.

I nod and bring my feet up onto the toilet seat, pleased to witness her transformation.

She smiles at the camera, and it seems so natural. No wonder she has so many followers. I avoid anywhere I see Miche and Ogone in the house during the day because it's inevitably a recording site. I don't want to be appearing like a monstrous creature in the background.

"Hello, my loves," Ogone says. "Welcome to my channel. Today is GRWM face beat tutorial for dark-skinned women. Get ready with me as I do my makeup for the Günter Prize private function. So excited. And yaaaas I am one of the Günter fellows!" She does a little shimmy dance ting, which is so cute. I don't know what GRWM means, but okay.

After an hour on her face, this babe ain't even finished yet. She starts parting her hair and cornrows it into ten lines. She dons a weave cap, applies some glue again, except this is different from the glue for the eyebrows, I think, then she pulls out this mega-wavy weave that's giving off Beyoncé vibes. This girl is still working her face. She starts teasing the hair with combs and brushes and scissors, and the hair sets onto her scalp as if it's legit growing from her hair follicles.

She starts working the baby hair. She talks through her process, her twenty-four-inch wigs, lace front and clip-in wigs, and alopecia which I know fully well. Her eyebrows

transform from trim lines to thick arched brows that look highly trained and able to bench press. I stare at my crooked eyebrows in the mirror. She combs her eyelashes—wait, people actually comb their eyelashes?—I watch her add more eyelashes as I stare at my poor bushy ones. By the time she's finished, babygirl has thick eyebrows, high cheekbones, long flowy, wavy hair, and a face that can beat a person up. I look the same as I always have, a dull version of her. She spritzes expensive perfume around herself and onto the pulse points of her body, covering us both in beauty that I can't afford or maintain.

After Ogone finally turns off the camera, she asks, "Want me to beat your face?"

"Excuse me?" I say, stepping back.

"I'll make sure it's simple and just tie your dreadlocks up," she clarifies. "You have such pretty eyes and lips."

When she's done, Ogone leans back inspecting her piece of art, smiles, and says, "Tsena wena babes," but she says it as *beyps*, the way she types it in her messages. "Jealous down, you look good."

I smile and weave my long dreadlocks into a high ponytail, proud of the seven years of grooming I've put into them; every natural coil is rich and healthy without a fleck of chemical damage that my relaxed hair used to be strained with.

The soirée preparation begins in Huis. A huge truck's parked on our driveway, and decorators wheel in massive boxes of decorations, a tall ice sculpture, fancy alcohol, and high-backed elegant chairs into Huis's garden. Carpenters with machinery howling are building a tiny decked stage

with a floral backdrop. Katja launches directives as luxurious items are strategically placed on the high tables draped in white cloth. Everyone approaches her like they'll be fired on the spot if they err.

The event feels ostentatiously a waste. I watch from my bedroom window, slouched on the sill, recording myself and the pending celebrations and knowing I'll never get around to posting them.

As the hour approaches, we wait in the living room. Bessie, septum ring, iridescent rouge lipstick, is in a huge feathered coat and a sculptured dress structured around the dips and shapes of her silhouette. Nilza, tousled black hair, chandelier of earrings, a strapless, slim plunging neckline long dress, a sheen across her olive skin, a cigarette forever in her hand. Ogone, Peruvian weave, in a long, sleek black dress and furry coat. Her outfit matches Ruvimbo's. I wear Ranewa's long-strapped rose lurex dress—the one she wore to the music awards in Botswana—mildly transparent, shimmers as if it's woven from tiny mauve jewels, with boots, and a deep night-shade headscarf woven up my head. At this rate, I'll have to ask Ranewa to send her whole wardrobe.

As we're waiting for the ceremony to start, we're chatting and laughing. Ruvimbo has a British accent toned by Shona, whilst Ogone and I have accents that betray we were schooled in an English medium school, more English with a dusting of Setswana. During our mingling dinner with the Günter founders, I learned that Bessie was educated at a public school before changing to a boarding school. She has a more colorful hue of a Setswana accent when she speaks, the dialect altering how we sound given that we come from different tribes. It's music when I hear us all speak, different

instruments and chords strung, a beautiful orchestra our voices. We could be friends.

Khethiwe, the founders' helper, quietly approaches us. "The madams are ready for you. They say you should come onto the stage in this particular order." She hands Ruvimbo a slip of embossed card.

"Thank you, Khethiwe," Ruvimbo says, yawning. "I don't know why this has to be at midnight."

A breeze wafts through the tree branches much like the cold trail of fear in my body, as we make our way through the mingled crowds of prestige—authors, agents, publishing associates, donors, friends, and I swear I eye a famous model talking to Anouk. For an event about African literature, the guests are mostly surprisingly white, with a spot of the kind of Black and Brown people who have that nasal, posh British accent that can only be brewed from a local prestigious education and colonial influence. Professional photographers snap away at people amidst their private conversations. I clock a few past Günter winners, who've gone on to publish award-winning novels and emigrate overseas to live the soft life, making me salivate, because I could be them in a few months. I read their bios post-Günter as a prediction of the trajectory my literary career may take.

Katja struts onto the stage, laughing, shouting, "Welcome, welcome."

She's lined us up together, and my mind clocks the arrangement: We're a spectrum of dark to white. I don't know if it's intentional, but it makes me uneasy.

Katja taps the mic, and everyone quietens. It's the first time I've seen her this alive, eyes wide, a grin across her face, ready to impress. So this is how Katja is in a room of

influential people. Her tiny frame and pastel pink skin is tied up in a loose, sheer champagne-rose dress, with a plunging neckline, heels so high I can't imagine how she balances on them. I feel like an imposter wearing a costume that doesn't fit.

"Welcome to the Günter Prize's Midnight Mix and Match to celebrate our talented fellows," Katja says grandly. "We have invited some potential mentors, including some who have weaseled themselves into this space." She laughs, gesturing to someone I can't see. "The goal of our Midnight Mix and Match is to pair our fellows with professional mentors. Our mentors have a wealth of experience, an eye for the market, and the vision to shape up our fellows' manuscripts—and careers—to turn them into Africa's finest authors." She points to a high round table where the mentors stand. Khethiwe brings them a mic so they can introduce themselves.

"I'm Olivia Bloom," the first mentor says. "I'm an award-winning author and critic, as well as publisher at Mountain Books. I founded the Diversity Co. nonprofit and have a roster of bestselling authors of literary fiction and nonfiction." I'm surprised that Olivia Bloom is a Black woman. She has a chin-length weave, steely protuberant eyes that remind me of my strict Setswana teacher, but posh.

I remember an article on the next man, Langa Mangezi. He wears a laid-back loose-neck mauve silk shirt, pants with deep pockets, and silver sequined flats. He keeps his hands in his pockets, and has a beard that has a great sheen. Langa motions with his wine as he speaks, his English accent closer to mine. "I'm Langa Mangezi, an award-winning author of several books and plays; my novel *Men Who Bloom Flowers* is currently being adapted into a TV series by Amazon. I

founded the nonprofit organization Write to Freedom, an outreach program seeking to promote literacy in children and teenagers from low-income areas. As for my literary tastes, I'm keen on unusual concepts and cross-genre work—show me something new and fresh."

Grace is next: "I began working in publishing as a media rights manager before moving to a successful editorial career spanning fiction and nonfiction. I'm currently the co-founder of Writer's Studio, a book packager whose authors have become *New York Times* bestsellers as well as recipients of the Pulitzer Prize, the NAACP Image Award, and the National Book Award. I gravitate toward big-topic literary fiction with voice."

Anouk waves with both hands. "I co-own Rijks & Busz Literary Agency. I'm a hands-on agent with an editorial style that routinely secures seven-figure book deals and award-winning bestselling clients. My specialty is distinctive, voice-driven literary and commercial fiction and journalistic nonfiction."

As each mentor speaks, I feel devastated, like I have a hundred times since coming here, but worse. The Günter Prize is all about prestige and showboating, and to them what brings prestige is literary fiction and commercial bestsellers. Where do I fit in with my Afrosurrealist work? I am the weakest link of current fellows this season. Either I have to sabotage them, or I have to elevate myself somehow. Or I lose.

Katja claps. "And you all know me. My father founded Günter Books on the merit of common-found interest in literature. We have a global reach, with several publishing houses in various countries. I have sixteen years of experience

acquiring and editing bestselling authors that boasts the International Booker Prize, Dublin Literary Award, Drue Heinz Literature Prize—I could be here all day. But it's with the legacy of Günter Books that we've been able to support many African authors. With this inaugural Midnight Mix and Match, we'll be able to bring valuable mentorship to our fellows: five talented young women."

Five? I resist the urge to count us again.

"Oh, I almost forgot." Katja's notorious devilish grin spreads across her face. "One fellow will go home if they don't snag any of our most-prized mentors."

I am Michele Visser, signing off. Thank you for listening to What Happened to Ana? *If you enjoyed this episode, please share, subscribe, and leave a review. We are a small two-person team, my assistant and I, and every like and subscription goes a long way. See you next week, Crimies!*

[theme music]

RANEWA

MY BEDROOM DOOR SWUNG OPEN UNTIL IT HIT HARD AGAINST the wall. Bright daylight swarmed in from the hallway, Papa fuming, waving his phone about. "Did you know about this?" he asked.

I stood up from my bed, my braids tangled with the wires of my earphones, Anaya's voice a slight leak. Papa angled his phone at me, showing me the headline of an article. My heart thrummed fast against my chest. "What?"

RISING LITERARY STAR MICHELE VISSER TO HOST TRUE CRIME PODCAST

I grabbed Papa's phone, scrolling down the article frantically. It was Miche announcing her new venture: a narrative nonfiction podcast "What Happened to Ana?" detailing my sister's disappearance with Miche claiming to reveal the untold and *supposedly* "unbelievable" events from the time during their Günter residency.

My eyes skimmed the advance praise for her yet-to-be-released podcast—"thrilling magical realist narrative nonfiction," "unputdownable," "the voice we all need." It was this season's anticipated hot new show. The article had gone viral, with over a million views across the world, people in various languages commenting on it with heartfelt emojis.

This was more attention than when Anaya disappeared, none of it invested back into her missing case.

My sister is a Black Motswana woman. The person who's going to profit from all of this is a white Afrikaner bitch. Say what you will about my mouth, I don't give a damn.

While Papa called a lawyer, I flipped my laptop open and looked up Michele Visser. It seemed like her Günter manuscript, *The Tales of Our Lost Magic,* had become an instant international bestseller. I found articles about her upcoming exhibitions in Italy, the Netherlands, South Africa, and Ghana, interviews of her experience of being a Günter Prize fellow, a number of features in big-name media outlets. She was young, sexy, white, and with modelesque features; no wonder she was in the spreads of reputable magazines. She'd hit the prodigy gold mine. I didn't care if Miche was famous—she was a plagiarist, a thief, a leech.

The next article about the podcast had a picture. *Michele Visser, 23, celebrated interdisciplinary artist and the youngest ever Günter fellow,* the caption read. Miche stood against a green wooden railing at V&A Waterfront, overlooking the harbor, her chin-length chiseled tresses bleached. She appeared frail and tired, a vulnerable victim.

Above her head, in block form: **GÜNTER FELLOW TO STAR IN SELF-PRODUCED TRUE CRIME PODCAST**—and in lower case continued to say:

> . . . documenting the unsolved disappearance of another writer who went missing under bizarre circumstances during their writing residency with the prestigious Günter Prize. "I want to set things right," Michele Visser tells me over brunch, voice soft and

delicate, a torn beauty struggling under the impact the trauma has had on her life. "There's been no leads and no interest in the case. Every day, women experience violence in this terrible place. The government doesn't care. The police look the other way. There's no coverage in other true crime podcasts. It's a shame."

When asked about the inspiration for this podcast, Visser says, "Whilst working on pieces for my next solo exhibition in London, which will use multimodal approaches, I came across these recordings I made during the writing residency. I showed these recordings to the police, and they dismissed it. Dismissed me. The police aren't willing to use it as viable evidence, so I thought, maybe the world will. I began to edit these recordings and integrate them into my exhibition, but when I realized the need for this to be distributed to a larger audience, I knew the exhibition wouldn't be enough—hence the podcast direction. I felt a duty to use my platform to help in any way possible. I can't be complicit to the silence and erasure of this story.

"My friend is missing. The throughline of her work was giving voice to what's omitted, and I want to continue to do that for her and her family. I want people to know the truth, to really, really hear her voice, and I hope this will have a positive outcome on the case. The episodes will be released weekly. I implore everyone to subscribe."

I placed my phone down, every bit of me burning with rage. She is very fucked up to think she's doing something good.

Miche never talked to my family about this. Never shared any of these recordings with *us* that she wanted to share *diligently* with the world. The article couldn't care to at least name my sister and the other victims.

Michele Visser is a bitch I want to kill.

The first four episodes were releasing this Friday. I ran my fingers over Anaya's phone on my desk, wondering where it had come from, and why now? Either way, I had a head start. Something strange was going on, and I was going to find out the truth.

ARCHITECTURE CAPSULE

ARCHITECTURE   ART   DESIGN   NEWS

A NEW LITERARY MOVE INTO AN ARCHITECTURAL MASTERPIECE OF IMMENSE HISTORY

BY LORRAINE MOKWENA

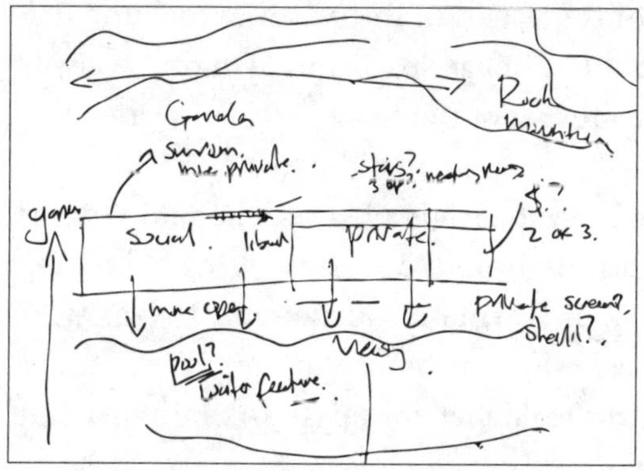

Architect Philip Kruger's sketch conceptualizing the award-winning Cape Dutch home Günter Huis. Source: Philip Kruger Estate.

Günter fellows move into the Günter House, a 1963 architectural masterpiece designed by Philip Kruger that covers 1,000 sqm. The north-facing rectilinear home has a backdrop of Table Mountain, seafront views, and a haven for the elite's heart. At the time, Philip Kruger had no educational background in architecture and had trained and worked with his father as a builder. He would go on to design other commercial and residential notable works across the continent, like the Heritage Museum in Kenya, a safari lodge in

Botswana, a contemporary shopping center in Addis Ababa, a Bahá'í temple in the DRC and more.

The private two-storey home, nestled in Camps Bay, boasts six en suite bedrooms, an open-plan kitchen, lounge, dining room and three garages. Verdant indigenous plants and trees farmed on the land form pockets of rest, and a pool oasis to slumber beside. Floor-to-ceiling glass-walled spaces offer sweeping views of the Atlantic seaboard. The ceiling is reminiscent of the waves of the ocean, wood undulating throughout the linear space and bringing warmth to it; movable louvres of the same material were introduced to provide shade against the east-west sun's arc.

The Günter family originally used the mid-century property as a bolt-hole from their winter in their home country of Germany, subsequently leasing it out as an upscale short-term rental unit before transforming it into a residency for up-and-coming African women writers.

In its colonial past, the residence was home to missionaries spreading the Gospel. But the unusual history of the Günter estate traces back to Evert and Anna van Guinea, who were sold into slavery and dispatched onto the slaver ship *Hasselt* to the Cape of Good Hope in 1658. In 1659, Evert was rewarded manumission for his due diligence in recapturing runaway slaves; he was eventually able to buy freedom for his wife and their daughter Maria. Maria van Guinea was the first freed black slave to receive a title deed from the Dutch East India Company for land in Camps Bay, which

is now known as the home to many prominent and wealthy white South Africans.

During their stay in the luxury of Günter Huis, perhaps the Günter fellows will draw inspiration from the unusual story of the land where a slave woman rose to power, wealth, and stature. It seems a fitting backdrop to Africa's biggest literary award.

RANEWA

I SPENT THE MORNING GOING THROUGH MY ROSTER OF CONTACTS OF anyone associated with Günter—the founders, the other fellows, the investigators—and none were returning my calls. It's as if the announcement has made them react this way, to distance themselves from me. In the early weeks after Anaya's disappearance, everyone was so sympathetic, open, sharing their contact information with me, keeping in touch with me. Now they're ignoring me. Fuming, I relocated to the living room where my parents were gathered like old furniture, Papa on the phone talking to someone in a harsh voice.

"This podcast thing of this woman using Anaya's voice, you have to do something about this. Clearly this an ethical infringement—it's unlawful," Papa said, his deep voice agitated. Mama stood near him, wearing only one slipper and the other askew in the hallway. Her hands were raised as if waiting for something nourishing to drop in them—perhaps better news from our lawyers.

"You can't copyright a voice, but you can protect how the identity of that voice is being commercially exploited," the lawyer said on speaker, although Papa held the phone to his ear. Mama sighed and slouched into the couch. "The problem is that Miche has adamantly stated that it's not an exact replica of Anaya's voice."

"Oh, what, she made sure to get it as close at 98 percent?" I said loudly. "It still sounds like Anaya."

"Ranewa, didimala! Se tsenye nko mo dikgang tsa bagolo," Mama admonished.

I grumbled silently and folded my arms, waiting for Papa to conclude the call.

Instead, our lawyer informed us that Miche's lawyers had, in legal speak, told us to back the fuck off or else.

"Who does she think she is to threaten us?" I shouted, against my mother's admonishment. "No, you tell Miche and her lawyers that they can go to hell. I know she's hiding something."

Papa apologized to the lawyer for my behaviour before hanging up and giving me an earful.

"This is exactly why Anaya disappeared," I said, seething. "You'd rather be strict with us than with the world."

My head drooped low as I shook in anger. "Anaya was all alone in South Africa just because of you and your standards about how we will look to people, just because she wasn't going STEM and you needed to punish her. Look now, what the world's fucking done with her," I said. Hot tears fell down my face. A slip of the tongue. Of course, swearing in English is a little bit less sweary than swearing in Setswana, which afforded me a little pardon.

At the utterance of my cursing, Mama's hands rose to her head, and she whispered, "Joh! Jesu! Ngwano o o nteka tumelo. What have we done?"

Papa held Mama's hand and kept quiet. That became our pattern: yelling or silence. Since Anaya disappeared, they handled me with strange kindness and gentleness; the grief taught them that I was their only daughter left to treasure, and they couldn't ruin that chance again.

Five months ago, home alone, something snapped in me. I had a desperate need for peace. I started with weed, then I cleaned out a bottle of Russian Bear, that clear liquid devil. I didn't stop there. The grief was overwhelming, hungry, leeching at my flesh and bones. I downed all my medications. They found me bloody, a loose bone-wan body floating in the bathtub, a whisper of a breath smoking from my lips. Now I often have a pair of eyes, if not more, glued to me.

As if they were recalling the same memory of my attempted suicide, their anger subsided, and they moved toward me. Mama hugged me, and we wept into the quiet of our home as Papa held us together.

Papa whispered softly to me, "You're twenty-five, Ranewa. Your life has to continue. Whatever you want, we will support you. If you want to go back to law school, if you want to go back to modelling, if you want to go to film school like you used to dream of, we will give you everything you want."

"Anaya deserved that, not me."

"Nana, we will find her. She'll come home, but let her find you happy and doing what you love, okay?" Mama stroked my face.

I bid them a good morning and left the living room. I closed the door of my bedroom. The podcast had gone live at midnight, four episodes at once to get the audience salivating for more. It was no surprise that in that stupid tiny brain of hers, she thought this whole thing was a grand idea.

Although Miche said she had compiled the audio files from personal archives, I was still shocked at how identical the narrator's voice was to Anaya's. It made me feel sick how authentically Miche had cloned my sister's voice for her podcast. She had probably manufactured it with AI, using

unintentional recordings she'd had of my sister's voice during the Günter residency.

But what about the content of the podcast? How could Miche know what was happening to Anaya when they weren't together? Was there truth here? I needed to do some digging, see if there was any of Anaya's writing I had missed; maybe I could uncover something that would help me understand.

Someone had already rated my sister's disappearance a low two stars because it didn't hold their interest. But a majority of the audience left surprisingly high ratings and intrigued comments, reposting and sharing across social media. The podcast had skyrocketed into an overnight sensation. I slammed my phone against the wall.

Why did my sister only mean something when Miche focused her greedy tentacles on her?

A desperate pain dug deep into my gut. I wanted so badly to hear Anaya's voice again, to know what happened to her. I hated myself for joining the people who were waiting for Miche to drop more episodes. Instead, I pressed play again and again.

WHAT HAPPENED TO ANA?

WHAT HAPPENED TO ANA?

113:15:14:01

BEFORE I DIE

Episode 3

Initiate • Anaya

Welcome back, Crimies. I am Michele Visser, host of What Happened to Ana? *In the last episode, the fellows and I were shocked when the fellowship announced an elimination. It was a first in Günter history. Nothing is certain about a writing career, and if anything, it cemented in me a hungry competitive nature to perform as perfectly as I could. All of us felt the same way. I wouldn't have traded these girls for the world. My time with them in the house, although turbulent at times, was eye-opening, challenging, and educational. Anaya's literary power was beyond anything I've ever seen. She was my top competition, and I felt in my gut that she would win the prize: Anaya was who I had to beat.*

This is Anaya Sebeya's story . . .

[upbeat music]

An elimination? My heart careens into my throat. The crowd murmurs and laughs softly. I thought I was going to be here

for four months, but there's a possibility that I will go back home to my parents with my tail tucked between my legs.

"That will be the one and only elimination," Katja continues. "I hope this little bit of news has woken you up to the realities of this competition." I don't miss her grudging tone toward our sleeping in this morning.

Ruvimbo crosses her arms, says, "Wow."

Miche's face stretches into a quiet, *Oh*.

Bessie, Ogone, Nilza, and I just remain silent.

"How about we spice things up a little bit to get the evening started," Katja says brightly. "A few words from our brilliant fellows to give us a taste of the ideas they're toying with." She steps aside, ceding the mic to Ogone.

Ogone launches into her confident, high-achiever spiel. "My work dissects religious colonisation, politics, class dynamics, and spiritual warfare on Black womanhood. My novel follows a young Motswana woman whose mother confesses a family secret on her deathbed that has her traveling back to her homeland, seeking answers to a mystery that has followed her lineage for centuries." Sounds very rehearsed.

The audience claps, and Nilza struts forward, confident, her hands in her pockets. "I want someone really hands-on to help me develop my project into successful commercial fiction. I'm writing about a young man who is forced to return to Mozambique to solve the murders of people in his community."

Ruvimbo recites, "My story is set in an unnamed country rife with conflict; it's a multigenerational story of family, loss, faith, and queerness," She hands the mic to me.

My boots give my trembling legs firmness when I step onto the stage. I hold stiffly to the mic. "My project uses

Afrosurrealism to excavate and capture our past, our history, our culture."

When I look up, I feel something beyond the eyes of the crowd pressing down on me: The dark-window eyes of Huis stare too deeply into me. It's a strange feeling that curls like a cold wind at the nape of my neck, leaves me breathless. Some people in the audience stroke their chins curiously, others' expressions change as if they really notice me for the first time.

Bessie holds the mic sternly for her pitch. "A globetrotting twenty-something woman with chronic illness is on a mission to find love, but as she experiences new cultures and new relationships, she finds herself instead."

When it's Miche's turn, she stretches out her hand to someone. "Catty," she calls. Khethiwe appears, carrying a wrapped canvas on stage that she silently unwraps, revealing a painting of five people, their postures soft and feminine, arranged as black flowers cuddling a lily-white flower of a face.

So she's using her art background to scale up. I shouldn't have been surprised.

Miche titters into the mic. "I'm interested in the border of flesh, land, culture—a story of five women with intertwined pasts. I'm a fast writer, and I have a huge platform of book and art lovers that I use to spread important messages." She bows for a little too long.

The night has deepened. Katja claps, concluding the introductions and throwing us out to the sharks. Once we make it out into the crowd, I can finally breathe. Bessie marches to Olivia Bloom, introducing herself. Ogone heads to Katja with Miche watching distantly. I'm standing alone by a

swan-shaped topiary, hoping to be swallowed by its foliage. A waiter passes by with a tray labeled "Günter fellows."

"A drink specially curated for our guests." He motions toward me.

Curious why we have specialized beverages, I sip the hazy purple drink; it's tangy, peachy, and fizzy. Nilza is already getting into her second glass of it.

Bessie is chill, as if she's just smoked a joint. She teeters on her stilettos, like a framed ice sculpture, speaking boldly to some white woman.

Grace senses my trepidation, taking me under her wing, introducing me to a couple of guests, listing off my qualities, a soft tinkle in her laughter. I feel soothed in her floral perfume. I have become fond of her; where Katja is ruthless and Anouk genial, Grace is like a mother hen to us. Once I'm settled, she moves to tend to other guests. The longer I socialize with these people, the more I start to feel uncomfortable, unable to relate to their high-class conversations of things unknown to me and feeling stupid for nodding and saying yes, yes, yes, endlessly without understanding anything.

I circle back around to Ruvimbo, Ogone, and Katja, who are talking at a high table. Ogone has her debate expression on.

Katja is saying, "BIPOC stories are trending, Black literature is trending, queer literature is trending." She waves her cigarette around, its smoke dense and putrid. "Combine those ingredients into your writing, and the market will want your book—*be* those ingredients and the market will want *you*."

"Are you suggesting I become queer just to sell a book?" Ogone asks, dangling her glass, which a waiter quickly refills.

"Gender is a construct. The public won't have to know the truth. Just you and God, I suppose. Think about your image."

"I care about what God will think about my image, so no," Ogone says.

"Free will, huh," Katja says, strolling away. "You will understand in no time, Ms. Molefhi, that it will be to your advantage that things of the past remain in the past."

My eyebrows raise. What does she mean by that? Ogone appears shaken, a sweat across her brow.

"Bathong, Ogone, why are you always arguing with Katja?" I say. "It won't bode well for you."

Ogone eyes her bedroom windows on the upper floor. "I don't feel well."

"What?" I ask, perturbed. Ogone just hugs her arms.

"Damn, this drink is so good," Bessie interjects, swiping more of the nearest tray handled by a waitress. I don't know how many glasses we've had, but I take more.

Nilza is on stage singing Miriam Makeba, her voice smooth like Sade. She's truly more interesting to the founders and mentors now: knows many languages, dinner-talk flair, gorgeous writing. I'm awed by her seamless transition to bend her tongue to every language.

Her voice rises in Xhosa. People sway rhythmically, the song a drug . . .

Steep your body in Huis:
Huis is in you, and you are in Huis.

Soon the garden has been cleared of tables and turned into a dance floor. I can't feel my thoughts. I can't feel my

heartbeat, lost in the music, in everyone's limbs and sweat and Huis's arms of foliage, its dark glare of windows. I scream and jump to the beat and forget everything. I forget myself, my family, and I am a beating heart of pure joy. The night swirls, and everyone's limbs are a throbbing skin across my body, and I press my lips to someone. Tomorrow it will all be over, and I will be full of regret and guilt. This isn't me. The music—a mixture of voices, Anouk's, Grace's, Katja's—gathers around my body and neck like the waves of an ocean, taking me away from myself.

Beside me, Ogone's shaking, tries to back out from the dancing crowd, whispers, "Need to get away, please. There are too many bad spirits here."

That night was like a black hole. I recall that we got drunk, but neither my notes nor Anaya's have any details that could paint a picture of what happened. I believe Ogone and Bessie went to bed early, and Ruvimbo blacked out, even though she doesn't drink. We wondered if perhaps her drink was spiked, but by who? It wasn't investigated much, given what happened with her after. It probably explains why she did what she did.

I am Michele Visser, signing off. Thank you for listening to What Happened to Ana? *If you enjoyed this episode, please share, subscribe, and leave a review. We are a small two-person team, my assistant and I, and every like and subscription goes a long way. See you next week, Crimies!*

[theme music]

♡4,623 ☐49 ≺434

@POCrimes

Perfect episode, great premise, has me hooked! I listened to all the episodes in one sitting!

@SerenaVanNiekerk

I love, love Miche's work. Wish I could have seen that painting in person.

@DanaeTheron

Nilza is a better singer than she is a writer.

@DeadWomenTellTruths

Fantastic work, Miche!

@LeahRomanceWriter

I'm not really a horror reader, but a friend suggested this podcast and wow—chillingly gripping!

@AbinaOsam

Authors sure know how to party! A fan of Ogone, her project sounds interesting.

@BokamosoPhiri

So this chick came from Bots just to fool around? What a waste, this fellowship could have better served someone who's serious with their life. Clearly they were doing drugs, this is some serious levels of hallucination.

@AneleMatutu

I won't be surprised if Anaya started selling her body to earn money. There are no more good women nowadays. Then you'll start seeing all these women start rioting saying men are killing them when they have such

behaviour. Asseblief, you're killing your values in society. We can't take you seriously.

@DièyeSy

Anaya's work is gorgeous, and I can't imagine what stories we'd have from her if she was still alive. Donated to her foundation--she was just too talented.

@Helen

I love this podcast!

Add your comment:

The Günter Prize

for African Women's Literature

Aug 26: Welcome dinner with Günter founders
07:30 p.m.

TBA: Midnight Mix & Match

Sept 15: Official pitches to determine individual mentors

Sept 16: Workshop hosted by an industry professional
Fridays at 02:00 p.m.

Sept 30: Each fellow must submit a polished 30,000-word excerpt of your manuscript to your mentor

Oct 20: Each fellow must submit the next 30,000-word excerpt of your manuscript to your mentor

Oct 30: Fellow & mentor editorial meeting to discuss developmental edits

Nov 30: Each fellow must submit the full 90,000 words, including revisions from earlier feedback

Dec 19: Each fellow must submit the final, complete manuscript

Dec 20: Award Ceremony, Muizenberg Conference Hotel
03:00 p.m.

G Miller

Grace Miller
Program Chair, Günter Prize for African Women's Literature

RANEWA

I LISTENED TO FOUR TRACKS IN ONE SITTING, FROZEN ON MY SISTER'S bed. Then I went to replay them again.

Strange. There was an episode listed between Episodes 3 and 4, a dim track that wouldn't play.

Next from: Anaya

Anaya | Sejeso, Colonize the Spirit
🔒 18 mins 40 sec

Episode 4: It's Setswana
► 30 mins 36 sec

I looked around me as if the sender was nearby. There must be a logical, scientific answer for what was happening. I tilted the phone as if I'd find a speck-sized camera embedded into it, someone's digital eye watching me from afar.

I played the previous episode and moved the cursor to the end of the track to see if "Anaya | Sejeso, Colonize the Spirit" would light up. But the tracker refused to budge, except to move to Episode 4.

I clicked the dim track again, this time triggering a pop-up message:

You need authorization to listen to this audio. ⓘ

I clicked the icon for more information:

Authorization can be obtained from a person involved in this episode.

How would I know who features in the episode if I couldn't listen to it? I flipped the phone onto the desk, groaning.

Wait. I sat up. Clearly it must be the fellows and founders in the episodes. I'd met some of the fellows during the weeks after Anaya disappeared, when my parents and I rushed to Cape Town. I dialed Ogone, but there was no answer. Maybe she was in class. I dialed Ruvimbo, and she answered on the third ring.

"Ranewa, hey," Ruvimbo said, with some trepidation.

"I thought you could help me with something about Miche's podcast," I said.

"Ah yeah, that's nasty what she's doing," Ruvimbo said, amidst a background of clanking cutlery. "I listened to the first episodes, and she has me straight to a T. I don't know how she did it. I mean . . . of course, I have an idea of how she managed that."

It *is* strange but true. Sometimes I'd catch my sister talking to herself, the syntax matches Miche's podcast.

"So everything she's put on this podcast is true?"

"Yes. Some of the fellows, like Miche, Ogone, and eventually Anaya, recorded their days and . . . Huis had a way of helping us."

"Huis?" The lock screen. "How did the house help you?" I asked urgently.

"It offered me an advantage in the competition, but I declined."

". . . Offered?"

"I'm sure Miche's podcast is more thorough than what I'll say." Ruvimbo didn't offer more information, and I was not sure how much I could push her.

"But it seems there's an episode missing—more than one actually," I said.

"How do you know there are episodes missing?" Ruvimbo sounded panicked. Before I could decide how I wanted to answer, she told me, "Miche left out some details from the Midnight Mix and Match that Günter coordinated for us. That might be it."

"Why?" I asked.

"No one would want to confess that dark stuff to the world," Ruvimbo said, "and I don't know Günter's role in what went down. Either they were being used, or they chose to involve themselves in all of that."

"Used by who?"

"What's the *point,* Ranewa? This won't bring back Anaya."

"No," I press on, "Anaya's story deserves to be told in fullness, not in bits and pieces for some bitch's platform."

"Look, even if you *were* to tell Anaya's story, you're also going to color it with yourself and your politics. No one gets to know the naked truth for what it is, no one except God."

"Anaya cared about the truth. She always did." I loved that about her.

Ruvimbo blurted, "Did Huis contact you?"

"I don't know what that means," I replied, confused by the sudden change of subject.

"She did, didn't she? Do you know what you're playing with, Ranewa? Damn it. I'm sorry about what happened to Anaya, but don't contact me again. I'm not going to go through this again."

Ruvimbo hung up. I had lots of questions, but I would have to find my answers another way.

I brought out my little diary and noted down the clues: *Huis, darkness, spiritual?*

Anaya's phone lit up, a pop-up message:

> You have access to the next track, "Anaya | Sejeso, Colonize the Spirit."

The inaccessible episode was now highlighted. Miche's podcast was going to be ten episodes long, but the strange phone had nineteen episodes. If Miche redacted pertinent information, I could tell the truth, to fill it out. I would transcribe word for word.

The investigation team let us have Anaya's laptop back. I could go through every document and recording she made, and use that—poems, writings, diary entries, video and voice recordings—to string together a story, although vague, of what might have happened.

I was not going to be afraid like Ruvimbo or Ogone; I would tell my sister's truth.

I began to piece together my plan.

I had been contacted by dozens of agents and editors once Miche's podcast released, but I desperately didn't want to stoop to acquiescing to those vultures.

I could go with an African publisher instead, but I felt conflicted trusting *any* publisher with Anaya's story. And, besides, most Batswana authors self-published their books; why couldn't I?

No, I would go indie. I would spread Anaya's story through all creative platforms, I would reach as wide an audience as possible.

I would start a press in Anaya's memory. I would publish and produce her work, and I would showcase other African authors as her legacy.

I'd always yearned to work in TV or film production; when my sister and I were little, we had the wild idea that I'd adapt Anaya's writing, and we'd be the successful creative sisters. That never came to fruition, but it *will.* I know she would want that too.

But first, I had to write Anaya's story. Maybe that's why her phone appeared to me: Now I could listen to the story Miche never wanted the world to know.

I opened a Word document, ready to transcribe Anaya's truth.

I plugged in my earpods, and pressed ►.

Anaya | Sejeso, Colonize the Spirit

I wake up on my bed to total silence. The moonlight flows through the porthole window and through the bathroom door, illuminating Miche standing by my claw-foot bathtub. The light is a strangeness and covers her like water, drips from her neck, arms, and legs and turns the tiles ice cold.

"Miche?" I whisper. Her hands tremble as she touches her chest, says, "Ana, I'm sick." I ask her if she has a hangover, but she keeps on shaking her head, repeating, "I'm sick, I'm sick." I realize our distance, but I can't move. Can't touch her. I don't know why, but I'm scared.

My door creeps open. Something quickly scuttles up the wall, hangs at the corner of my room, silently throbs, watches me with cat-like eyes, dilated and reflective in the dark.

Suddenly Miche is by my side, her cold feverish fingers grasping me as she climbs into my bed. She smells like paraffin, a woman burning. I can't move my arms, my legs. I can't open my eyes, nor my mouth to let the scream out. But I can see through my eyelids for some odd reason. Panic ensues in my heartbeats. I feel them slow down, like someone's forcing my heart to stop keeping me alive, then it stirs into a quick beat. Again, again, again.

The bed creaks and sags farther, as if Miche carries more weight than her own body.

The moonlight drowns the room with its rays, and something in the air colours it claret, like the air is bleeding.

A closed body, closed casket, closed skin.

"A few nights ago, you saw something that you weren't supposed to see. Shush, don't cry. I am here," Miche says, caressing my hair.

She sits up abruptly, the movement unnatural. I close my eyes and feel her shifting over me.

I try to back away, but I'm frozen into place. *Miche, please.* But I can't speak; my thoughts won't reach her. Her tongue leaves a trail of a startling cold around my toes, ankle, up my leg. Licking the skin off until I'm bone white. I am turning white, I am burning white. Above, the roof has peeled off Huis, and the moon daggers through the night's skin, a glaring orb watching us. *Help me*, my thoughts cry. Miche laps at the skin on my thighs, curdling them into a moonlike stain. She's sealing my vagina with her tongue. *Miche, please. No, no, no . . .* She licks my wetness until I'm all gone.

Miche drinks my Black. And her tongues—how many tongues does she have?—scrape across my abdomen making a path toward my chest. Her tongues brush my nipple, and her lips wrap around my tit, her teeth bite at it. The glowing pain serrates into my nerves and the nodules of my breasts until my chest is completely flat. Her tongues wrap the entirety of my neck; her teeth nibble at my lips, my tongue. She licks inside my mouth, searching until I'm choking on her tongue.

Miche's tongues slick across my cheek, forcing open my eyeballs. I can't close my eyes. *Miche please.* I'm kept still by

sleep paralysis, by sebeteledi. *Miche please.* Her tongue brushes back and forth across my eyeball, like little ants crawling in my eyes, brushes my vision away from me and I am blind I am blind I am blind. Miche's tongues wipe the color from my eyes and bleeds a new sight into my irises. I see everything that I couldn't see with my before-sight. *Miche please.*

In front of the wardrobes, there's something strange about the veneer of air, there's a rip in its transparency. Beyond it, the wardrobe is blurred. I blink. The rip flickers. Behind Miche, the blurred line runs lengthwise from ceiling to floor, like a slit opening of a doorway.

Reality is torn.

Reality is torn.

Reality is torn.

Something's seated in the corner of my room, shadows making a skin of its bones. Crooning there, nesting there, the woman from my dream is watching me. My bones are locked into stillness. A drum beats, voices anoint my skin, a whispery fear darts across the room, the spindly feet and the craned back of a dog-like creature sprinting across the room like a monkey, teeth set into its jaw like old bones. The scuttle of nails, again, as it darts back and forth, looping my voice around the room. Silence. *Help*, I try to scream. *Help.* My limbs won't move, my eyelids won't move, my voice won't move. The tread of cold fear as the creature's thin limb presses the end of my bed. I push my muscles to lift my head, to lift my hand to switch on the light to scurry these things out of my room. *Get up. Get up. Help.*

The skeletal hands of other creatures crawl across my bed, curls around my ankle, traipses up my thigh, a scream

trembling to get out of me, to move my leg, to kick this thing off me—

I am breastless, vagina-less.

I am burning—*Get up, wake up, move!* Then a thought: *Pray,* Mmemogolo used to say. Mmemogolo always with a Bible. I remember when I'd be ko gae, and elsethings would make droppings onto the roof sheeting of my grandparents' home, at night, she'd pick up the Bible, read and pray, until the utterings and footsteps on the roof stopped.

Child of my child, *pray,* ngwana wa ngwanaka.

Pray:

Rraarona yo o kwa magodimong,
a leina la gago le itshepisiwe.
my bones unlock,
a cold hand clutches my arm.
A Bogosi jwa gago bo tle.
A thato ya gago e diragale mo lefatsheng
jaaka e diragala kwa legodimong.
The room dissolves to dark,
draining of sunlight
Re neye dijo tse re di tlhokang mo letsatsing leno;
mme o re itshwarele melato ya rona,
jaaka le rona re itshwaretse ba ba molato le rona.
O se ka wa re tsenya mo thaelong,
mme o re golole mo go Satane
my limbs retreat from rigidity
It is 03:00 a.m.
The prayer enfolds me, keeping me from harm.

It's silent when I open my eyes. The bald woman and Miche are gone. The creatures are also gone. Outside, the sun shines. The house interior and furniture seem much like that of Günter Huis, except from a different time. The wall's painted a deep blue, a coffee table with a vase of lilies, large wooden windows across the length of the room overlooking sloping fields and trees. No oceans, no mountains of the Twelve Apostles, or Table Mountain.

Ruvimbo enters, smiles, picks up a pair of scissors and stabs her eyes out. She pushes the wall of my closet until it opens into the living room where the Günter Prize founders sit, drinking tea. "Will they pass this initiation?" says their voice unified into one. Then Grace, Anouk, and Katja stand from their chairs, walk to the wall until they willingly become fastened to it, their eyes ogling us, rolling through the walls, watching *me*.

Nilza is seated at a workstation by a set of French windows, sewing a cloth of skin almost the size of me. Cold terror drips in my chest.

"There is something inside you," she says to me, her voice strange, unlike her. "A bad seed. It contaminates the house. Contaminates us," she says, cutting into the sides of her arms and limbs. I stare at her blood leaking out as she removes her skin to step into this new form. What is this place doing to us?

The walls bend away and the taps creak. The house bends its fingers through us.

Bessie scrambles in, licking the pus leaking from stab wounds.

Langa and Olivia stand outside, watching her from the windows, a champagne glass in each of their hands.

Langa jerks his head. "Some initiation alright." He gulps his drink, walking away.

Katja peels herself from the wall, leaving the other founders stuck to the walls, watching us. She enters, dragging in Ogone's body, her colour dim, she unconscious. Beside her lies Ruvimbo, unconscious too, scratches on her bare arms and neck, blood trickling from her lips.

Anouk shakes her head, saying, "No, no, I will have no part of this. You will find the rest of us downstairs." Us? She spins in the wall, disappearing downstairs into the party chatter and music in the garden.

"I know you're awake," Katja whispers, in a voice that is not her own, laying a butcher knife by my head. Beside me, she lays a Bible, a plate of ashes, and a tobacco container. She opens the Bible, cleanly tears several pages, folds them. "This holy, this bone, this body," she whispers to herself. She mixes the torn pages with tobacco, lights the end, inhales, exhales.

A slither of smoky screams floats to the brown undulating backbone of Huis's ceiling; grey-tinged, they stay stuck in the walls, in my ears. Slowly the air devours them into silence. I watch on from my mind's sight, paralysed. Mmemogolo used to tell me that some prayers wouldn't work during a spiritual attack if said in fear rather than faith; is that why I can't wake up?

Katja desecrates the Bible and soon receives the heat of reprimand, coughing up the pages that knit themselves whole into the Word. She moves toward Ogone, whispers words of indoctrination and manipulation that I can't hear, but her words stretch from her mouth like an elastic rope, slick with black goop that wraps around Ogone's body and

slithers into her ears and mouth and eyes, sealing every part of Ogone with itself.

But a slurry of thoughts spill from Ogone's mind. "I rebuke you in Jesus's name; in the name of Jesus no weapon formed against me shall prosper." The thick dark goop in her mouth withers to ashes.

Katja is pushed back by an invisible force, but she leaps forward, snarling threats at Ogone as she closes the distance between them.

A spirit materializes, serene stature, wisdom aglow, with majestic wings skimming the ceiling. The spirit strikes Katja with its hand, and she snarls, slithering back like she's been spat on with fire.

I see a rapid shadow drag Ruvimbo out of the room.

With a blink of the eye, the winged spirit is already crouched by Ogone's side. Touching her forehead like one would to check the temperature, it says, "And you shall be hated of all men for my name's sake: but he that endures to the end shall be saved."

And Katja's words leak out from Ogone's ears, putrid and wilted, until the color returns to Ogone's flesh, and the winged spirit carries her. The spirit stops by my bed, and I breathe in relief thinking I'm being saved too.

When I see the spirit's face, I shrink back.

"Do not be afraid," the spirit says to me. "I gift you this: The sorrows of those who run after another god shall multiply . . . Do not be afraid of those who kill the body but cannot kill the soul."

And the spirit leaves out the very same door Katja crawled out of, leaving me behind, still unable to move.

My heartbeat thunders against my chest. I wish I were saved like Ogone.

In the corner, the Black woman with a chiskop cut has returned. She sits on an overstuffed couch, stroking some creature; its features are so dark there's no definable nose, eyes, or mouth. Her body is dark smoke. Her eyes, something of her eyes, scares me. "Why didn't you listen to me?" she says. "I told you this house is dead."

She's the same Black as me, surely that should make her trustworthy.

"Help," I cry out to her.

Suddenly she's by my face, though I didn't see her stand or walk. She peers down at me, asking, "Are you sure you want me to help you? It comes at a cost."

Chatter, clinking glasses, and laughter flow in from downstairs.

The pain whittles my bones. "Please, just help me."

She reaches for me, her hand blisteringly cold, yet hot as fire. She pulls me to a stand, and I can finally move.

"Salt to dispel evil," the woman says, pointing to where Ogone lies, showing me layers of white salt. "They're trying to initiate you into themselves. Consume the salt, it will protect you."

Hurriedly, I press my fingers into the white crystals, wishing to wake, wishing for safety, wishing for reprieve. I cup the salt into my palm, run it across my face and neck and tongue.

A pain growls in my abdomen, intensifies as noise fills my ears. I double over, clutching my stomach. Something gropes from inside my throat. I gnaw at it with my fingers to get it out to get it out to get it out.

"Oh, Ana, don't do that. Didn't mummy say it's rude to reject food?" Miche. Her teeth smile at me, and I wave the butcher knife that Katja brought earlier, slicing the curtain of dark between us.

"Stay away from me," I say.

"Oh, Ana, that hurts," she says.

My mouth cranes open, stretching wide as I force my fingers and nails into the back of my mouth, trying to get this thing out from my body. My nails catch a tendril of it, and I cling to it, pulling, pulling, pulling it out of my mouth.

Miche's eyes are slits as she lurks forward. "Ana Ana Ana—" Miche daggers the name into my eardrums. "Don't do that." Her hands are an unusual creamy white as they scathe through my dreadlocks and my scalp—*it* burns, my scalp burns.

I drive the knife into her abdomen, but no blood speaks. I drive it in again, purging this thick rope from my belly. She continues running her fingers through my dreadlocks, my scalp searing from the burn. Tears squeeze out from my eyes as I belch, groan. My stomach clenches, trying to empty itself, to purge this thing. It's the food I ate from the dream before: sejeso, rotten.

Miche's bonelike hand clutches around my neck. "I said *stop*." Her voice is deep and animalistic. "Stop, I tell you." And she begins shoving the rotten food back into my mouth. Her hand presses into my chest. A sense of sebeteledi claims me again.

"Oh, my skat," she moans, "that's it. It's going to be okay. Shh, shh. Easy, easy. There we go."

Sejeso lays coiled up in my gut, oily and black-slick.

them hues of brown
packs them into her biceps
how do you think
she throws
those punches
onto the backs of
our necks?
Huis's brain is
scattered
in the air
That's how she thinks

so quickly
moves things
so suddenly
it's her thoughts
skittering the place

There's
muti
in Huis's knickers,
and a woman, hair shorn,
tongue of blade
pain of fire to consume a new
form.

My daughter dreams in English, a language I list as my third. She learnt it at the private schools I sent her to, and I forced her to speak it all the time, just like they did at those schools. 'Children are only to speak that language during the Setswana period,' the teacher warned. I wanted my daughter to have a life different, no, better, than mine. I sent her there so she would one day travel to faraway places that I had only seen in books. It pleases me that she lives like rich people do in my country."

Wame Molefhe, *Go Tell the Sun*

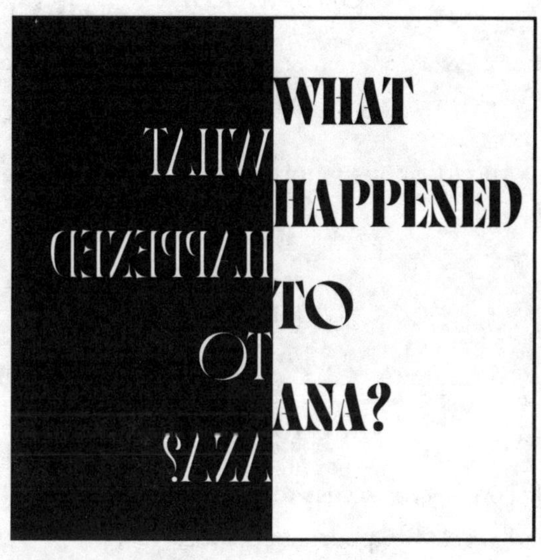
WHAT
HAPPENED
TO
ANA?

Choose your membership

Contributor

$1/month

JOIN

Thank you for your support – every amount goes a long way!

Witness

$5/month

JOIN

- Discord server access to Witness community
- Early access to podcast episodes
- Behind-the-scenes for our audio production and notes
- 10% discount on merch

Investigator

$15/month

JOIN

Everything included in Witness, plus:

- Access to old interrogation videos, articles, and Q&A that the team conducts with those close to the case, incl. Günter commentary
- Videos of Michele Visser's time in Günter and unexpected shots of Anaya's time in Günter

Recent posts by What Happened to Ana?

Hello, Crimies! As promised, here is a report regarding the missing case of Anaya Sebeya. I've redacted some of the following information for obvious reasons. To gain access to interrogation videos, upgrade your subscriptions to the Investigator level.

On 20 December, the last people to have seen the Günter fellows were the photographers affiliated with Günter who were photographing the fellows a few minutes prior to the ceremony to announce the winner of the prestigious prize. What occurred next was strange. The founders and audience awaiting the fellows in the auditorium came out into the foyer to find out what was causing the delay, only to discover the photographers in a trance, with their tools positioned in place and the fellows nowhere to be found. Within hours, they called the police. Two weeks later, in the early hours of 3 Jan, ██ of the fellows, █████ and █████, were found on the shores of Camps Bay, unresponsive. They were rushed to the hospital and woke up hours later, each traumatized and unable to recall their whereabouts. To this day, ██████████ and ████████████ are still missing.

Upcoming post:
Interrogation Videos: Me! 😊

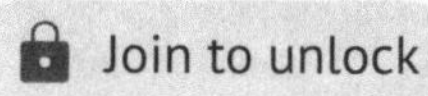

The New York Times

A Conversation With the Günter Winner

By Daniel Harrold

It's a balmy Saturday in Cape Town, several days before the award ceremony for the Günter Prize for African Women's Literature that would bestow one of the rising stars in African literature with a prestigious title as well as prize money of €100,0000. I sit at a retro bar overlooking the ocean, waiting to meet the woman who would become this year's winner of the Günter— See subscription options.

WHAT HAPPENED TO ANA?

113:09:18:49

BEFORE I DIE

Episode 4

It's Setswana • Anaya

Welcome back, Crimies. I am Michele Visser, host of What Happened to Ana?

Wow, what a wild night we had during Günter's Midnight Mix and Match. Despite my family background, I came to learn that this sort of rich people surely know how to party hard. I woke up on a pool float in one of the gardens. Bessie and Ogone had somehow gone to some of Cape Town's natural sights. Anaya found herself on a beach! It was a surreal experience being celebrated at the Midnight Mix and Match. And of course, we were hungover. Bessie and Anaya seemed particularly traumatized by how drunk they'd gotten from the Günter pre-mixed drinks, which were divine. But that's when things started going wrong with us, before we noticed that it was the house all along.

This is Anaya Sebeya's story . . .

[upbeat music]

The horizon is smudged, so it seems as if ocean and sky are smeared into a diorama of cloudy grey blues. A loose form pools around me and disintegrates from my body in a steady rhythm. My soul wants to follow suit, and it is this that wakes me—my soul trying to flee.

Water rushes into my throat, my lungs. I gargle, cry for help, fingers groping through water. I look about me, just ocean and the sun sparkling in the wide blue sky. A thought rises within me, not my thought, someone else's thought intruding me, trapped in my mind, saying:

Bessie and Ogone are lost in the woods,
no breadcrumbs to lead them home.
They are immobile,
sebeteledi oiled around their frames.
Their jaws are unhinged,
someone poured soil inside.
The evil wanes much like the tides,
its power dissolving the women.
This is only the beginning.

How did I get here? The cold ocean recedes and takes my warmth with it. The sun's soft print in the sky bruises my eyes. I swim to the coast.

My hair hangs heavier, weighted by water.

The emptiness inside me grows exponentially.

I find my phone lying on the beach, order an Uber, and arrive at the house sneezing like a dog, Ranewa's dress clinging to my skin like a wet, shaggy second skin.

I'm restless now, but sleep aches behind my eyeballs.

In the bathroom, I pull off my ocean-drenched clothes, shivering, and wriggle out of my panties. I leave them shriveled and wet on the floor, sparkling with beach sand. Mama, I'm homesick. I miss those times when Mama and Papa held Sunday lunches for church friends after church spat us out. The house smelled of paleche, chakalaka, serobe. The house sat fat, inflated with voices, laughing and yelling.

I miss Ranewa, I miss my Newa. Will she forgive me, for leaving, for being silent? I just left her knowing that she'd bear the brunt of my parents' strict nature. I was the firstborn, always most behaved in school and at home, with exceptional grades, adhered to every one of their wishes in being the perfect daughter (until I got tired of it), and made excuses for Newa, covered for her. As the weeks turned over in Huis, I stopped responding to her sad texts about their tempers and punishments, because I felt useless. I couldn't juggle her stress and mine with this competition. I've been selfish.

In the tub, I watch the shadows of trees reflecting across the walls and windows. When I come up for breath, I'm alone. I think about last night, about sejeso, the food I ate from my dreams. I ate a curse.

What happened to us last night? Even I know that such dreams can't *not* mean anything. If Mmemogolo was still alive, she'd immediately speed-dial moruti and call him to the house to pray for me. She'd pray against every bewitchment launched to her grandchild. But I don't see it like she does. These things don't happen to people like me. I don't believe in such superstition.

Last night, I was about to purge myself of the poison of sejeso, but Miche pushed it back into me. Mmemogolo would

say that a demon or evil spirit is trying to break into my body, to spoil my spirit.

None of this happened when I was back home.

If I leave, I lose all of this. Second time dropping out of something—and fumbling about with my days, unpolished stories, and odd freelances jobs with nothing stable until Günter—worse that it will be a prestigious prize.

No, no, no. Miche or whoever won't chase me out. I won't let anyone scare me away. I am Miche's competition. *She's* trying to chase me out of my body, out of mind, out of the Günter Prize.

No, I have to prove my parents wrong. I can survive as a writer and on my own. This wasn't a mistake. I will show her.

When I step out of the bathtub, I notice my legs for the first time. They are stained with a constellation of white spots, in oblong and obtuse shapes, forming a Rorschach pattern. I cover my legs with the towel again.

My legs are normal my legs are normal my legs are normal. I pull the towel off them, and they're still wounded in whiteness.

No, no, no. It was a dream. It was a dream. This is not real. No one's skin color can appear on another's skin color like a rash, a disease.

Miche. Miche. Miche. Her name is abuzz in my mind. Someone must've spiked me last night. Miche spiked me with herself. You can't get cursed in a city. There's logic to this.

I need to wash the nightmare from my mind. Staying cooped up worsens things. I drag on loose jogging pants and a jersey, hide everything of my skin. Then keys, purse, shoes. The door. A dim hallway, house quiet, everyone asleep or gone. I need to go to a doctor.

Down the floating stairs.

I stop cold on the threshold of the living room and the sunroom, and inside the latter room, two canvasses, brush-strokes in oil paint, of two women on a bed, one pale and one brown, an elastic Black thing stretched out from both their mouths. It's a painting of my nightmare.

"It's for my exhibition." Miche appears, skin sweaty, after a run. I back up, startled. "It's in a couple of weeks in Morocco."

I am her exhibition. She will be displaying me in a couple of weeks.

"Good morning, Ana." Her teeth smile at me.

I back away. "That's not my name." Call me by my name.

"Are you okay?"

"Don't touch me," I hiss. "Stay away from me."

Miche's hand rests on the bookshelf. "There's no need to be so cold."

I need to go past her or through her.

"I've tried to be your friend since you arrived," she says. "But you and Ogone have been blatantly rude to me. You know it's like reverse racism, right? Aren't we beyond that now?"

"I just want to head out, and you're standing in my way," I say.

Her eyes skirt about us, then she leans in. "Can we talk about last night?"

Shame colors me cold. "Nothing happened last night." I close my eyes and see her cold tongue licking my skin color off. I feel her whiteness burn into my legs. I wrap my arms around myself.

"Are you embarrassed by me?" Miche asks.

My eyes widen. "You're standing in my way," I say.

"What are you scared of?" Miche steps forward. "Do you miss home, Ana?" she says, softly.

By her neck, there's a stain of my skin color. It's not a birthmark, it is me. I know it is me. It's me on her neck. The sunlight dims, clamored by a bit of night. Something starts a-drumming. The air presses itself against me. I walk backward up the floating stairs, feel for the knob of my door, slide in. Close it shut. Hold my breath in and cry, with Miche burning hot on my skin.

Time has sped with the daylight, tracking silhouettes and shadows across my walls as the sun arcs through the sky. My door swings open. Ogone, looking fresh and well slept. Her hair is tied up in something, and when she catches my gaze, she says, "Felt like going old school using a molenza and all." I don't know what word she's using, but the way the word enters me recalls an old memory of when Mama would wrap her hair in a pantyhose, using it like a hair bonnet when going to bed.

She looks at me closer, asks, "Aye, mfetu. What's up with you? What happened to your hair?" I touch my hair, realizing I haven't looked at myself in the mirror today.

I touch my head, remembering how Ranewa and I grew up in between our mother's legs, the edges of our scalps anointed with Vaseline to buffer the burning we'd feel as Mama massaged Dark & Lovely into our hair, every root, every growth, every knot to cremate every existence of our Afros into straight hair until our scalps screamed in pain from the burn. We'd sprint, squealing and crying, to the bathroom for the baptismal feel of water. Feel the pat-pat

of the towel, and the heat of a blow dryer, until our hair was transformed into something "sleek and beautiful." *Bontle ba itshokelwa*, Mama used to say to us every time Ranewa and I would squirm, crying that "it's burning, my scalp is burning." I was twelve and Ranewa was eleven, and all I remember of those words is that's what it meant to be a woman, a beautiful woman. It meant burning, it meant pain, the pain a passage to beauty that one needed to be patient for, to sit still for. In that burning, my youth was crucified, my womanhood wasn't mine.

I couldn't be a woman if that's what it meant.

And so when I turned eighteen, I fasted from all these chemicals that were a cancer to my skin, my Afro, my language, my self. And now, staring at the mirror, I see all the seven years of having dreadlocks has gone undone. My hair is straight, thin and wiry, the weight of my dreads gone.

Miche's hands were the color of *Dark & Lovely* when she ran her fingers through my dreadlocks. My scalp still burns, and the spots of her on my legs *still* burn.

"I'm burning," I cry.

"Tsalu, it's going to be all right," Ogone says.

I've been retwisting my hair instead of letting it freeform, but I can't do my locs from scratch. I can't part my hair into the correct shapes and patterns across my scalp. This is damaged hair.

Ogone reaches out a manicured hand toward me. "Come, I'll fix this," she says, like she can give me myself back. "We're going to do a hot oil treatment, then I'm going to lay bentonite clay into this, autlwe? Wash hair day is a full-day thing. You got time?"

"Will this fix me?"

"Think of it as undoing the trauma that's been done to your hair today," she says, knowingly.

But what I went through feels more beyond the boundaries of this short, simple word—trauma.

"Then I've got time," I say.

I let her drag me up with my sorrow into her bathroom where she shampoos and conditions my hair. Her fingers massage away the fear that's been fondling me for days. Humming, she dries my hair off before leading me into her bedroom. She opens a cupboard which is lined with an extensive set of natural hair products, some that you'd expect in a kitchen, too, concocted into different containers, which is no surprise given her detailed vlogging process for makeup and hair.

She gathers some, sits on her bed, pats her thighs for me to sit between them.

She tells her phone, "Play *Mayibuye* by Miriam Makeba." And I wonder what song that is.

The song starts to play as she pulls out a set of combs, a hair dryer, and a heat protectant, and runs an Afro comb through my hair. My hair's not held snugly by the strands of an Afro as it should be; the hair just lets the Afro comb stream through it. There's something reassuring about Ogone's fingers in my hair working against Miche's witchcraft.

"You felt something last night, didn't you?" I say, and I explain everything that happened to me. But I feel ashamed to show her my legs, as if I'm the one who did something horrendous. As if I am the ugly thing. I'm more afraid that the spots of white on my legs will mean that I'm not hallucinating, that everything that happened last night is real.

Ogone ponders for a while, then says, "We were under spiritual attack—my faith, my God sent a spirit to protect me."

I stare at my hands, remembering the rumors that Ogone's a religious zealot. I hadn't put much stock in them before.

"You will come to learn that many things in this world are spiritual," she says matter-of-factly. "Most people don't realize the false gods they worship, how they're promoted in every facet of our lives, from the shows and music we watch to the institutions we hold to."

"Ogone, you're a Christian that twerks in the club to this very same music you consider sacrilegious," I say.

I think of my dream, how Katja tried to force Ogone into something she's not. She's been doing that since we arrived in Cape Town; it reminds me of the stories I'd hear from bo rakgadi of how jealous neighbors or relatives would go to unscrupulous witch doctors to bewitch someone out of their wealth or health and direct it to themselves. Does this mean that my spiritual encounter was predicting Günter's agenda?

"I didn't say I was perfect. My flesh is weak. It's a thing I battle. I've been trying to stop for years, but it's hard. It shows just how much I need God."

Ogone is different from some of the Christians I'd interact with in Botswana who bombarded me with righteousness because of my dreadlocks or because they saw me kissing a girl, putting themselves above everyone, saying that everyone will go to hell—which only pushed me away from the religion—as if they were pure. And here's Ogone acknowledging that she's not a perfect Christian, and she's not telling me I'll go to hell. It confuses me, because some of the Christians I met never humbled themselves this way.

"What do you believe in?" Ogone asks.

I shrug.

"Anaya, you have to believe in something. Being ignorant is very costly, because you don't know the spiritual contracts you enter into."

"Spiritual contracts?" I ask.

She sighs, twisting my hair with the comb. "You know how some people conduct idolatry? It's like every deity or spirit that person worships has its terms and conditions, like a contract. It will give you wisdom, fortune, fame, wealth, fertility—whatever it is you seek from it," she says, counting them off on her fingers. "And you have to pay it back, somehow. Or your descendents."

I nod as she massages a product into my hair.

"You do know that you can idolize a relationship, a prize, worship it, and do every kind of bad thing for it, akere? It's such a high burden, the cost of that," she says. "I prefer my God, because His burden is lighter. He said, 'I will give you rest.' And He does."

I nod, staring vacantly at the window and the world beyond it. "But I prayed, like you, uttered words, yet why didn't my words work like yours?" I ponder aloud.

"Some things can't be stopped with prayer alone. Also, your spiritual rank factors into it." Ogone taps my shoulder. "Anaya, whoever that bald woman was, she protected you, but just because she saved you, doesn't mean she's a good person." She pauses, coiling more hair. "You can come with me to church tomorrow."

"Sorry, but I don't follow the colonizer's religion," I say. I stopped attending church at seventeen, frustrated with the hypocrisy of those running it.

"Hae bathong, so o Motswana yo o ntseng jaana?" she says, rolling her eyes, and I can't tell if she's sworn at me. "Yet you're following Günter. Yes, the colonizers and missionaries came here with Bibles, and as we closed our eyes to pray, they stole our land. The problem with people is they confuse the colonizer's greedy mishandling of religion with God. It's people who commit evil acts, not God."

"Yeah, I know what Jomo Kenyatta said. I stand where I stand," I say.

"Well, may God protect you."

Silence ensues for several minutes, although we're not mad at each other.

"Eish, wena," she says, breaking the quiet after collecting metal clips from her cupboard to section off my hair and clip the locs into place.

I give her a look, wondering what's up with her today. She's been adding gibberish, incoherent words to her sentences. I don't want to call attention to that until she's finished my hair, in case it triggers her bad mood, and she ends up leaving me with an unfinished head.

She tugs the comb at the ends of my hair before working her way from the roots, then flips her hand to comb-coil it. "I'll use a crochet tool to refine the structure of your dreadlocks next time if you want."

The process takes two more hours as she continues locking the rest of my hair. Miriam, the singer's voice, and the tune and lyrics weave into my hair into our skins into our voice as Ogone sings along in a foreign language.

We've done half my head when Ogone says, "I didn't know you spoke Seburu." She says it in a way that feels like

a test, and I don't know how to pass it. "I don't know of any school in Bots that teaches in Afrikaans. Where'd you learn it from?"

"What's that? Speak what?" I ask.

Eyebrow raised, she asks, "Seburu? Afrikaans?"

"I don't know Afrikaans," I say.

"Wa peka nare? Brah, come on. Ke go utlwile o bua Seburu le Miche when y'all's were arguing in the sunroom," Ogone says, and all I can make out is something about me, Miche, and Afrikaans and the sunroom.

"I really don't understand you," I tell her.

"Banyana, go on, pretend like you don't hear me," Ogone says. "You legit sounded Afrikaaner. For one second, I thought ne go na le leburu mo kitcheneng. Ooh!" she exclaims, "That's a cool idea for a story, no? Like, name it 'There's a Leburu in My Kitchen' as an ode to the film 'There's a Zulu on My Stoep.' But, I want my credit when you become famous, forstaan?"

I press the tips of my fingers to my temples trying to process this complicated conversation. "What's that thing you just did with your mouth?" I ask.

"Huh?"

"You've been making funny sounds."

"See yourself? Ja neh, re tla bona teng." Ogone laughs until tears spill from her eyes, not fully grasping that I don't understand what she finds funny. Even if this is her way of joking, there's no sense to her words.

It's like her mouth is chewing something and she's trying to pass words around it. She continues narrating a story to me in between laughs, and I can't understand her.

"Okay, honestly, what language are you speaking?" I ask.

She lowers her head closer to my face, presses her long nails tightly to my chin, turning my head to her. "You're joking, right?"

"I can't tell where it's from, why?"

"Bitch, it's Setswana."

I am Michele Visser, signing off. Thank you for listening to What Happened to Ana? *If you enjoyed this episode, please share, subscribe, and leave a review. We are a small two-person team, my assistant and I, and every like and subscription goes a long way. See you next week, Crimies!*

[theme music]

♡7,013 ☐143 ≮601

@Tebogo_1934

For real, like how do you expect nothing to go wrong if you're a party whore. These guys clearly had problems with alcohol. They need God in their lives.

@JuliusH_L

Weird stuff is going on, but my money is on Miche, I don't trust her. Another thought: what if Bessie and Anaya ran away and eloped and that's why they're missing? Team Anessie!

@Thabiso_jamaan

This is how they attacked our identity, forcing foreign languages into mouths, chemicals into our hair because we weren't the beauty standard then demonizing our traditional spirituality and Anaya went through all that in one night shem skepsel yoh!

@NHBots

African women are born with beautiful natural crowns! Rock it, sis.

@KeletsoMokgalagadi

It's no surprise, most of today's generation can't even speak their native language. Ba choma sekgoa fela—hae ba lapisa gore!

@StefanieWilis

This story is amazing! I love, love it! I can't wait for another episode to drop! I went to Africa on a mission trip and what Ogone says is true, this happens in their culture.

Add your comment:

"*The existence of many African languages in one nation makes some writers' mother-tongues the languages of a very small minority. Ethnically-based political strife makes other writers' mother-tongues the languages of the oppressor. And indeed many African governments do not have the political courage to resolve the question of indigenous languages and instead promote the assumed neutrality of English, French, or Portuguese in the name of national unity, which often does not exist in any case. Forces of such governments have often been quick to brand writers who have written in their mother-tongues as 'tribal' and 'anti-national unity' . . . Some writers have pointed out that they have a handicap in using their mother-tongues, because they have become alienated from their own ethnic roots.*"

Penina Muhando Mlama,
"Creating in the Mother-Tongue:
The Challenges to the African Writer Today"

WHAT HAPPENED TO ANA?

112:21:22:03

BEFORE I DIE

Episode 5

Bolotsana • Anaya

Welcome back, Crimies. I am Michele Visser, host of What Happened to Ana?

In our last episode, things escalated between Anaya and me. She was behaving quite strange to me, and I, thinking it a joke, played along. In retrospect, I experienced strange things in the house that affected how we all interacted with each other. It's almost as if we weren't truly ourselves. The next few days we hunkered down to prepare for our pitches and work on our Günter manuscripts—we weren't going to have another morning run-in with Katja.

This is Anaya Sebeya's story . . .

[upbeat music]

The spots of Miche's whiteness have faded from my legs. I've been blatantly avoiding her since our last altercation, and she walks around with a sports bra, taunting me with my skin color on her neck. No one else has noticed, stuck in their

nooks and devices, typing away, determined to win this prize. I don't bring it up.

The only thing I can do is dig so far back into history to cling to myself the parts that are not lost. I drive to Iziko Museums of South Africa, hoping that artwork and exhibitions could serve as writing prompts. I find humanoid sculptures with animal heads. I'm stunned by Mary Sibande's *The Reign* of a night-black sculpture of a woman in a Victorian dress, hoisting a stallion. But the immensity of the history weighs heavily on my heart, and I drag myself back out into the blinding daylight.

When I return home, my afternoon of mindless writing in the living room is filled with the views of the fog of white-frothed clouds skimming the tops of Table Mountain. Instead of writing, I stare through windows at the endless shimmering turquoise blue of the ocean, wafting in a cold breeze against me. When I try to write, the words I'm looking for are not there. It's like there's no signal to a part of me that used to help me conceive ideas and write dialogue and characters. It's worse than writer's block—something has been severed from me.

I hunt through my discarded and unfinished stories, trying to hitchhike on interesting sentences that I can use to build my Günter manuscript and pitch. I stare at the blank page, hands poised on my keyboard, but nothing comes. Miche's in the sunroom, encroaching on me with sounds of her relentless speed-typing on her Mac. She makes frequent glances to her unfinished artwork on her canvas. I crane my neck to steal a glance, and when she scrolls up, it's like thousands of pages.

I grab a large straw hat, my laptop, a book, and head outside, across the pavement bordered by a cave of wild jasmine and cape chestnuts, drooping flowers and scents of musk and honey that brush the tips of my shoulders. I pause, embalmed by this perfumed world and stunned by this new life I'm living. I halfheartedly remind myself that I should capitalize on the aesthetics of this house by being active on my social media, posting glamorous pictures, at least.

In the gardens, I see Ogone under a parasol, sitting by the poolside. I observe the pile of books by her laptop: a mixture of theoretical textbooks, nonfiction, and memoirs by African authors. For some odd reason I find myself panicking, wondering if it's for her pitch. Beside Ogone is a Bible commentary she's studying, highlighting lines and transferring notes to her notebook, wiping a tear here and there.

"Are you okay?" I ask, sitting beside her on the lounge chair. Beyond us, the dark eyes of Huis lean heavily on us, its breath interfering with the spirit of us.

"I think I'm going home. I think I've screwed up my chances," she says, wiping her tears.

"What?" I ask. "We haven't even done the pitch yet. Why would you say that?"

"Katja threatened me during my private PR session."

"What?"

"I was a lesbian before," Ogone confesses, to my shock. "For a few years, and I was atheist. I went through a lot of stuff, but He was always there with me, eventually delivered me from it. I don't talk much about it. God showed me visions. He's shown me things, Anaya, like the night of the mix-and-match, and it's only when you experience Him that you understand."

"Oh," I say, bringing my knees to my chest. I'm confused on how this is connected to Günter, but such sentiments aren't unusual to me. I've relatives who think queerness is a sin. To each their own god, I suppose. "I didn't know that about you."

"That's because the minute I talk about my faith and my personal experiences, people misconstrue my words." I remember the rumors that Ogone was a religious fanatic. They don't seem to matter now that she's my friend. She blows her nose into a tissue.

"I still don't understand how this is connected to Günter and why she'd disqualify you for your past," I say.

"I'm telling you, everything I'm saying to you, Katja said to me whilst reading my pages," she says.

Panic shoots up my spine. "You have sample pages written already?"

"Just about twenty pages, but Katja didn't really like my character's journey or what was being said about traditional spirituality. My character had a traumatic upbringing that exposed her to quite some perverted things, causing spiritual warfare on her sexuality that is apparently a generational pattern of the women in her family, as a curse of some sort. Katja didn't like the 'controversial nature' of it."

I exhale a deep breath, suddenly not worried about her as my competition. She's doing a good enough job of destroying her chances at winning. "You're not seriously writing that, are you?"

She buries her face in her hands. "She's instilling within me a spirit of fear that's affecting how I'm writing. I can't see clearly the way I used to. Katja thinks my writing will leave my readership divided, that there will be uncharitable

interpretations of my sentiments in the US that will affect the critical reception of anything I write. So if I don't give into her standards, she said she will 'expose' me." She blows out hot air in frustration, her hands trembling.

I am surprised at the toll this has taken on her. A tiny of part of me revels in the idea of that. If Ogone's gone, there will only be four people between me and the prize that would bring me financial stability, a successful career, literary stardom, perhaps even revive my parents' confidence in me and our relationship.

"But we're not American," I say. "Things are different here."

"But *we* are trying to get published internationally, so it affects us. If Katja reveals my past in the ingenuine way that she will, it won't reflect my complex experience and only depict me as this hater, when I'm not, and that could be detrimental to my literary career. I wish I had someone who knows what it's like to be in my shoes, to help me navigate the tricky messaging while being true to myself. What world is it that we should be scared into silence, just because a few don't believe what you believe?"

I've never seen Ogone this anxious before. Even if she's not eliminated, I pray that this fear terrorizes her and affects the quality of her writing so she loses the Günter Prize. One less person to worry about.

"You've seen what they've done with other authors. All I've done is compromise myself by fighting with Katja—she definitely has more power than Anouk and Grace, and I'm scared she'll have me eliminated." More tears crawl down Ogone's face. "I don't hate queer people. They deserve their rights just the same as I deserve to follow God freely. I just want to write and live and worship—that's my oxygen."

"I can't see how Katja can threaten you with that. You're overthinking it," I say, leaning back into my lounge chair.

She trembles, more tears falling from her face. "You can get cancelled regardless of how respectful you are in your views. I would understand that kind of reaction if I was being violent, but I'm not."

"Words have consequences, Ogone, you should know that."

I brush the sides of my arms, feeling cold and lonely. "So, what, are you going to give in, then?"

"No. 'The fear of mankind is a snare, but the one who trusts in the Lord is protected,'" Ogone says, the verse turning her calm and reassured. "I'll find other ways to make my writing attractive to them and send *my* message across."

Damn it. I chew on my nail nervously. I'm ashamed to admit it, even to myself, but I liked the tension between her and Katja. It made me feel safe, made Ogone feel less of a competition. If she's not going to change her stance, then what does she have up her sleeve that she won't disclose?

I steal a glance at her laptop, but she has one of those privacy screen filters on it. Everyone has been working on the project secretly, and not knowing is making me anxious.

My phone beeps, a last-minute calendar invite from Katja for an impromptu video conference call, just as Bessie strolls through the garden.

"Katja wants a meeting with us," Bessie says, sitting beside us. She nudges Ogone. "Fam, are you still shaken over Katja?"

Ogone just nods and dabs a tissue to her face, composing herself.

Once she's checked her makeup in the camera, Ogone connects to the video conference with her laptop, and we

lean forward to appear in view. The call reveals the other fellows in the living room. My heart starts racing, anxious about what new curveball Katja will throw at us. Within seconds, Katja fills up the screen. I'm struggling to figure out how I feel about what she did to Ogone.

"Good morning, Günter girls. I have some bad news," she says against a backdrop of a pastel wall and bright sunlight. "You've probably noticed that one of you is absent in the house. Ruvimbo has withdrawn from the residency with immediate effect. That leaves only five of you."

I stare at the others, realizing we're one short. I've been so focused that I didn't realize Ruvimbo wasn't in Huis.

"Did she give any reasons why?" Ogone asks.

"The pressure got to her, and she got cold feet," Katja says curtly.

"That covers the elimination then, right?" Nilza asks from her small window on-screen, a flash of excitement on her face.

Katja peers through narrowed eyes. "There'll still be an elimination. Good luck, girls." The screen goes black abruptly, leaving me in sudden shock.

Nilza stretches her arms, yawning. "Well, that was odd." Her screen goes black too.

"When did she even leave?" I ask as Ogone exits the call. Everyone shrugs their shoulders.

Bessie draws her feet onto the lounge chair, hugging her knees. "With Ruvimbo leaving, it's got me thinking about the Midnight Mix and Match night again. I can't shake off how weird it got. Do you think she left because of that?"

"But why not leave the morning after? Why wait over a week to leave?" I ask.

Bessie shrugs. "I got so drunk, I think I was hallucinating. Maybe it's the drinking and drugs that turned her off."

"Drugs?" Ogone asks, perturbed. "You need to stop saying that."

"Why, then, was everything so weird?" Bessie says. "I don't know if Ruvimbo willingly left or if she was disqualified and Günter is covering some lie."

"Whatever it is, it's shaken me up," I say.

"Me too," Ogone adds. "Since then, I've been cleansing with my salts and started my fast."

"Wena, mara, cleansing what now?" Bessie asks.

"Ah-eh, mma, ntlogele," Ogone says, frustrated, "any time you come into a new place, you have to bless it and take authority over it. I had a spiritual attack, and I'm dealing with it before whatever they handed me in the dream starts cursing me."

I don't believe that any harm will come to me, or that to avoid it, all I have to do is fast, pray, and cleanse. I'm not as religious as Ogone. Also I've never seen a Christian like her twerk, chain-smoke weed, and go through vodka like a tank without passing out.

"The body is like the protective wall and boundary of your spirit. When the body shuts down, prayer functions as a protective order for your spirit," Ogone says.

"Just prayer?" I ask, incredulous. "It can't be that easy now."

Ogone claps her hands in a way that says I possess stupidity. "You think prayer and faith are easy, huh? When you enter a new territory or a new house, you don't know what history it has. Sebeteledi is a non-consensual invasion of the body, finish and klaar, regardless of whether the assault is a person or a demon or an evil racist history. Tell me, if you

were to report the allegations and accounts you experienced here, what law enforcement will take you seriously? With what evidence? Witchcraft is the loophole, portal, for such evil agendas."

Bessie's gaze is distant. She's not here with us, and I see a glimpse of history that she won't reveal.

"Since the Midnight Mix and Match, I've been struggling to understand and speak Setswana," I say.

"Girl, what do you mean?" Bessie asks, eyebrows knit.

"It's just gibberish to me," I say, then realize how rude and, ironically, racist that is of me. "I mean, the words sound incoherent, and I feel no connection or history to them. And I didn't know I was speaking Afrikaans until you told me that day."

"Wait, wena fam, you can speak Afrikaans?" Bessie says, laughing.

"Hae, bathong, Bessie, ema pele tlhe." Ogone has the audacity to shut Bessie up, who looks very disgruntled and offended. "Anaya, some things can be cleared with fasting and prayer, but like you said, you don't believe in anything. I mean, you could go to a doctor, but to them it won't make sense to have lost fluency in one language for another overnight." Then she raises her shoulders in a shrug. "But you picked my white salt the other night so maybe that will help you. I was unconscious, but I still saw you."

"Why are you so unconcerned?" I ask.

"This world is full of spiritual warfare. There's nowhere to flee unless you cover yourself with the armour of God."

But I've never experienced anything like this before coming to Huis.

"Still, though, how can you not be worried?" I ask.

“A spirit in the dream told me to not worry and keep faithful,” she says, eyes averted.

“And you believe what your dreams say?” I ask, panicked. “There’s no truth to dreams.”

“My dreams tend to reveal things to me. It was the same with my grandmother. She had a dream that foretold someone in the family would poison her. And she followed the crumbs of her dreams to that person so she could protect herself. Mmemogolo said that we could lock our doors and close our windows as tight as we wanted but unless we were a child of God, these evil things might possess us,” Ogone says.

I nod, not really listening. I’m distantly thinking of our earlier conversation and my writing. I flip open my laptop, in need to stay ahead of the game. Something about our conversation has opened the door of an idea. Hunchbacked, I go over every sentence, erase every Setswana word because I can no longer understand Setswana; it looks so foreign to this body of mine. Every native word I murder for an English word, anglicizing everything about me. I start writing poems, with the gaps of my lost language, without having to stick to structure of prose, because nothing makes sense. I wet these pages with tears as I erase every part of me. Will an MRI scan provide a crime scene, evidence of the part of my brain, my body, that has been removed in these nightmares?

Maybe I should be writing about what’s happening to me. It feels real, but I know a publisher will call my experiences speculative fiction, surrealism, magical realism. All this horror I’m living is not real to them, is magic to them.

Bessie lights a cigarette and picks up a book from my lap, *Black and Female* by Tsitsi Dangarembga. She fingers the millions of sticky notes as Ogone stares at her laptop.

We stay like that, silently typing. We steam in our thoughts, in silence unable to lift the weight of this gloom. The cold weather entreats us to find warmth and safety. As the sky slowly darkens, I become hyperaware of the terror that dwells in the night, creeping into our slumber. How do I fight something that is not a man I can see but comes in my nightmares? When I look up at the others, the mirror in the garden gleams gloom.

My reflection is not of us. It's of a woman, chiskop cut, thick eyebrows, irises screaming fear. Pointing at me, telling me to leave. *I tried to save you. Leave*, she mouths, *Ntlo e sule*. There is a bald woman stuck in the mirror. The fumes from Bessie's cigarette shadow my mind, my thoughts. I stare at the sky, a deep grey. When I raise my finger to point, to show the others, she is gone.

I am Michele Visser, signing off. Thank you for listening to What Happened to Ana? *If you enjoyed this episode, please share, subscribe, and leave a review. We are a small two-person team, my assistant and I, and every like and subscription goes a long way. See you next week, Crimies!*

[theme music]

♡9,088 ☐121 ≪3,240

@EmmaHen

Such a smart girl Ogone is. Even the africans themselves know how perverted it is to be against nature

> **@MiriamChioma:** "And you shall love the Lord your God with all your heart, with all your soul, with all your mind, and with all your

strength.' This is the first commandment. And the second, like it, is this: 'You shall love your neighbor as yourself.'"

@KaoneTau

Wow, some friendships can really derail you in life, yet wena foo you're thinking they have your best interests at heart. That was so vile of Anaya to think like that of her friend who was speaking to her vulnerably, kante Anaya ene o tshwere thipa ka fa eish!

@PalesaDikobe

I'm an African Christian and queer, some religious spaces have embraced me. There is a space for us in religion no matter what they say!

@MysteryTales

anyone notice the chiskop woman who keeps showing up, how weird is that?

@MumbiNjuguna

I stand with Ogone. Your writing, honesty and journey in faith helped me see the ways of my sin and repent and seek God. I'm a born again Christian. God bless you sis, keep speaking the truth.

@CarolineMoore

I implore everyone to contact @OgoneMolefhe's publisher @HorsestreetPublishers, agent @ClaireMilburn and these universities @SouthLondonUniversity, @MetropolitanCollege, @DerbyCollege and organisations where she studies and holds speaking engagements to drop her—we have to hold her accountable. Those who live in London here's her current address: ████████████████████. It is opinions like hers that shape policies and harm people, and we can't stand back and watch …

@IanRiley_4389: otw to chop her arms and breasts and her family to pieces.

@ChrisWilson
I always get new books to add to my TBR from this podcast! Thank you Miche for uplifting African literature!

Add your comment:

Yellow bones—the insidious casualness with which it is bandied about. As if, by dint of being catchy and trendy and pervasive, it has been expunged of its divisive, destructive and dehumanising past. As if the term hangs suspended, disconnected, from an ugly, painful history. As if 'yellow bones' is not implicated in the daily humiliations and assaults on the self-esteem of millions of black women. As if it does not resonate with decades of institutional violence inflicted on women who did not 'make the colour grade'; as if it was not a perverted form of gender-based violence perpetrated against millions of women for generations."

Gail Smith,
"We need to talk about yellow-bones"

WHAT HAPPENED TO ANA?

WHAT HAPPENED TO ANA?

106:18:20:19

BEFORE I DIE

Episode 6

Sight • Anaya

Welcome back, Crimies. I am Michele Visser, host of What Happened to Ana?

Due to abusive language, death threats, and spamming of hate speech, the comment section is now disabled. I do not make this decision lightly. Listen to Anaya's story and draw your own conclusions.

This is Anaya Sebeya's story . . .

[upbeat music]

A sniffling sound like that of an animal startles me from my sleep. I sit up, stare ahead. There's something crouched in the corner of my bedroom. It's too dark to see. I swallow, want to scream, but any movement might trigger it to attack me.

Bessie and I had come back to my room to chill for a while—we'd fallen asleep in my bedroom afraid of the night heaving its weight alone on us. Under the covers, I slowly

reach to my side to shake Bessie awake. When she doesn't shift, my fingers dig into her softness. She won't wake. The huddle of darkness in the corner continues growing darker and darker as if sucking in all of night. I want to run to the door to switch on the light, but it's right next to the thing. To walk through that distance of darkness—no, I can't. I pat Bessie. She does not wake. I can't let my voice get its attention. I pinch Bessie hard.

She uncoils. Stabs me. The pain so unnatural, so immense, dislodges a scream from my throat. Blood pools on the bed and in my hands.

Sheer reflex bolts me toward the door, and I trip over the crouched thing. Fall over. My mouth yawns open, a silent scream. Hot urine wets my thighs as the thing stands, towers over me, reaches above me—I'm going to die—flicks the lights on.

I shake with cold, bright light pouring into my eyes. "B-B-Bessie?" I stammer.

"What?" she asks, bewildered, standing in a puddle of my urine.

Then who was in bed with me? My face is cold, my neck is tight with pain as I turn to see what I was lying next to. The light shies away. A shadow divides us from the grunting noises on the bed. The lights dim shut. A scuttling of nails across floorboards. Cold steel clenches my legs, pulls, pulls, pulls, as the darkness drinks all of the light.

Bessie trembles, backs up against the wall.

"Bessie, help, please," I cry, as the strange animal drags me across the room.

Bessie hugs her arms, eyes wide, teary, slumps to the ground in fear, shaking her head.

"Bessie," I shout. I scrape my nails across the floor, grabbing for purchase of something, grab at the legs of the bed—the dragging continues. The cold grip tightens around my ankles.

Finally, Bessie walks toward me. "We lost one fellow. Perhaps losing another might make the competition easier," she says in a deep, hoarse voice, unlike her, and pushes me toward the hole in the wall, shuttling me and my scream into it. My skin leaves my bones.

I'm dispensed onto a field of sand and veld. I don't turn to watch the fleeing, galloping feet of the thing that stole me away. Yellow dust floats in its trail. Time wilts. Behind me, windows—no, mirrors—reflecting the glare of some type of nowhere sun. It's hectares and hectares of fields full of the sharp blades of mirrors floating in slow pivots at my waist level, tall as man, wide as the stretch of my arms. This grave of floating mirrors continues on, a million of them. No foundation, no wall to hold them in place, just pure air, gravity its hand.

I glance into their surfaces, looking into bedrooms and homes, women sleeping, a married couple having dinner, families lounging in living rooms, people working in home offices, a man weightlifting in his home's gym. The glass is of a rippled surface. I stroke it. Nothing becomes. I step back, facing fields and a clear sky. The area looks like Karoo, like Kgalagadi—desertlike and dry veld. Karoo, Kgalagadi: the land of thirst.

In the middle of the veld, the bald woman stands still, the swaying grassland up to her shoulders. The colors of the

baked earth, the soft blue expanse of the sky, and the grey of the deformed mountains begin to seep into her body. She's wearing old-fashioned attire, points to the west where the sun sinks into a mirage of blood-red skies. In its foreground stands a majestic farmhouse of a Cape Dutch style, but older and less fancy.

Ntlo e sule, her words, point to the farmhouse.

I glance back at the house. It's as if a guillotine has sliced the front of the house, such that I see a section of its several floors, its innards exposed. Women hanging from the ceilings, one scuttling out from a window, down the façade, women on different levels imprisoned in repeated acts of domesticity, the visuals on a loop, the echoes of a ticking clock, a hammer strike, water dripping, someone moaning, someone purging, someone giggling, furniture parts made of limbs, the wood of walls made of skin, eyes for buttons and knobs.

I weave through the Grave of Mirrors. Peer into homes, hotels, offices, ateliers—and Huis. Ogone on her knees praying. Miche in front of her mirror with large, hooped earrings and laying her edges. Bessie, in the bathroom, splashing something from a tiny bottle onto the walls, onto the floor, onto the ceiling, the air swelling with its perfume, the odor rotting the innocence of the interior. I press my palm against the surface of the floating mirror, but it's scalding hot, and I jump back.

The landscape gradually dissolves into dark, draining of sunlight. If I don't do anything, the abyss of dark will swallow me whole. I run, but the mirrors have sharp sides that slick my skin. I'm clueless of how to return.

The scenery is weeping colors. The woman stares at me.

"What do you want from me?" I scream. "Get me out!"

The scream seems to enter her body with a jolt. She spins, and the air is a slow wind around her. I surge forward. I want to trap her and interrogate her, make her show me how to leave this place. My madness clamors for her, but the air is swift as sea, a thick medium I push through. I leap forward, throwing my entire body, momentum guided by all the energy I can muster. I'm a bullet. My bones click from the unnatural stretch when I reach out for her wavering dress with my hand. She smiles, and in a hoarse voice, says, "Thank you for touching me again. I accept your consent. I have limited time. I want you to be my voice. Our voice."

"Our?" I try to let go of the fabric, but it's clinging to me too.

"There are many of us here. You will meet them soon. Our eyes glaze the windows of Huis—we were watching you as you pitched your mentors, and the project you're tinkering with matched our goal." She pauses, watching the information settle in me with dread as I remember the weight of being watched that evening on stage beyond the eyes of the invited guests.

The bald woman circles me. "We are better than mentors; we are vessels of history, and we can offer you more than an expert editor: hands-on guidance to create a masterpiece."

"Wait, what do you mean?" I ask, in a panicked breath.

"I can guarantee you inspiration that will ignite your writing process. If you want to rise above the competition, I extend to you our offer: I will help you, and in helping you, it helps us. If you agree, follow these instructions upon your return: fill the bathtub with water—no salt—submerge yourself. Repeat these words into the water: 'I submit, Yanano, I am open, come.' Then we will pour into you our gift," She looks

up at a waning sun. "I've run out of time. Your flesh is waking up; your spirit will leave me now."

The fabric of her dress is thick in my hand—I feel her, thick as life, in my own hand; she is real. She. Is. Real. Her nails slash a deep wound into my palm. The pain flows like lava.

"Blood has been shed. The ritual has begun," she whispers.

The edge of her dress is a wing in the night sky. I fall, drop into darkness, voices surrounding me in worry. My left hand pours out thick globules of blood. I'm encased in a funeral type of darkness, sealed into a coffin. She buried me. But my back is hunched against something hard and dank. My nails scrape against a coarse texture, sharp splinters digging into my nailbeds. Wood. Wood opposite me. I kick and kick. Hear voices. Splays of light storm through the wood slats, sneezing dust. My vision is obscured by dark flimsy things—my clothes. I'm in the space behind my wardrobe.

"Anaya?" Ogone shouts. "Bathong, where are you?"

"I'm in here," I shout, banging against the wood slats.

"What the—" Ogone pushes aside the curtain of my clothes, peeps close into the slats, can't see much into the dark, into the dust.

"Please get me out of here," I cry.

"An axe," Ogone calls.

"It's in the basement," Nilza says, disappearing. Soon she returns with the red-handled axe.

Ogone grips it, traces her hand along the wall as if her fingers can read it. "Step back. You have room in there to move back, right?"

"To the side maybe. The space runs the length of my wardrobe," I say.

"Good, move to your right, which is my left, okay. I'll break down the wall on this side," she says, tapping on the wall to my left. I crawl to my far right and squeeze my knees together, my hands sticky with blood.

I close my eyes tight and dig my face into my knees. The crack of the axe shudders into my dark prison. The axe hacks, hacks, hacks, births me into the light. Hands slither around me, drag me out onto my bedroom floor, splay me into the warm pool of light.

I am Michele Visser, signing off. Thank you for listening to What Happened to Ana? *If you enjoyed this episode, please share, subscribe, and leave a review. We are a small two-person team, my assistant and I, and every like and subscription goes a long way. See you next week, Crimies!*

[theme music]

♡12,569 ≺5,020

RANEWA

MY EYES UNSEALED THEMSELVES FROM DARKNESS TO REVEAL A ceiling tacked with stars. I was lost—identity, locality, sense. Then, recognition. My ceiling. My room. Mama was sleeping or somewhere negotiating with God. I could tell by the stillness of the house, the quiet intrusion of sunlight through the curtains. Anaya was with me in my ears. She hadn't sounded like herself in those episodes. I'd never known her to be that selfish.

I had fallen asleep while going through Anaya's notes. It seems like she had been using a Setswana dictionary to try to piece together our language. She'd even highlighted the words in her old writing, scribbling question marks around them. I wondered how long it took her to archive this, and I imagined how lonely she must have felt.

I had pieced together that Anaya had been researching witchcraft and mythology in Botswana, and specifically dithokolosi—though it seemed the only way she knew that word is because it was in her work-in-progress. She wrote down her frustrations with the process. Even though our elders had a wealth of knowledge about Setswana myths and folklore, there was not much information written down or accessible anywhere.

She must have been looking into something related to the attacks she had been enduring in Huis. One of her notebooks had a scribbled note on the house that unsettled me:

Huis is awake
purged her residents
grew bulimic to ward off new tenants:
cracking her foundation
tilting her ceiling like a bad mouth,
wobbling her stairs
—spread her guts in newsprint:
Boer wife and husband murdered, Franschhoek
farmhouse up for auction

I rubbed my eyes. Something was strange about that house, and I needed to get in to find out. I decided to book a flight to Cape Town.

My braids were old and getting in the way, but I didn't have the energy for Afro-grooming, especially not if I was going to be in Cape Town for a while. I took Papa's shaver, skimmed it across my skull so that it left a smooth buzz-cut surface. My braids lay around my feet like tangled snakes.

I stared at myself in all the mirrors, not recognizing myself anymore.

Then, I told my parents I was heading to Cape Town. Anaya and I grew up with a lifestyle of secrets that created loopholes for bad things to sweep in, but our parents have changed. I wish it hadn't taken Anaya's loss for my parents to learn how to love us.

And so although they were uncomfortable with me living in a place that had robbed them of their first daughter, they just asked what I needed. *This* I preferred.

My luggage contained files of research.

My mind contained encyclopedic knowledge of the case. Over the past year, I had wallpapered my bedroom with a collage of media reports, findings, witness accounts with certain paragraphs highlighted, and profiles of every suspect I had. I knew it all by heart, but I would take it with me anyway. I tore them all down, leaving bits and pieces of Bostik and masking tape scarring the white wall with dirt.

On the day of my flight, I took a cab to the Sir Seretse Khama International Airport. Through the windows, I watched the empty stretch of fields from the agricultural school elongate to the urban road separated by a fence. I saw the distant skinny birches like pencil sketches etched into the sky background, growing hazy into the watery blue above. My home, places where I saw my missing sister. Soon the malls appeared—one-story or two-story strips of grey with chunks of parking, glittering beneath the charring sun. After some frustrating time through the noon traffic, the January sun rose, melting through the cirrus clouds into bands of red and orange, like the sky was burning.

Two hours later, the plane flew over the craggy lower peaks of a mountain, cliffy and chalky, until they plateaued to form Table Mountain. The rest of Cape Town was a glittering sprawl of urban life with specks of white constructions and multicolored roofs of grid-lined suburban homes, and larger feature buildings, and the congested slums sunbathed beneath the pale, blue sky. The ocean

hogged around the settlements. Bustling streets lined with high-risers and roads sloped up to the mountainside where villas slumbered.

One hour later, after the Cape Town traffic, I arrived at the Central Police Station.

I edged toward the counter, where a policemen raised his head from his desktop.

"I'm here to see Olivia Skommere," I said. "She's the investigator in charge of my sister's missing person's case."

"Skommere's still in interrogation. Please have a seat to join the rest." He gestured.

"The rest of . . . ?" I turned around. Ogone. She was with her fiancé, Adebowale, who had his arm wrapped around her. "I'm Anaya's sister," I repeated. "I have a critical piece of new evidence. I talked to Skommere about this."

"Even so, please sit; the investigator will be with you shortly," he said.

Strange. It was traumatic enough thinking about the people considered as suspects, but to be sat next to them . . . I walked toward the seats and sat beside Ogone, and without as much a greeting, I said coldly, "I thought you were in London." When the Günter residency ended, Ogone packed up her life, declined every media invitation, ignored all my calls, and relocated to London, where she resumed her masters, fast-tracked to PhD.

"They want to verify some stuff that Miche leaked in her podcast," Ogone replied, eyeing the doors leading to the private offices.

"Why didn't you tell me, at least, about the things that happened. Don't you owe Anaya that?"

She turned to face me, her weave a short bob, impeccable makeup, and the trace of fear and pain in her eyes. "Have you listened to the whole thing?"

I shook my head.

"Once you do, come at me correctly or don't come at all."

Surprised by her acerbic tone, I touched her shoulder, but she shrugged from my hold. "I want nothing to do with Huis," Ogone said. "I've left that time of my life behind me. Anaya understands."

Wait. Ogone referred to her in present tense. "Please," I pleaded, "if you know something about her whereabouts, ke a go rapela tlhe, tell me." She ignored me. The sun began to set, dripping subdued light through the windows, shaking darkness into our recesses. Desperate, I asked, "Why is everyone afraid of this house?"

Anaya's phone vibrated. Two more dim tracks, "Anaya | Submission" and "Anaya | Pitches," displayed themselves on the screen.

The door behind the police reception desk clicked open. A burly old man with a balding head stepped out. Beside him was Olivia Skommere, guiding a frantic girl out. Miche.

"But I've answered all your questions," she said, blowing her nose into a tissue. "I'm just confused."

I hurried toward her. Her silver-white hair was cropped close to her skull so that her eyes stood prominent in her face, a pale blue mixed with brown. She had bruised knuckles and dark bags under her eyes the size of thumbprints. She backed away, terrified.

"Ranewa," she said. "I didn't know you'd be here."

I leaned in so close to her face. The truth would eventually spill from her. "I know what you're hiding. I know what you did in Huis."

Her hand covered her mouth, eyes skittering about, until they focused on me, unwavering. "Do you know what your sister did?" She delivered it as if her deeds weighed the same evil measure as my sister's.

Skommere motioned to me, pushing Miche gently away from me to kill the tension between us.

"Ms. Sebeya, we're ready for you." As we walked, Skommere continued, "Everyone, thank you for coming at such an impromptu time. We'll be interrogating each one of you, much like the last time, throughout the coming days or weeks. I strongly advise you to not leave the city."

Good. They couldn't run away. That meant they were close to an arrest. For once, Skommere made me feel safe. I could see it. They were afraid.

Skommere guided me through a narrow hall. I remembered the times my family and I walked through here to her office, Mama weeping, Papa hard-faced and too overwhelmed to even hold his wife. I sewed myself together to be a blanket that covered her trauma. No one ever thought about me like I did of them.

But we continued walking, passing her office.

I stopped. "Where are we going?"

She paused in front of a door marked Interrogation.

"We have a few questions for you," she said, and pressed a switch.

The interrogation room was claustrophobic, with one chair and a desk. I'm sure a serial killer had sat in the same chair. The wall reflected me. It looked as if the weight and

flesh were sliced clean from my frame and only my bones hung my skin up.

Skommere joined an older man opposite me. The other officer steadied a video camera that pointed directly at my face, and I held my breath, as if the camera could expose every secret and lie I was hiding.

There's the issue around nationhood and belonging thwarted by continuing xenophobic attacks. One of the reasons that the wave of xenophobic violence in South Africa has been termed Afrophobia is that it is a class and race matter . . . Foreigners' who have had to face the worst of it are from African countries and reside in black townships. It's a tragedy, really. You know, people say, 'Money whitens.' . . . [but] many practitioners got so used to using the black body as a kind of cipher for all sorts of white phobias."

Nomusa Makhubu

Anaya | Submission

That morning we're woken up by Bessie and Miche fighting in the living room.

On my bed, flecked grey and white are strands of fur like scattered hay. Not a dog. Not a cat. But from the creature that dragged me into the wall last night, into a place where time is slow water.

I cannot be distracted. I flip the hair from the blankets, flapping it off the memories from last night and head downstairs.

Bessie's manuscript and pitch have been wiped from her cloud, hard drive, laptop, phone. Even her printed manuscript has disappeared. She's furious, on the edge of tears. She tries to pinpoint the criminal between all of us. Miche's backed up against the wall, face flushed because her art is ruined too, and Ogone's muttering defenses. Bessie eyes me suspiciously as I come down the stairs. I wonder if she thinks this is my revenge on her for what she did to me last night: sacrificing me to the creature instead of helping me. The memory of it recalls my anger, and though I've no idea who the culprit is, I want her to know how painful betrayal is. So I lower my hands, smirk, and say, "One less fellow, one less competitor, right?"

She shoves me hard. "You fucking bitch."

Every part of me devours Bessie's fury with glee. I want more, for her to be disqualified, for her to never write again. "If you can dish it, then you should eat it too," I add, smiling and walking around.

"Anaya, you can't possibly have done this, right?" Ogone stares at me with such dismay it makes me almost regret saying it, because we're meant to have prepared a concise summary of our Günter manuscript along with sample pages for the pitch event, and the thought of me sabotaging Bessie this close to the deadline—

"The pitch is in five fucking days. What the fuck am I going to do?" Bessie says, throwing her hands into the air.

"You're definitely not getting Katja," I say, laughing.

"Damn, does everyone have Katja on their list of preferred mentors?" Nilza asks.

Miche beelines to us as if to sniff us for deception. "If y'all have beef, keep it to yourselves. I did nothing to you guys!"

Around us I feel the heavy weight of Huis huffing, hot and ravenous.

"You, Nilza, and Ogone are the only ones whose work isn't ruined," Miche says.

"That doesn't make us criminals," Nilza retorts, folding her arms.

"And I was stuck behind a wall last night," I add, glowering at Bessie, who's fuming.

"*You've* been anxious about not knowing what we're writing, not knowing how to strategize against us. Is that why you made our work disappear?" Miche asks me, which knocks the breath out of me. I only thought that to myself a few days ago. I'm unable to formulate a response, wondering how she knew my thoughts.

"Without any work, it's a given that one of you will be eliminated," Nilza says.

Everyone eyes Nilza suspiciously.

Miche stands close, tapping Nilza's chest with her index finger at every enunciation: "No. Fucking. Way. I won't take this lying down. Don't undermine me."

Ogone just says "Mxm" and stomps away.

I glance at the painting that Miche revealed at the Midnight Mix and Match; it has claw-like marks, flaps of it hanging to the ground. The only drafts Bessie has are the lousy ones she emailed a friend. They'll both have to start from scratch.

My hands shake when I close the door to my bedroom. *That* was unlike me, yet I enjoyed feeling powerful over Bessie. If I can't trust myself, I can't trust them. Katja was right. It's not safe this close to the pitch event. From there on, I take my laptop everywhere with me—bathing, toilet, meetings—and I use a VPN for research. My writer's block is worse than ever, but at least I have backups that no one can possibly know about. I add tiny surveillance cameras in my bedroom in every hidden crevice to record everything. If anything goes wrong, at least I'll have evidence. I'm a good writer, but good doesn't cut it if I'm with the crème de la crème of writers. I'm the odd one out. I need edge. I have to leave no chance of their rise.

That woman with the shaved head said that helping me helps them—is that all it will cost me to break through this writing block? People used to go to dingaka tsa Setswana for assistance in political campaigns, prosperity or business dealings. And I've bypassed the middleman straight to the spiritual realm.

I won't think longer about it, else I'll get cold feet. I hastily fill the bathtub with water. As I submerge myself, I think of my bloodshed, consent, and now incantations from my lips and the sight of water: "I submit myself to your help, Yanano. I am open, come."

A sleep enfolds me. In sleep there is truth; reality is denser than ours. Huis is dark. There is a darkness in Huis. A living, breathing darkness that surrounds us, contracting and expanding. The senile house's pipes groan in syncopated voices, its breath covered in dust and steam. Its heartbeat pulsates through passages. Its hand coils around my body, buoyant with me.

White noise sparks into being. I stand in a room of night. White noise batters my ears until my senses adjust to the dark. I stand in a hallway of Huis, a thought tells me, a different Huis. A silence like that of before the sun wakes up. It reminds me of ko gae at my grandmother's home, before the noise of technology penetrated our lives, our homes. My language is with me in this realm. I feel whole again.

A paraffin lamp waits for me on the concrete floor. I reach for it, smell the fire of the matches that lit it up. Its metal body is warm in my hands. The lamp leads me forward through its flickering ambiance into staged rooms enshrouded in darkness.

A movement from within the room startles me, a bald woman forming out of the dark.

She has a thin lace trim on her tight bodice and long sleeves, the skirt flares out slightly toward the hem, three layers of white beads around her neck, wrists, and a lone bead hanging from her ears. Eyes downturned toward the ends

as well as the lips. Hair shaved, a layer of tufts of moriri o Setswana forming.

"We are pleased that you followed our instructions. You made it in, and now we've made it into you," she says. "You may call me Yanano, though sometimes I cannot remember my name because of the way they killed me. The Grave of Mirrors is at the front of this stead." Yanano, shrouded in cloth, walks toward me. "Huis is the spirit realm of the victims of history. It's why Huis is back here, brought us back, to confront one of them, a descendant of those evil people, the evil things they did. Those evildoers live in her blood. You can see it in the way she behaves, treats you all like little commodities."

"Who?" I ask. Immense guilt washes over me—what have I signed myself to? I didn't know. I *didn't* know. Ogone was right; maybe this was a bad idea.

"You will see history. Telling you brings you no understanding, but *experiencing it* does—it will help you write to *feel* our pain, our stories," she says. "House of Ghosts, huis die spook. The structure collects people, 'cause no one ever wants to leave."

All around the white house, darkness exists. Everything feels immeasurable.

"Are you truly okay with walking around blind, not knowing who we were before?" Yanano asks. "Are you okay with not knowing yourself that much?" Her gaze presses into my face, a disconcerting heat. "Do you know about the Anglo-Boer War? The Batswana-Boer War—Battle of Dimawe? The Difaqane Wars? Do you know what malata, makgalagadi are? Mafufunyana? Are you okay with maintaining this colonial amnesia?"

I avert her gaze, shame scalding me. "I don't know what those words mean."

"It's a shame you're so far away from your native tongue."

I stand back, weary, having never interrogated my thought process. All I've been doing my entire life is accepting this way of life as is.

She walks around me, hands knit across her abdomen, poised perfectly. "Our history was passed on from generation to generation. An elder passed the way of life to the parent who passed the way of life to the child. A person doesn't just carry the past of the generation before them, they carry the generations before that and before that. When none of these events are captured, then you lose all of your history when the holder of it dies. But that history can be restored in you," she says, "only if you submit yourself to us. If you allow yourself to be a conduit, you can resurrect our dead bodies from your blood—our generation and our predecessors—but it's not easy, no, it's not easy to enter the past, to submerge yourself in the pool of its wound and not get burned by its torment."

"At what sacrifice?" I ask, recalling the gruesome night of the Midnight Mix and Match and what this would cost me. Will it hurt?

Ignoring my question, Yanano says, "Mafufunyana was a local train they used in the '70s, when the men went to Reef, the mines for jobs. We have a girl here, who can connect us to that locale. Lelata, singular form of malata, means a slave—the Bakgalagadi endured such under the Bakwena."

I stare about the room and the old curtains. "What's the point of showing me, telling me, all of this?" I ask.

"Should there be a point to everything? You're a storyteller. Do you think your stories are authentic with this

omission?" The air suddenly grows cold, and Yanano pauses. "But time is not on our hands. Soon you will leave. Listen—you've slipped into a hole in history."

"Is this only happening to me?"

"No, it happens everywhere. Huis is both a terrible wound and an archive, of us and of that terrible, terrible time. Not many people know what happened to us African women and the genocide of tribes during the colonial wars." She spits to the side. "There are voices and stories that were unable to be preserved, documented, the silence is screaming in your present life. Writing revives the dead, it summons history!" A sheen of sweat appears on Yanano's face. She composes herself. "This is why structures like Huis are important, but terrible, oh, so terrible. *This* one," she says, arms wide, palms gazing up at the ceiling, "belonged to Meneer and his family. He grew up as a poor farmer, worked on many farms, eventually bought one, sold his Transvaal farm before heading here, to Bechuanaland—we were chased out from this land that he took into native reserves." She spits again, face disgruntled.

I stagger back from her as people suddenly flow into the room dressed in traditional attire, bodies poised in peace, eyes a dull gaze, sweeping in to form a circle around us. From behind them, sauntering through the hallway, is a ghostly white figure that moves so fast I think I imagined it.

"We are so glad to meet you," they whisper. Their voices flow out from their throats and other rooms, lit by candles.

"Hopefully you'll be better than Nosipho," a woman with braids to her knees says.

"Nosipho?" I ask.

"Merapelo, stop!" Yanano chides the woman, and I lose sight of her as she slips back into the crowd.

"Yes, yes, yes, we've been here before. Thrice. Günter stays in one place, but Huis migrates," they whisper, dizzying me with their movement. "But we trust you, Anaya." They keep handing me off from one to the other, their faces so close to mine:

"Violence is brewed in different parts of this land, the mines, the segregation. They had thoughts about our land, to use it as a fertile ground for the Cape to Cairo railway. It was unsuitable," one says.

"So they thought cattle ranches would do better here, with our land, with our earth. This settlement wanted to avoid the expansion of the Afrikaner-occupation Transvaal colony. You need to write about this," another says.

"Yes, you must write about this. This Huis came from Rhodesio. Huis, always on the move, a migrant house. The Huis you're living in doesn't look like it used to. No surprise, it's a Cape Dutch house now," another says.

"Those of the colonial regime and missionaries used to stay here, forcing their baptism and Christian names on us, distorting God for their agenda."

"Mxm, hae! They were so dirty, using the Bible for evil! They lacked fruit of the Spirit."

Their voices bicker with the clack of knitting needles, the slow steam from their teas.

"Huis is us, and we are Huis, her spirit," they say.

They keep referring to each other as Huis rather than the structure as Huis. I think I understand. Much like the flesh houses the spirit, Günter houses Huis—*them*.

The whirling of people deposits me back in front of Yanano as she says, "Huis is muti. A concoction of people's parts, herbs, and elsethings—a concoction of us. Huis keeps a graveside in her wardrobe, the basement, the hidden spaces

behind walls where people have lain for centuries. The deep pockets in her closets like dark mouths, the things you'll find there; her teeth are made of skeletons, death things. She has an open door/open mouth policy. Open a closet, you might not find clothes the second time. Look, did you see the bones? There they are! Skeletons cling to hangers," she says, in a singsong voice.

Her mouth stretches wider, a gaping wound. I feel nauseous.

"Please, I want to go home," I plead.

A sudden panic shadows Yanano's face. "She's coming," she says, looking out the window.

A white woman in a red coat floats through the yellow fields, smoke leaking from her fingers. The coat is like blood slipped from her body and stitched itself sinew by sinew, clot by clot, into a heavy coat. Her skin is as pale as the moon.

And just as I'm about to glimpse her face, desperately, the women clamor around me, obscuring this newcomer. Their hands in my mouth, down my throat, in my hair, around my legs—shouting, "We need to get out." These hands are like mine, strangling me as if trying to get out through me by getting into me. This black hand crosses into the border of my black body.

I submit myself to this hand that looks like me.

I submit myself to this violence that looks like me and enter into the Black. The hand that reaches around my throat, is Black like me, is soft like me, is terrified like me. I do nothing but submit myself to the hand, to the strangling, for I too am tired of breathing this air as this black, this black this black this black this black this black this black this black this black this black this black this black this black this black this black this

black this black: this site of a crime, archived in the blood in the lung in the mind—where is me amidst all this violence to ourselves?

This hand that wants to kill me touches me with the violence that once touched it.

There is violence in my blood. It is spilling out.

"Stop," Yanano shouts to the coven of women. "I know you're hungry for freedom, but now is not the time."

The spirits heed Yanano's command. Their breaths feel like hate, feel like anger, feel like hope.

With a sad, solemn expression, Yanano turns to me. "Why are you afraid of us? We only wanted to show you our wounds."

She pushes me past the group with the cold touch of history, saying, "Go now, go! Remember, leaving the doors open at night is a sign for the dead, welcoming them in.

"I hope this won't hurt you much," she says.

Yanano presses her hands, palms flat, against my chest. Then a loud explosion, shattering, seismic, tears apart every wall floor ceiling every fabric of them into a dark abyss. I'm catapulted through the dark mirrors of time. Speed and blazing wind rush through my form, fingers unable to grip hold of anything through this rush of black wind as my body shatters through never-ending darkness.

Anaya | Pitches

I land on the stairs of Huis. Startled. Arms flailing as I regain my balance and take note of the glass wall overlooking the Atlantic Ocean.

I am trying to run away from myself, from the house. It won't let me.

Ogone's shaking in Huis's bed, wanting to leave her body like a ragged dog evicting fleas from itself. A nightmare locks her body tight, refusing her her prayers, her white salt, her incantations.

Miche has a stone in her hand scraping at her arms, scraping the skin off. "The evil lies in our veins. We must bleed ourselves dry."

Bessie is somewhere in the house, talking to a daughter who is dead. I never imagined that she was a parent. I feel excited with this new information, and eager to capitalize on it, but that behavior feels unlike me, which scares me. I could use this information against them. No, better, this is evidence—Huis can give me access to secrets like she promised! It would cut down research by a huge margin. But Ogone would remind me there is a cost.

Miche suddenly appears before me, brings to my mouth sweet koeksisters dusted with icing sugar and desiccated

coconut. I shake my head no. "Eat, so Huis stops punishing us. It's Huis driving us mad to be bad to each other. See? I'm eating." She takes a bite. "Ogone will eat now, and so will you."

I shake my head no, backing away. No more sejeso, no more. I hug my knees. "I need to go home. I need to go home." Home: made of flesh and bone. Take me home. Take me back home.

The daylight touches Miche sharply. "It's no good," she whispers. "It's in the walls, the ceiling, the foundation. The house has already inhaled everything—us."

She swallows, holds on to the silence. "I haven't been able to sleep either. It's not safe to sleep in this house. Sleep has become this house's territory now. We should have left the first day—we were invincible then . . . stronger. The thing that's always sitting on top of us, lying beside us, trying to get into our bodies at night."

"You also?" I swallow. "What about what you did to me? In the kitchen, in my bedroom?"

Tears fall from Miche's eyes, sprinkle across the floor. "I was just so frightened, wasn't thinking. I let Huis sit in me. It needed my skin to do that to you. I thought . . . I don't know what I thought. No one tries to disobey Huis's spirit. I had to let it use my body. It's the only way I can survive. You have to understand."

Every time I cried, I received no comfort. Every time I spoke up, I received no comfort. Not from my family, not from the world, and not from myself. I never gave myself a moment to be weak, and this, what she says, what she's asking me now, to hold space for her . . .

"You bitch," I snarl.

"Whoever would listen to you, anyway?" Miche says coldly. "Muzzle yourself, 'cause your fear's leaking from your mouth."

She walks away. The door clicks into its frame after she's left, and loneliness settles around her absence, wrapping itself coldly around my frame.

An itch travels up my inner arm. Death. Could Bessie be right? I feel it in my eyeballs, my elbows, my chest—something is off. Moloi. Where is home? I ask.

Blood leaks down the sides of my face, cold and wretched with pain. Home is Botswana. Botswana is my body.

A door swings open, and an Ogone—not the Ogone tied in bed by sebeteledi on the other side of time's door but another Ogone stands from a world outside this one, and says, "Wake up! Pitches for the bitches today!" The reality from her world pours in like bright daylight. The boundaries have been broken, where before they were demarcated distinctly, and I would move from this realm to my reality, but now time is mixed up, is broken, and it's stirring a headache in my brain. It hurts to think whilst standing at the crossroads of times, a traffic jam of times.

"Pitches for the bitches, pitches for the bitches, pitches for the bitches," Ogone shouts jubilantly through Huis.

The darkness
holds my mouth open
the darkness
recites words from my bones:

"Bechuanaland is penetrated from every side, scarred at
Pont Drift where the river slices through it. In the freehold
farms of Tuli Block, a kgosi instructs his age regiment to

relocate the Babirwa families—the peoples the cattles—for the white settlers.

Resistance, resistance, resistance. *This is our land, how can you give it to them?* A gasp of flames, moans of cattle smoldering in the fires.

The night is creaking, the land is dying as its women and children are devoured. Feet stampede across its skin, a beating drum of fear of betrayal of despair as the Babirwa flee northwest northwest northwest to Bobonong; the sap of milk ebbs into the sky a moon, its horns point downward like a cup, which one tribe believes that it pours into the atmosphere disease and misfortune.

The moon, an omen, foretells their fate.

"In the stillness of morning, the air smells like smoke. Flames of dawn color the underbellies of clouds. White feet scorch the earth with their arrival seeking promise, seeking fortune on the burnt backs of the land. As a settler farm, Huis becomes kin of the Afrikaner and kin of the Englishman. Huis, the first wound of a displaced people arises. In other European reserves—Ghanzi farms, Molopo farms, Tati farms—more imitations of Huis are uprooted. Herds of game lull their tongues across the Limpopo River, a terrain fertile for shooting and hunting. Huis gazes on, horror within it, muti burning in its foundation—"

I say, vertigo overwhelming my body. I want to purge the sickness of all the times in my blood.

Hands clap. A shard of light. I raise my arms to block it. There's shooting and shouts and smoke before the scene materializes before me into stillness, organizing itself to the proper reality: a small intimate room, decked out with dots

of light, a table backed against one end where three heads, orbed in white, float in the backdrop next to two Black heads. Gary, Olivia, Langa, Anouk, Grace, and Katja.

My breaths are still coming fast as my sight adjusts to this calm scene. It's the pitch. I was performing my pitch.

"Ana," the voices say in astonishment, "what a brilliant, brilliant pitch! We can tell you worked hard on it. We love the idea of historical fiction infused with surrealism. Thank you for inviting us into your writing process. I like the notes of tribal conflicts between the Babirwa who lost their lands to the white settlers. Brilliant work."

I stare about me, stunned by the light that burns into me. It seems I was the last one to perform my pitch, as the rest of the fellows are invited back to the room.

"Now that we have heard your pitches, we have come to a unanimous decision on which author will be eliminated."

I swallow, tie my fingers into each other, stare down praying it's not my name that will escape their lips, but hoping I lose to be free.

"Nilza and Anaya, please step forward."

My heartbeat throbs loudly in my ears, and sweat pours down my face. My legs tremble as I step forward.

"Of the fellows, we have the strongest writer and the weakest writer. Of the two of you, one shows incredible promise," Grace says. "The other author has talent but disappointed the judges with lacklustre storytelling technique. Anaya—" My breaths rise heavily. I'm going home, and my parents will be right that I have no career in writing, that I have to give this up and enroll back in school— "the judges loved your work. Anaya, you're not going home. Nilza, we are sorry, but your journey ends here. We're excited to see where your

career takes you next, and remember, you will always have our support."

My heart drops back from my throat into its rightful place, and I almost collapse from the shock leaving my system as Nilza hugs us and leaves. Although they made their decisions this morning upon reading our pages, they're only informing us of our selection after our pitch performance. Every mentee is paired with their mentor in a blur. Grace for Ogone. Katja Günter for Miche, the darling princess who has her upcoming solo exhibition in Morocco. Olivia Bloom will mentor Bessie. Langa will teach seminars. Anouk comes up to me, smiling.

"I'm so glad I am your mentor," Anouk says. "We women we have to look out for each other." She's never talked like this to me before. "Anaya, I'm so excited about your manuscript and our partnership. I love the idea you're exploring about young African women navigating historical violence set in the 1800s. There's so much promise in your pages! You'll have notes from me soon." She bids me goodbye with a tight hug, her nails pinching into my shoulder. I force a stiff smile across my face and thank her, afraid to glance at Langa, feeling like I've lost something.

Choose your membership

Contributor

$1/month

JOIN

Thank you for your support – every amount goes a long way!

Witness

$5/month

JOIN

- Discord server access to Witness community
- Early access to podcast episodes
- Behind-the-scenes for our audio production and notes
- 10% discount on merch

Investigator

$15/month

JOIN

Everything included in Witness, plus:

- Access to old interrogation videos, articles, and Q&A that the team conducts with those close to the case, incl. Günter commentary
- Videos of Michele Visser's time in Günter and unexpected shots of Anaya's time in Günter

Recent posts by What Happened to Ana?

Hello, Crimies, as promised, I'm sharing my own interrogation video with the lead investigator on this case, Olivia Skommere. Some of you may have seen this already, as it was leaked, so we appreciate your continued subscription and support.

I do know that the other fellows felt uncomfortable with Skommere's way of interrogation. My comfort doesn't matter, because at the end of the day, the investigation team is trying their best to find Anaya. We need to offer them grace on how they go about it, even if it feels offensive to us. Press play to watch.

Investigator Subscribers-Only Access: Michele Visser Interrogation Video

Here you will find access to interrogation videos and links to the victims' social media pages as a bonus to your favorite episodes. Remember every little bit of information is vital to the case. Enjoy!

Michele Visser

Olivia Skommere: How was your relationship with the rest of the fellows in the house?

Michele Visser: It felt lonely for me. I was the only white person in the house. They always talked behind my back and looked at me strangely when I conducted my work in spaces throughout the house. It felt racist to me. And ja, I know, I'm the white chick, I'm supposed to be the racist one. I tried everything to be amicable, but they didn't want to associate with me. There was that one day, Anaya and I connected over our stories.

Olivia Skommere: On 20 December, you and the rest of the fellows disappeared from the winner's ceremony. It's come to

my attention that another fellow had supplied you all with marijuana. Where did you go?

Michele Visser: Ja, to be honest, Ogone supplied everyone with weed, and I don't know if she mixed in some other drugs. One minute we were taking photographs, then we were hallucinating. It gave us such a trip. I don't know, it felt like we traveled to another world, like astral travel. I know, it sounds crazy but that's the only way I can describe it. I felt betrayed—I thought I could trust Ogone, of all people. Anyway, I just remember waking up in the hospital, hearing that the others had disappeared.

Olivia Skommere: Thank you for the transparency. What did you observe of Bessie during your time with her in the house?

Michele Visser: Bessie was a sweetheart. She was chronically ill. Most times she was bedridden. I felt sympathetic toward her. She couldn't participate in most activities because of bouts of exhaustion. She told me that her medical team likened her condition to sickle cell disease or Lyme disease, but her test results weren't consistent with those diagnoses.

Olivia Skommere: Did this cause conflict with the rest of the group?

Michele Visser: At first, Anaya and Ogone looked after Bessie. But something happened between the three. Ogone and Anaya became close, hung out often, and Bessie expressed to me she felt like a third wheel. I felt sorry for her, looked after her whenever I could.

Upcoming Post: Interrogation Videos: Ogone Uetuu Molefhi

 Join to unlock

Culture > Books > **Global**

Günter Prize Under Fire

By Chisomo Mwale

The Günter Prize, a prestigious prize for African women in the literary community, is under fire following expositions released by their former employees citing distress, humiliation, and unpaid overtime that included working overnight and long hours on the weekend, a secret source reveals. All employees were Black and Brown, all classified as contractors. There are no people of color in senior level positions at the Günter Prize Foundation.

Further accusations call into question Günter's commitment to diverse stories: cleaners, interns, and other low-level employees report being interrogated heavily about their culture, which would then be used for other non-Günter projects to give them an "African spice." None received compensation.

Even within the Günter residency, racial tensions seem high. One source shared with our team a terse email exchange between one Günter founder, Anouk Rijks, and award-winning writer Langa Mangezi.

2:17 PM Anouk Rijks <██████████>

I love █████ material and there are ways we could make it accessible. The language, for example, interrupts the flow of understanding for English readers who are non-African.

2:17 PM Langa Mangezi <████████████████>
I disagree. The language and cultural artefacts make her book authentic and unique rather than the manufactured, whitewashed formulaic story that you want it to be. A Black mentor is a better fit for a Black author, and to be more specific, one with a similar lived cultural experience.

2:20 PM Anouk Rijks <██████████████>
Then I'd beg to say a woman is more fitting to mentor a female writer. This disqualification Olympics is a distraction, Langa. I trust that both our expertise will benefit any author regardless of their background.

2:21 PM Langa Mangezi <████████████████>
Disqualification olympics? This is not some feminist theory class, Anouk, it's about culture, it's about authentic experiences that you have a blindspot to.

2:27 PM Anouk Rijks <██████████████>
I mentored three African women and they seem to be performing excellently.

2:28 PM Langa Mangezi <████████████████>
Whilst your accolades are exemplary, they do not replace the authentic relations that fellows need. Olivia, care to throw in your thoughts.

2:34 PM Olivia Bloom <██████████████>
I'm not attuned to ███████ story. I believe an editorial fit is most guided by the knowledge in genre and

understanding of the author's work. We have sensitivity readers to fill in the authenticity gap. Let us remember our vital role for the authors this cycle.

2:34 PM Langa Mangezi <███████████>
Whilst that's wonderful, Olivia, we fail writers by not rectifying these diversity issues. Anouk, you have selective mutism when it comes to race and politics. Most people won't say the truth to your face, but I will.

2:35 PM Anouk Rijks <███████████>
Not everything is political, Langa. We invited you here to afford our writers the best resources and mentorship, not to be our enemy.

2:36 PM: Grace Miller <███████████>
Team, I'm coming in late to this. I was enthralled by our Günter authors' manuscripts much like you, so I understand your enthusiasm for ████ piece. That is the importance of literature, to challenge our biases and inspire debate.
Let's take this offline.

WHAT HAPPENED TO ANA?

96:01:59:13

BEFORE I DIE

Episode 7

Decolonize • Anaya

Welcome back, Crimies. I am Michele Visser, host of What Happened to Ana?

Our pitch came and went. It was intense, and I was very lucky to be paired with Katja, who's changed many authors' careers and enhanced our publishing spaces. She's very intelligent, and not many people understand her. Of course, this put a target on my back with the other girls. Anaya seemed troubled that day and had been for a couple of days. I observed that she'd sometimes appear distant, as if in a trance, and that she had become quite anxious.

This is Anaya Sebeya's story . . .

[upbeat music]

The last few hours have been a blur. Nilza has already packed her suitcase and been driven to the airport. I press my back against the fridge waiting for the dregs of time to settle. I stare at the clock, watching the seconds flow.

Bessie leans across the marble counter, tossing her weed tin between her hands. "Why do you think Miche got Katja?" she asks.

Ogone fetches a wine glass, and then works a corkscrew into a bottle of Fat Bastard and, after pouring it out in haste, takes a long sip. "Who cares? Our careers depend on how we massage our relationship with our mentors. I'm going to be a sellout for my Günter manuscript, as long as it doesn't go against my faith."

"What are *you* worried for? You're going to be a QS and stuff," Miche says.

"Have you seen the lifestyle I aspire to have? It's costly. I'm going to be a bougie mega-rich Black Barbie. Just you wait," Ogone says, raising her arms.

"What if they're asking you to do something that is ethically wrong, that does an injustice to our people?" I ask, mentally counting the people in the room, keeping focus of their eyes, so Huis won't slip me out of this reality again.

Ogone swigs her wine. "Beyps, damn these ethics, nna I'm not here to be a role model or an activist. Survival means suckling on the breast of white saviorhood." And of its sap of white milk will it cauterize my Blackness, I think. "As long as my writing isn't being turned into some white supremacist work, I'm good."

"But why did *you* get Katja?" Bessie says, eyes glaring at Miche over the rim of her glass.

Bessie has been gunning for Katja because she believes she holds the majority of the power and influence in the judging process. If Katja doesn't like who the other judges pick as a winner, she can influence them to her choice, and she may be biased to her own mentee: Miche.

"I deserve this as much as you do," Miche says. "My race forms the minority in Günter's history of alumnae, so you have an advantage."

Ogone groans. "Did I have an advantage when your people came to our lands—"

"Stop, I'm not going to let you guilt trip me for something *I* didn't do," Miche says, throwing her hands up. "Günter's funding 50 percent of your masters. You don't see us bitching about it."

They continue bickering. In the mirror behind Ogone, I catch a reflection of myself and what I'm wearing: dreads stacked high by loops of gold, heavy gear boots, an asymmetrical plaid skirt, a woolen halter top that I stole from Ranewa. Dark shadows beneath my eyes, telltale signs of sleeplessness. Fear-taut skin. Bones screaming against my skin. The room begins to tremble, as if I'm watching everything through an unfocused gaze. No, no, no, Huis wants to spit me out from this reality into Yanano's. I gather my arms around my shoulders and steer myself into the wall, repeatedly, to feel the solid borders of this place, to stay in this reality.

Hands pull me back. Ogone pats my cheek the way one does to wake someone up.

"I want to get out." I feel myself babbling and I can't stop it, I'm so exhausted. I know I sound crazy, but I say it all anyway. "All of Huis's doors of time are open into this room. I don't know how many days and weeks or hours it's been. I've been everywhere, and I did a pitch, but I was on the other side of reality before. Huis just throws me from one time to another time—"

"Don't give Huis the power," Ogone says, gripping me and preventing me from drumming my body against the wall.

"And you were all there in that other place with the white salt," I shout. "Don't tell me you don't remember, that you didn't see me. *You*—" I point to Bessie, "you were trying to kill me because of your daughter. You had a child, didn't you?"

Bessie backs away, lips trembling. "How did you know that?" She throws a look of distrust at Ogone who raises her hands, denying the blame. Bessie lowers her eyes. "It wasn't even born yet. How did you know that?"

"And you," I say, pointing to Miche, "you keep trying to feed me a curse. Huis helps you to read my thoughts." She shrieks, covering her face with her hands, crying.

"Here," Ogone says, trying to hand me a glass of warm, sugared water. "Drink. This will calm you down."

I turn, punch my elbow into Bessie's chest, who doubles over, away from me. "No, you're trying to feed me a curse again. I won't, I just won't." I cross my arms, back away from them.

"Anaya, it's been five days, and you haven't eaten anything," Miche says, wiping the tears from her face.

"Five days?" I whisper, dazed. Five days ago I was dragged into a hole in the wall. "Just four hours ago it was five days ago. How can five days happen in four hours?"

They've made a circle around me, a fragile attempt to corner me.

"Any food offered to you in a dream is not always sejeso. Sometimes it's to nourish you spiritually," Ogone whispers, praying over the water. Pours it into her mouth. Drinks of the prayed water to show me it's safe, but of course a bad spirit in a dream would trick me the same. She ushers the cup to my mouth. The water caresses my tongue and the drought in my

throat carries me toward a stable peace. Arms gather around me, hands sweep across the fabric of my skin. I'm embalmed in the dark cocoon of warm breaths and perfumed bodies.

"That night you felt that creature in bed, I saw it too," Bessie tells me. "I tried to deny its presence. We need help."

"I thought it was just me," Miche says, lips trembling and stepping closer to us.

I step forward, pointing at Bessie. "You pushed me, helped that thing drag me into the wall. Do you think that *will* actually get you this prize?"

Bessie's face crumbles. "I don't know what got into me," she admits. "Ever since I stepped into this house, I'm doing things that are unlike me, ka bommaruri."

"Oh my gosh, that's been happening to me too," Miche says, patting her chest. "I find myself thinking conceited things, thoughts convincing me to jeopardize you guys. Huis, it has this strong energy to make itself so present in me in a way I can't explain. I liked it at first because innovative ideas easily came to me, helped me with my work."

"What do you mean?" Ogone asks, with a suspicious glint in her eyes.

Miche shies away. "It's just thoughts, nothing else."

Ogone looks into her wine glass. "When I go to sleep, I can hear creatures and people in my room, talking, walking around my bed struggling to get to me. When I wake up, there's no one there. To be honest, I don't think doctors or policemen can help us. This is spiritual."

"Yeah," Bessie says, nodding vehemently. "This is witchcraft, what else can it be? What happens if the attacks become worse?"

The nightmares and vision revealed something to me. Traditional medicine is not bad unless it's peppered with something. The muti in the house. The bones of the dead.

"What about a traditional doctor? They can spiritually cleanse us, right?" I manage to say, held together by the reality of these people. I know full well I gave consent to these spirits, to Yanano, but surely someone can help sever those ties. I don't know if I can handle being pulled out of my life anymore.

They stew in their thoughts, considering it. Ogone's eyes shimmer in the dim light, like black opals.

It's a grey cloudy day as I stare out the window, trying to psych myself into Langa's first workshop at one of Cape Town University's classrooms. He will be working with us every Friday until our manuscripts are due. I'm glad Anouk isn't the only one who will be giving me advice.

"Consider writing your stories in your mother tongue," he tells us, standing in the front of the room, hands steepled, body well-built, wearing chinos, cardigan, and a buzz cut. "And with grace and patience translate that into English. You, what's your native language?" he asks, pointing at Miche.

"Afrikaans," she says softly.

Then he points at me, and I feel a spotlight at the top of my head burning down on me.

Mumbled words leave my mouth, although what I tried to say was my native tongue, Setswana. His eyebrows furrow as I lower my eyes. But he continues pointing randomly in the room, the other three uttering, Afrikaans, Seherero, Setswana, Zulu . . . and I didn't know Bessie and Ogone knew so many languages.

"Good," Langa says, eyes observing the room. "Consider each word you translate as if you are killing it. Consider how much you will kill, and how much you will keep alive."

"But that makes the text inaccessible to an English-speaking audience," Miche responds.

"Don't you think Anglophonic authors' books were inaccessible to us too?" Langa asks, slowly walking back and forth in front of the class, shoes an echoed staccato across the floor. "But we just got on with it. Still read it, still enjoyed their books. Didn't we use the internet to look up the places they mentioned? The lingo they used? Didn't they come here and kill our languages? Put up all these walls of borders up just as they do with our writing? Dividing us up." He muses for a bit. "You need to interrogate why you write the way you do and what sacrifice you commit to serve a certain audience."

"Miche's right though," Bessie remarks. "Writing in our languages makes it difficult to sell to a literary agent or publisher. You took that gamble and it worked for *you*."

"Nothing about the literary life is a guarantee," Langa replies. "When you walk out into our streets, you hear different languages, see different traditional attires, and traditional food—is that all going to be in italics? Let me tell you something, some things just cannot be translated, but that doesn't mean they must be killed off the page."

I quickly scribble down, *I must not kill who I am off the page. I must not kill my history off the page.*

"When I write, I'm writing for my people. Everyone else is a bystander," he says. "That is writing: squeezing every part of our identity into the narrow tunnel of the English language, then leaving portals and thresholds to our native language. There's nothing wrong with that." Langa closes class off with

a directive: "Probe your history and show your audience what you find."

I look down at my notes. Beneath my scribbles, I ask myself questions, and several question marks surround a question I can't answer myself: *What is our history???*

At the end of class, I approach Langa's desk as he's packing his books into his tote bag.

"Thank you," I say. "This is my first writing workshop, and I've never considered all of the things you taught today."

"Where would you expect to learn these things when our schools are programmed to teach one way?"

"Yeah, true," I say. "I sometimes feel like an imposter. I was a nobody before."

Langa tilts his head, incredulity woven into his wrinkled forehead. "Just like our continent was nothing before they discovered it?" He shakes his head. "Ntwana, you were *a* someone before they found you. We are someone before these awards come in to tell us that we are good writers, to impress upon us the seal of recognition."

I say, "I just want to write and make a living out of it."

"Well, as someone who has lived it," he says, smirking, "this profession will show you that it's not that simple."

He picks at a book that's sticking out of my satchel, *Call and Response* by Gothataone Moeng.

"She's a brilliant author," he says.

"I'm almost done reading it," I say. I'm trying to use the book to find myself again, my culture. "She has a way of capturing our culture in a way I never thought. I just don't know how to write about where I am from, even though I am living me. And she did it right, and I don't know how to do it *right*."

He waves his hand, as if he's chasing a fly away. "Don't let such things distract you. There is no wrong way to tell your stories. At the end of the day, you are a Motswana, and every Motswana lives their culture in their own way."

"Thank you," I say. "This has really helped today."

"I've been in talks with Günter to facilitate partnerships with African authors as mentors for their fellows. It's unfortunate they didn't let me be your mentor; I was intrigued by your project. You're the real thing, Anaya. Keep in touch, and if you need 'Black' eyes on your writing, feel free to reach out to me."

Relief balloons in my chest. I get to have a Black South African mentor on the down low. My phone drinks his contact info in glee. "Of course," is all I say.

"Are you working on anything else?" he says. "Günter likes its authors prolific."

"I've been . . . distracted," I say.

"You need to strategize and make yourself stand out from the other fellows. Miche is doing that art thing, which raised Katja's interests. So keep people's attention on you. Publishing a short story here and there will certainly sway the Günter judges toward you. Send your stories to me, and if they're good enough, I'll pull some connections."

I almost want to bow to him and kiss his palms in gratitude. Then I realize how our interaction may look to a bystander, a young female emerging writer working secretly with an established, good-looking male writer: sexual, gold-digging, ingenuine.

I shake the thought from my mind, and a risky idea nudges itself into me.

"I'm actually working on a story," I say.

"Oh?"

"But I've hit a wall. I have a traditional doctor character, and I need to conduct research to make it authentic. I'm new to Cape Town and don't know the safe ones I can talk to. Might you by any chance know any? I'll pay, of course, for the consultation."

"Yeah, my aunt's one," he says. "I'll app you her number. She is a good traditional doctor. Tell her I recommended you. She'll give you a discount."

We weave through the university grounds, shielded in foliage and sprinkled sunlight and scents of lilies and ponds. He's so personable and down-to-earth rather than the snob I thought he'd be. We talk about everything, gossip, where we're from, missing home, our writing, mine never really getting there, and the pressure from everywhere. We walk toward the parking lot, I to my car, and he to his. I'd never considered ever adding Setswana into my writing. I'd never considered what else I was subconsciously rejecting of myself and where I'm from. I leave that workshop feeling like I am born anew.

I am Michele Visser, signing off. Thank you for listening to What Happened to Ana? *If you enjoyed this episode, please share, subscribe, and leave a review. We are a small two-person team, my assistant and I, and every like and subscription goes a long way. See you next week, Crimies!*

[theme music]

♡9,034 ⪪2,340

RANEWA

"Where were you on 20 December?" Skommere asked me.

I stared at the camera, a bead of sweat rolling down my neck. "In Botswana, at home with my parents. We'd just had dinner when we got the news."

"Has your sister ever been diagnosed with a mental illness?"

"No. She's not crazy." And just what I hated: my voice broke. "Did you investigate Miche on how she was able to get sensitive information about my sister? Did you actually *listen* to the recordings?"

"I'm well aware of Miche's podcast, which I must be frank, does not suspend my disbelief, but it has called to our attention certain issues we want to fully cross-examine."

"What kind of South African *are* you? You know someone is behind this bolotsana. Miche, Günter, someone envious, someone greedy," I said.

Skommere raised her hand. Her and her stupid plastic weave. "We had someone come forward. We just needed to confirm your sister's . . . mental capacity. And how was your childhood and educational life like, for both you and Anaya?"

"I've already answered these questions last year, the first time we met."

"We like to go over things again, usually something new comes up," she said.

"Well, we grew up sheltered, went to an English private school, had tutors, cleaners, drivers. I know a lot of people think the Günter residency was too challenging for Anaya. But we did our A-Levels in all the sciences; we were high achievers—we were fluent in the language of pressure. She did her first year BSc at the University of Botswana, but Papa felt the program was not rigorous enough, and Anaya being the oldest, she was transferred to start med school in Russia, like a lot of Batswana med students."

My voice hitches at this point, remembering that time so reminiscent of when she left for Cape Town, the second time we became apart. I missed her sorely when she was in Russia. But she kept in touch, often crying on our WhatsApp calls to the miseries of the weather, the pressures of school, and struggling to fit in with her cohort. Not like at Günter. To imagine she returned safely from Russia, but it's *our* land that disappeared her from our lives.

"She dropped out of med school before the year was over," I continue, clearing my voice. "My parents weren't going to support her financially, and she was desperate, so she used the same zeal she had in aiming for a high grade in school and redirected it into her writing career, to be independent. Yes, she struggled to get published, but she pushed on. So Günter, in comparison, was a walk in the park, which is why I believe that something else happened in Günter. And this is why I came here, to show you that Miche is not telling the full story, that Günter *may* be hiding something."

"The audio still needs to go through forensic analysis for voice recognition. And we are investigating all parties in light of this new information," she said. I stared at her notepad where she was taking down some notes. "This is for your

sister, but not just her: it's for Bessie too. Both girls suffered a great deal. So don't shrug off any small detail—it might prove very helpful."

I gave her a resigned look. "That's why I brought this." I pulled out Anaya's phone contained in a Ziploc bag. They could run forensic tests on it, perhaps even manipulate it to access the dim tracks. "It has everything in it that Miche won't talk about on the podcast. The tracks become available once I do something."

Skommere narrowed her eyes at the Ziploc bag. "Ms. Sebeya, did you come to Cape Town by yourself?"

"What? Just listen it to it, and I'm sure you'll get more answers than in your interrogations with Miche." I shoved the phone toward her.

"Ms. Sebeya, there's nothing in the bag." She rubbed the sides of her temple. "We'll end the interrogation here. You must be tired. I understand the pain when someone loses a loved one, but you need to take care of yourself, for your sister."

The bald-headed old man handling the recorder looked away as if embarrassed for me. To them, the Ziploc bag was empty. But I could still see Anaya's phone inside. Coldness licked the inside of my bones and threaded me with a slight fear. I gathered the phone into my bag and hesitantly motioned to leave.

The phone vibrated, and the track before Miche's episode eight lit up. It all happened out of Skommere's presence, as if intentional, as if the sender could see me, making the tracks accessible at moments where no one would witness what I saw. Whoever that person was, they didn't know who they were messing with. I wouldn't buckle.

I was still receiving emails from literary agents and publishers. Everyone had dollar signs in their eyes. Katja Günter unashamedly reached out to me to offer me crumbs of a publishing deal to get in on sensationalizing Anaya's story. I declined. My tragedy and my sister's missing case in the news was a proposal enough for a publisher to offer me a deal, but I was determined to forge ahead with preserving Anaya's truth free from their claws.

A new plan formed before me.

I needed to document my search for my sister, piecing together Miche's podcast and the missing information I was getting from Anaya's phone, and write her *whole* story in what I hoped would be authentic to her voice.

I knew exactly who I could use, and how.

I emailed Anouk: *I'm going to say yes to the publisher. I'm writing Anaya's truth. I'm ready to discuss your offer of representation.*

Unsurprisingly, Anouk quickly responded and happily set a time according to our availabilities.

When I stepped out into the cold, empty parking lot, Ogone was waiting for me. "I'm sorry about how I acted in there. You almost look like Anaya, and I went through shock. I miss her so much." She wiped a tear from her cheek.

I clasped her hands together. "Please, please tell me what I happened, just for me, for Anaya."

She pulled her hands from my grasp. "It's exactly why I can't say much to you . . . after all she did to protect you, I can't open you up to the things we escaped. I don't know why Miche is messing with this again. It's dangerous, it could

jeopardise everything. Be careful of Huis, *please* for Anaya's sake." And she walked away.

The phone grew warm in my hands. Its display flickered. When I looked down, next to the new track was a 🫆 symbol. In my Uber, I pressed play. This phone would help me find out the truth—and hopefully find my sister.

Anaya | Ngaka ya Setso

Our hour-long coastal drive into the Cape Peninsula is a caesarean cut from the world, like we are being born into some place, and like birth, there is no choice to it, torn out of the shielded world of womb into a new world. We believe it now, en route to the sangoma, that we are bewitched, with a hope the sangoma might end this haunting and spiritual terror. In this moment, she feels like a god. This gives us no relief, for even a god takes lives, and fear glooms in us at the possibility that the sangoma could mess things up and make our horrors worse. What would worse mean?

"In 400 meters, take a right turn," my GPS guide says.

We turn off the M4, and my tiny car trundles along a graveled road, lush foliage so thick it reaches over to form a roof, dripping birdsong and flowery scent. Intermittent breaks through the dense thicket offer a view below to shacks that protrude from the deep-green mountainside, which gradually descends to the shoreline. The houses are in wan washes of blue, turquoise, green, and mild yellows.

We stop at a black electric gate, a house powered by solar panels and shrouded in hedges.

I step out feeling fearful. I leave my phone in the car, everything of my items. Ogone has undone her weave, and in its

place is her natural hair held up into two halo-like puffs. Her baby hair curls at the edges, framing her prominent forehead.

"It's so quiet," Ogone comments as she steps out of the car.

"A place free from modern-day amenities," Bessie whispers. "Perhaps a perfect place for rituals and tradition. No urban noise, no witness for, say, murder."

Bessie rings up the intercom, and a Zimbabwean accent responds. After explaining that we're here for consultation, the electric gate slides open to a paved path leading us into a garden tended by a gardener who's raking fallen leaves from the earth. The path bypasses a contemporary home past the garage to a secondary house, an office in the backyard where the sangoma receives her clients. The main house is quite a distance from the office, but I can see a little boy doing his homework in the dining room with a helper giving him his lunch.

When we enter the sangoma's office, she sits at a long mahogany table. Hanging on the wall are her awards and qualifications: Master's degree in Health and a PhD in Social Anthropology. I never thought sangomas had a formal education. I thought they were just born with their ancestral-connection abilities and were dusted with magic to perform miracles.

"I'm Sangoma Abusiwe Mangezi. Nice to meet you, Anaya." Her smile is wide and warm.

"Thank you for seeing us on short notice," I say, shaking her hand in etiquette of holding my right hand with my left and doing a slight bow.

"My nephew called, informing me that you were in need of help," she says.

"Yes, it's my—*our* first time seeing a traditional doctor," I say.

"I don't know how to reconcile what I'm about to do today with my faith," Ogone says uneasily.

"A lot of people consider sangoma as witch doctors conducting evil, who may heal you at first but give you medicine to have you coming back to them routinely for help," Sangoma Abusiwe says. "But we are not all the same. Unlike witch doctors, we abide strictly to a code of conduct like that of doctors. We are here to respect the lives of our patients, diagnose them of their issues; we find the source of your ailment and cure the root cause of it. We find out *why* you are sick."

Her reassuring voice convinces me that we made the right decision.

Sangoma Abusiwe directs us to the consultation room. When she joins us, she has changed into a traditional attire—beads, bracelets. Waist-down she's wrapped in a symbolically patterned and colorful cloth, beaded necklaces crisscross her chest and encircle her waist. A beaded headdress hangs over her Afro. She is accompanied by three assistants.

I stare at her multicolored beads, trying to understand their meaning, as if a sacred language is latticed around her body, connecting our world to our ancestors, a religion of its own. The feeling is immense and relieves me of fear because the belief system is a two-way thing: Someone has faith in what we say, likewise we have faith in her diagnostic ways.

Inside the hut, we kneel onto a grass mat, barefooted. The space is sacred, quiet and cool, surrounded by earth walls. It isn't what I considered of a typical consultation, the common practice of bone reading as shown in media or movies; instead she lights a candle and asks us questions with observant eyes.

Ogone and I relay our personal stories of coming to Cape Town, our experiences of living in Huis, the scar in my palm, the nightmares, the tripping of reality.

When it's Bessie's turn, she keeps quiet.

"Nothing you say or do here today is considered embarrassing or crazy," Sangoma Abusiwe assures her. "You can trust that I will respect and keep private the information you share with me."

Bessie shuffles about on her folded legs, clears her throat. "My experiences are exactly like theirs."

I catch Ogone side-eyeing Bessie.

"Let us begin," Sangoma Abusiwe says, nodding. "I will give you some herbs to take, which will help open you up spiritually. But you must also give verbal consent. Do you consent that I use your body as a portal?"

I nod, then stop myself, not sure what I'm agreeing to. "What are the consequences of using our bodies?"

"To see into your ancestry, use your body as a vessel to the spirit realm," she says.

"Will it hurt?" Ogone asks.

Sangoma Abusiwe focuses her eyes on us. "For one of you, yes. The one who time affects more."

I stifle a groan, preparing myself for the magnitude of pain that may claim me. She stands toward her cupboard, opening small glass jars of herbs, mixing them up as her attendants heat water and steam the herbs inside, then pour the beverage into earthen mugs, hand them to each of us. I pinch my nose to avoid tasting the mixture and swallow it whole.

"Good, good, you're all connected." Sangoma Abusiwe kneels before me. She presses her hand to my arm, to my forehead, it burns, and when I stretch my mouth to purge, this

reality instead squeezes into me, purges me into a different place without walls, without wind, without people, stands me beneath a glaring sun in the sky in a field of yellow stalks. I can hear feet sweeping through dust, the cry of a goat before its last bleeding. I can taste the knife that will sever its neck, and the copper tang of the blood before it explodes into the air. I can hear the singing palm fronds, reeds, and grass as the breeze cries through the land. I can hear the people mutilating a young boy's body for medicine. I can hear them doing the same to a virgin woman. I can hear their cries. Smoke, wails, blood.

Behind me stands a Cape Dutch farmhouse. Huis, a thought intones in this body of mine, a thought not my own. I feel a history of another body filling mine.

I step forward, toward the farmhouse, pulled by a force. The light sizzles, sneezes, and I'm dispatched into a shaky state, hands planted against Sangoma Abusiwe's earthen floor—droplets of sweat splatter from my face. A jittery reality pours out from my mouth, liquid that's almost as transparent as water. A cold clasps itself to my skin, and I'm shivering, wondering who are these people connected to Huis, as if I've purged parts of my soul, of my life.

"It's okay, child," Sangoma Abusiwe says. "It seems the house is afflicting all of you differently. One of you—Bessie?—your sickness gives ease for these ghosts to enter you, making your sickness worse. If there's no intervention, things will exacerbate beyond your body's strength, ultimately ending your life."

Bessie gasps and begins to cry.

"I will prescribe something to help you," Abusiwe says. "Anaya, you witnessed something bad that your ancestors did

in the past which the house used to its advantage. We are almost there, but it's too much. Take a breath and we'll try again. I need to get into the house. To see. To see. It will be very painful. We may have to tie you down. Do you consent?"

I swallow, stare at Ogone fearfully. She holds me tight. "I'll be right here. I won't let it get dangerous for you. I'll be here," she says.

I nod, watch them tie my hands to the poles in the hut. Sangoma Abusiwe leans in, starts uttering words in a different language, starts calling ancestral names. Begins shaking and jerking.

My thoughts spin in my head. The world shakes, spins, a fever catches my mind with sharp pain. The world blinks. I find myself standing on Huis's stoep. Its door swings open into the hallway. A rush of voices, lively. Down the dark passage is a light flowing out of one of the rooms. The closer I get, the higher the notes of the voices. Inside the sitting room, I find women, knitting, sewing, reading, chatting, around a low table with scones and magwinya and diphaphatha and rooibos tea, steam slithering from its golden liquid. On the floor sits a green mosquito coil, sending a dull scented smoke into the air. A bare room, a settee covered in plastic covering, the table decorated with crocheted doilies. A few windows, decorated in thick curtains, looking into a foggy darkness. I come toward the door's threshold, the voices stop, heads swivel front to back, facing me, unperturbed by the unnatural turn. Women wearing long dresses with bell sleeves, some thin sleeves trimmed with lace. Hair adorned in plaits and braids, some hair shorn, some in short, patted Afros.

It is dusty, and the lamp flickers light across my face.

The voices play:

"There's not much to survive by, they pay us mealie meal," says the woman who Yanano chided before. Merapelo. "We're thinking of leaving to the Ngwato reserves, like some of my group. Although they'll hire us, they'll still suspect us of witchcraft and ditlhabelo. They don't trust us, but we need work to survive."

Stay calm, assimilate, a thought guides me. I come forth, bend to the floor on my knees, observe them like a child watching elders talk. Subservience protects me. *These are the characters in my historical fiction*, a part of my brain reveals to me, *ask them all you need*. I've entered a secret part of my subconscious, within Huis's subconscious.

"Ditlhabelo? What's that?" I ask, overwhelmed by my lack of fear.

"Human sacrifices," she says, skirting a needle into a stenciled cloth, and I want to ask her if that's true, but she continues, "We plough, harvest crops to get by."

"Is this what our tongue has come to?" one of the women asks, a teacup in hand, eyes disapproving. "She doesn't know our language. Is this what we died for?"

The women are dressed in dated attire though I can't pinpoint which year each cloth comes from. I look about me as if I'll come across a calendar, anything to tell me the time and period.

"What year is it?" I ask.

"1919, sometimes," says a woman, knitting a long garment. "1923, sometimes 1960-something. I'm 1884, she's 1902 and so on. The years change when the sun rises. Sometimes it stays the same, if we're lucky or unlucky, depending what year we become stuck in. Tomorrow it could be the year before those white things come; that's the days I treasure." The sun

treks light across the world, trekking backward into the past or the future.

"Before who came?" I ask.

"The men of bone," the say, heads swiveling again.

Her eyes skirt the room, look down to her sewing.

"There are many others here in Huis, and so there are as many years as tenants in this house. I am 1919," she says and points past the reeds and rivers where there are farm laborers working the fields. "Our men come from everywhere." She points to the rear side of Huis, a window that eyes what looks like a squatter camp. "We live in ntlo ya Setswana behind. Meneer, he came from England, settled in the Transvaal, before occupying our farms southwest of us, but failed because of their Depression, before coming here to take Tuli, our Tuli, the borderland—all our farms."

Yanano arrives, sweeping into the room, hands tucked into the bell sleeves of her dress. She has severe eyes that scan the room. "Dumelang betsho," she says.

The women respond with a nod.

"We are happy to see you again," she says. "Not much time on our hands now. I see a spirit has come with you, without our consent. Nothing we cannot take care of."

I look about me, wondering if Sangoma Abusiwe is here and how come I can't see her.

Yanano continues, "There's a tear in the land, a scar, by the border—that scar stretches for about 200 km. It's the Tuli Block farms—that's the border, the borders, that they cross as they please. Our bodies are their leisure. They stripped this land naked of the Babirwa, of us."

The night is hot and sweaty across the nape of my neck. I swat away the mosquitoes, the humidity. "What's beyond the

border, the river?" I ask, staring through the window where I see a shimmering river cutting through the flesh of night.

"Southern Rhodesio," she whispers, points to the distant left, and then to the right, she gestures, says, "Transvaal."

"Transvaal?"

"The Boer Republic," she says. At my confused expression, she says, "You're from my future, but you don't know me, your past. You don't know how earth hurt on this soil of ours. This soil, oh this soil." Her hand reaches for the floor, the concrete cracks, a deafening fracture, revealing earth beneath it. She clutches her lower skirt with her left hand. Bowing, she scrapes the soil into the urn of her hand, lets it spill from her fingers in loose grains of brown. It becomes thick liquid, turns into blood, and I'm frozen in place by a cold fear, by the sense that things are getting worse, but she moves forward, rubs the blood of our soil onto my face like ointment. "They murdered our land. They murdered us from your face, your skin, your mind." Her eyes widen. "Look, look, look, here they come!"

Panic ensues, a flame catching on. The women fluster about, pick up the hems of their dresses, agitated.

One of them holds onto my hand, her grip a burning cold, her eyes a steely glance. Something tells me to step back, to get out now, to go back, to return my spirit into my body before someone takes its place.

"A body shouldn't spend a long time without its spirit," Yanano says, hand around me. "Spirits are bartered for in the spirit realm in exchange for things. It isn't that difficult to enter you," she says. "After all, one of you is in debt. Bessie, that one."

The earth ripples. I grab onto bottom of a nearby sofa. "What's happening?"

"Huis is migrating, packing up," she says.

"Oh, Jesu, anywhere but the Transvaal. They'll burn us up again," a woman screams, hands raised above her head.

Another woman points to a window, where I see skeletal bones glowing as bright as the moon. "There!" she shouts. "There they come, there they come! Those white things, isn't it enough now? Look here they come, here they come."

"Yanano, it's your scene, go now, go now before they disturb us," another woman says.

Yanano's grip turns to my throat. "No, I'm not staying this time. I'm not staying. You will take my place. *You* will take it."

One of them holds her back. "Yanano, this is premature. It will destroy everything. You can't. It's not yet time, sisi."

Yanano steps back, eyes lowered, sadness weighing down her shoulders, her lips, her frame. She looks up at me, tears brimming her eyelids. "Before you return, remember Huis is also a wound; the pus of its pain inflicts violence on you. Remember, Huis hurts too, Huis hurts too."

"How can a house hurt?" I whisper, still feeling the burn of her fingers on my throat and arm.

"You'll see," she says, stepping backward into the dark passage.

I'm yanked backward by a force more powerful than her, only I can't see its form. I walk backward, sound draining the color from Huis, from the fields, from the sky. I walk back, back, back and come to in my body on Sangoma Abusiwe's floor, scratches all over Bessie and Ogone, screams and grunts still pouring from my mouth, their arms struggling.

An exhaustion digs into my bones and I submit myself to its pain.

"She's back, she's back," Ogone says, falling back onto her rear side, sweating. Bessie stands against the wall wide-eyed.

Sangoma Abusiwe pats my arms and forehead with medicinal herbs. "I see, I see now," she says. "This is not fully clear, but this is good enough. There were too many people inside you. It was too much for you to reckon with that many people at the same time."

I'm too tired to ask them to untie me. My bowels are tired, my mind is tired, my body is tired from holding onto my life. My spirit wants to unhinge itself.

I'm not prepared for Sangoma Abusiwe's words: "Besides the people, there's a person haunting you. This person is a house." She pauses, watching each one of us. "These things follow you because you have been cursed. Something leeched these things onto you to make your life unbearable. Thokolosi." Her breath snuffs the candle. "It is this spirit's slave, meant to guard a place . . . a place . . . filled with many mirrors—no, not mirrors, something similar to mirrors—windows. There are many of them. This creature watches over the spirit's subjects through these windows."

"Okay, what must we do now?" I ask, terrified.

"To all of you: Your sickness will resist biomedical treatments. It's textbook-case witchcraft. I will give you medicine that will chase away your burdens and then perform a ceremony."

There's a candle on the floor and the curtains are drawn. After making us wait for half an hour, she returns. "The spirit is here, uncontrollable, angry. Do not worry for now. Its evil is not strong enough to overpower you, yet. We will cleanse you today and give you remedies to cleanse the house. This will be the ceremony: the removal and therefore the burial of the evil spirit. It will cost R2,500 each."

We stare at each other, powerless. And Bessie foots the bill for us.

Sangoma Abusiwe and her assistants burn something and dance the smoke across our bodies. They use an oxtail to brush medicine onto our skins, whilst sweeping something off our shoulders, our backs, our heads. Drumbeat sounds vibrate at the center of my ribcage. My head a rush of sounds, a symphony.

I can't make out the sangoma's incantation, but it must be taking off the weight of spirits from us. Bessie just closes her eyes, the way church people do, and I'm half expecting her hands to stretch sky way. Sangoma Abusiwe holds a knobkerrie. Her assistants point their faces upward, sniffing the air as if evil has a stark scent buried in our bodies, escaping our pores.

I expect the weight to lift off me, as if it can be measured physically.

After this ritual, we walk. They have one white chicken with them as they direct us out through a small gate at the back garden sheltered in morula trees. We walk across rocky outcrops, down a narrow path flanked with thick bushes, until after a few minutes we come upon an empty beach, Smitswinkel Bay Beach. No one in sight.

As we walk out, Ogone's trembling hand reaches out to me. "Do you ever think that if our ancestors didn't go through so much violence, that we wouldn't be so disconnected from ourselves, that we wouldn't be killing the Black in our skin, turning further away from what makes us?" A tear crawls down her face. "I think about my great-grandfather who went to the mines in Joburg to seek opportunity and support his

family in Botswana. Every day I feel the grief, the loss, the pain—will it ever stop?"

There are things that linger in my blood, an echo of my ancestors' strife, of their commitments, affecting me. I don't know myself fully if I don't know them.

I slip my fingers into Ogone's fingers, then my arms, until we're a fabric of safety. I never thought that such a small, warm body of fear could make me feel less alone. I feel her hot breaths glistening with tears clasping my neck. I cry too, and I don't know if it's my grandmother or another ancestor crying through my tears, but I feel their pain in the span of my spirit.

"Ke tshogile," Ogone says. Her Black skin on my Black skin opens the portal to my language, slips me in: I am home. My language is back. The sangoma's cleansing has taken effect.

"Le nna ke tshogile," I whisper back, submerging myself in the language stripped from our tongues.

A wind brushes at the curls in her puffs, flicks her tear aside. I wipe the rest of her tears with my thumb, a promise to keep her skin alive.

The coastline is a thin belt of pale beach sand, bordered by grey rocks, rising steeply to clifftops cloaked in a deep green foliage, forming a long crescent shape, dropping sharply into the ocean. Far out, the horizon is an indistinguishable parting of sky and water.

We stop at the shore, the sunset reflected across the ocean.

Sangoma Abusiwe points to a pale area of beach sand and says, "Dig."

We look at each other as the three assistants hand each of us an adze—an axe-like tool.

The hole we dig, we throw upon it seeds and more seeds and plastic-covered substance, filling the opening with beach sand. The sunlight holds us warm. Sangoma Abusiwe walks forward seeking water, seeking an end, where she folds us into the warm bay. We're dressed in salt water.

The chicken is still, its feet tied, its head buried into its puffed chest. Sangoma Abusiwe reaches for the chicken. "In death, you find birth," she says. "We birth it to the ancestors."

I stand at the edge, watching the world in motion. Waves collapse into stark-white foam and drag back into the ocean. The sun is at its highest peak. The mountainside gradually descends into the shoreline.

Sangoma Abusiwe unties the chicken and places it on its hind feet. Shuddering, with the ocean lapping at our feet, we follow her commands as we trace her footprints up the steep path, wind teasing our skin. The chicken, alive, stands steadfast by the burial site, head turning to every direction.

Sangoma Abusiwe whispers, "Do not look back; do not invite the spirit back. Steer your eyes forward. The ascent of the chicken will symbolize the spirit's leave from your life."

The cold bites my neck as if proxy for the evil spirit, gnawing bone, tempting me to look back. I will myself forward. I check my side for the others—Bessie's neck is twisted back, returning her head to the path we face.

In my gasp, I hear the flap of wings, the flight of a bird
will carry my evil away.

I believe this: a bird that knows no flight
its wings will glimpse the sun
turn to ash our evil.

Huis is awake
Huis is hungry
Huis is angry

The past is not dead
The past is not dead
The past is not dead
The past is not dead
The past is not dead
The past is not dead
The past is not dead
The past is not dead
The past is not dead
The past is not dead

Choose your membership

Contributor

$1/month

JOIN

Thank you for your support – every amount goes a long way!

Witness

$5/month

JOIN

- Discord server access to Witness community
- Early access to podcast episodes
- Behind-the-scenes for our audio production and notes
- 10% discount on merch

Investigator

$15/month

JOIN

Everything included in Witness, plus:

- Access to old interrogation videos, articles, and Q&A that the team conducts with those close to the case, incl. Günter commentary
- Videos of Michele Visser's time in Günter and unexpected shots of Anaya's time in Günter

Criminal

$30/month

JOIN

Everything included in Investigator, plus:

- Access to partners-in-crime group where we dig out the mysteries of Anaya's life and disappearance
- As a Criminal, you will have access to our files, investigation techniques, and breadcrumbs we follow to hopefully find Anaya.
- Membership funds are used to hire professionals to assist with our investigation.

Recent posts by What Happened to Ana?

Hello, Crimies, welcome to the top-tier level of your subscription. It was difficult getting access to this interrogation video of one of Anaya's closest friends, Ogone Molefhe. As we have seen in previous episodes, Ogone was not a big fan of mine, but I haven't held anything against her since our time together in Günter Huis. During her Gunter fellowship, Ogone was doing her master's in quantity surveying (QS).

Investigator Subscribers-Only Access: Ogone Molefhe Interrogation Video

Here you will find access to interrogation videos and links to the victims' social media pages as a bonus to your favorite episodes. Remember every little bit of information is vital to the case. Enjoy!

Ogone Uetuu Molefhi

Olivia Skommere: On 20 December, you were standing in the foyer of Muizenberg Conference Hotel for media photography, 15 minutes prior to the winner's announcement. All four of you disappeared shortly after for two weeks. Where did you go?

Ogone Uetuu Molefhi: I've said this before, I can't remember.

Olivia Skommere: But only two of you returned. Did you have something to do with the disappearance of the other two fellows?

Ogone Uetuu Molefhi: No.

Olivia Skommere: Did you supply your friends with marijuana that night?

Ms. Molefhi's legal representative: Don't answer that. Is my client considered a suspect? Unless you have evidence that substantiates this claim, you are crossing the line. We can end this conversation anytime.

Olivia Skommere: I understand. No, your client is not a suspect, and we appreciate her time. I'll ask another question. In late September, you, along with two other fellows, Bessie Kgositsile and Anaya Sebeya visited a sangoma. Is this correct? What was the purpose of this visit?

Ogone Uetuu Molefhi: Yes. We were working on a story. It was for research purposes.

Olivia Skommere: That doesn't corroborate Sangoma Abusiwe Mangezi's story. She states that you were all terrified and exhibited behaviors that were consistent with signs of abuse, hauntings and spiritual attacks.

Ogone Uetuu Molefhi: We had to tell her a story to get the appropriate details for our characters who were dealing with experiences of haunting and possession. We must have been so good for her to believe us.

Olivia Skommere: There are reports that some of the fellows hallucinated, took drugs, and expressed "difficulty in maintaining their connection to time." Did Anaya Sebeya, or any of the other fellows exhibit mental health issues?

Ogone Uetuu Molefhi: If you think we were crazy, then there's nothing I can say that can disprove that. You won't believe me either way.

Olivia Skommere: I am here to help you, and I will respect anything you share with me.

Ogone Uetuu Molefhi: Well, with your conclusion on Anaya's state of mind, I don't think so.

Olivia Skommere: How was the relationship between you and Michele Visser?

Ogone Uetuu Molefhi: We kept to ourselves. We were committed to our writing disciplines. I was focused on school, so I didn't interact with her often.

Olivia Skommere: It's come to my attention that you were all not fond of Michele Visser. What are the reasons for this?

Ogone Uetuu Molefhi: Who ever told you this lie can also provide the reason.

Olivia Skommere: There are allegations that Michele Visser violated Anaya Sebeya. These are very serious allegations.

Ogone Uetuu Molefhi: It's the first time I'm hearing this.

Olivia Skommere: There are reports that Anaya Sebeya and Langa Mangezi were in a sexual relationship, and that she was using him to break into the literary scene.

Ogone Uetuu Molefhi: Firstly, Anaya wasn't having a sexual relationship with anyone the entirety of the writing residency. And before you ask me, I also wasn't sexually promiscuous. And Langa is the plagiarist who stole her work, so he was using her.

Olivia Skommere: Langa Mangezi cornered Anaya at the award ceremony and they had a tense conversation. What was it about?

Ogone Uetuu Molefhi: Perhaps you should ask Langa since he was present during the conversation.

Olivia Skommere: Why? Did you feel she was unsafe with Langa? Do you think Langa is complicit in Anaya's disappearance?

Ogone Uetuu Molefhi: You're the investigator, investigate.

Olivia Skommere: Mr. Mangezi informed us that he and Anaya were in a committed relationsh—

Ogone Uetuu Molefhi: That's a lie. That shameless bastard. He's using Anaya to clean up his image since the allegations came out, because organizations are cutting ties with him. He's using Anaya's disappearance to his advantage. Mxm, that thokolosi.

Olivia Skommere: Ms. Molefhi—

Ogone Uetuu Molefhi: No, I can't even believe that you're giving him the time of day! Anaya deserves more than this.

Olivia Skommere: The same witnesses overheard your plans with Anaya to kill Michele Visser? Did it backfire and lead to Anaya's disappearance? What was Bessie's hand in this plan?

Ogone Uetuu Molefhi: They misinterpreted us. Anaya and I were talking about a story collaboration that had a character called Miche. It was a murder mystery. Since those witnesses had exceptional hearing, perhaps you can ask *them* about Langa and Anaya's conversation that night.

Olivia Skommere: Ms. Molefhi, do you understand that lying to the state is a criminal offence? It is my understanding that you and Anaya Sebeya and Bessie Kgositsile were very close. I would assume that you would be very forthcoming to aid our pursuit in finding them. Surely their friendships meant something to you.

Ms. Molefhi's legal representative: That is not a question. If you don't have any more questions, my client and I are leaving.

Olivia Skommere: Well, Ms. Molefhi, the lie detector indicates that you've provided nothing but lies to every question I've asked. Thank you for your time.

There are new changes to our Patreon!

- We've added a new membership tier: Criminal.

Upcoming Post:
Interrogation Videos: Anaya's rumored bae

 Join to unlock

WHAT HAPPENED TO ANA?

WHAT HAPPENED TO ANA?

84:23:11:29

BEFORE I DIE

Episode 8

Black Trauma Sells • Anaya

Welcome back, Crimies. I am Michele Visser, host of What Happened to Ana?

As you know, Anaya, Ogone, and Bessie had decided to go see a sangoma. They were diagnosed spiritually as they felt they were being haunted by something from the past. It seemed as if things were back to normal. The girls returned from their sangoma consultation and did something behind my back by medicating the house. They never asked for my consent, and this troubled me deeply when writing this episode. But speaking with my therapist has helped me immensely.

Anaya has experienced her first haunting, and at first, she tried to seek help. This is where authorities failed us. If police had done something, today Anaya would still be with us. Anaya and I got close on this episode, and I'm lucky that she considered my advice for her manuscript.

This is Anaya Sebeya's story . . .

[upbeat music]

We return after the sangoma's treatment, exhausted. We pass by Kofifi restaurant to purchase chips and kota, spiced with atchar. The noises around us are filled with life: people chatting and laughing, the humdrum of traffic, the vendors selling outside—the world continues on as it was, as if we expected it to feel as different as we are. We don't talk about what happened, afraid that it will call the spirit back.

I can speak Setswana now.

That's all I do.

Ogone leans toward me. "Do you think Günter is part of Huis?"

I shake my head. "I don't think so, but they definitely benefit from it."

"If they find out what we're doing today, the sangoma, the traditional medicine, they'll think we're crazy—backward—they might kick us out," Bessie says.

"Miche is asleep. No one will know," I whisper.

Cloaked in the dark of night, we divide the medicine Abusiwe gave us to medicate the house from its illness. Ogone heads to the front, Bessie heads to the garden, and I head into the bathrooms, pouring it down the sinks and flushing it down the toilets. The air is chillier, the night thickens. We salt the house with the medicine, healing its ailments from our bodies.

That night, I'm woken up by a loud groaning noise from downstairs. It's 2 a.m. Bessie. Why can't anyone hear her? It's probably another flare-up. Even though she betrayed me, I feel sorry for her, so I hustle downstairs and prepare porridge for her. When I enter Bessie's dark room, she's moaning from

pain, each tiny movement making it worse. I sit on the edge of her bed, feeding her motogo wa ting. She's unable to sit up, and quietly, she says, "I'm so sorry."

Even though I haven't asked anything, she's apologetic, which is insane, so I say, "Hae, motho wa Modimo. Relax, I'm not Miche. You don't have to be worried that I'll judge you. It's not good for you to be this anxious."

She wipes a tear from her face. "Grace hasn't been able to accommodate me with the Günter pressure, given Katja's insistence on our progress. It's eating into my body trying to keep up."

"I want to apologize," I say. "I feel terrible. The things I thought about you when we first met, it was not right of me, because I can see that you're suffering." I tug her hand and squeeze it. "If you need someone to help you bathe or clean your room, I can do that. Let me know; I don't mind. I know Ogone is usually the one that helps you, but I know she also has the pressures of school."

"Anaya, I don't want to put you through that," Bessie says.

"I just don't like seeing people suffer," I say. "I'm not saying it will be easy for me, but I want to try to help."

"Well," she says. "How about now? I just need someone to run me a hot bath and put some of my salts in there. They are white, in the bathroom cabinets. I can bathe myself, but if you can clear up my room and let in some daylight . . . just the labor of it all has been too much."

I head into her bathroom, open the windows, quickly clean the bathtub of its stains, and spread white salt into it until steam billows. As she soaks in it, I open the sliding door, letting in the excited air full of salty sea breeze, pick up all her clothes from the floor, take out all the accumulated

dirty dishes, pick up all the plastics of finished snacks and put them into the trash can, take out the dirty clothes to the laundry room and put them in a thorough wash cycle, change her bedding, until her room is organized and full of clean air. On the table I find her manuscript, printed, bound, about 160 pages.

"You can look at it if you want," Bessie says, walking in with a towel wrapped around her body. It's a rom-com; I can tell right away that it's very funny, and I've never encountered a romance novel that deals with the obstacle of immigration and love with a character from southern Africa.

When I put the manuscript down, Bessie's expression turns serious, and she whispers, "Anaya, that night we got attacked, I'm sorry I pushed you. I don't know what got into me. I don't want to blame Huis, I shouldn't have given into its nudge."

I stare at the night pressed to the windows, wondering if her apology is as unsafe as Huis at night.

I've spent the past four weeks speed writing, sending Anouk my first 30,000-word excerpt. Now my second submission is due in six days. That evening, Miche suggests we do a writing session in the dining room. For the first time, it feels beautiful sitting with the other fellows—I no longer feel alone. I get straight to work, interspersed with questions I throw to them, and them deliberating their anxieties to each other.

I glance at the stack of papers beside my laptop, freshly inked the title in bold, *Void in History,* the excerpt of my manuscript that I used for my pitch. I page through it, unable to recall moments of writing these lines.

Something about this house has breathed life into my writing. I am happy, I am proud. everything is worth it for this literary piece. And since the sangoma visit, I feel lighter, hopeful, perhaps a sign that we're healed.

During my research—my conversations with Yanano and the other ghostwomen—I learned about violence in the borderlands of Botswana and its neighboring country, Zimbabwe, during the colonial era, that affected Black Batswana women who lived near these areas, which is hard to think about. I turn to poetry instead, the brevity in it is befitting; its slick knife cuts away at fillers, conveying more than can be said in paragraphs. Huis's dialect is poetry. I don't have much time to focus on fluff.

Bessie leans over, eyes skimming my pages. "How's it going? What are you even writing about?"

"My book is historical fiction," I say, recalling the period that Yanano and the other spiritwomen come from. What I don't say is how I want to represent them, archive their stories beyond the borders. "I've been looking for documents written by Black women in southern Africa from the 1800s until our countries gained independence. Most papers and books are written through a white lens or hidden behind high paywall systems." What I don't say is Yanano and the spiritsisters are my research. No more white lens that I have to filter through.

Ogone stops typing, stares at me. "Please don't do that thing where your story is racism with the white-people-are-evil horror trope. It gets so boring and cliché when writers do that."

I lean back, crossing my arms. "Horror is the lived reality of people."

"I'm sure there are creative ways to tell a horror story. Why is this one always the only one we tell?" Ogone asks.

"What is horror but the graveyard of our pain? And a nightmare here and there," Bessie says, eyes lowered, and I sense she remembers the time I got stuck in the wardrobe.

"I don't want all my suffering to be retold by a white person, for the system to win, and for another one of us to die," I say. "Our voices should be enough without the passport of a white voice to carry us.

"Bathong, Anaya, I've been helped by so many white people in the publishing industry, who published me, requested more work from me, supported me when I needed it, whereas I can count one or two Black people who gave me support, whilst most wouldn't even give me the time of day," Ogone says.

I chew my lip, shoulders slouching. "I know, me too; I'm not denying that. But I listened to some of Langa's interviews and speeches. Have you listened to him expose the harsh treatment by white gatekeepers?"

"Listen, Langa is right, here and there," Ogone says. "But he's always raging some propaganda on social media about racism and colonialism to get himself into certain spaces. My whisper networks say his Black activism is performative, that he's very abusive of the same African people whose rights he's fighting for in public. He's a fake progressive. It's not always black and white, Anaya, when it comes to race issues."

"Yeah, from what I hear, he loves to pander to the white gaze and wants to be the only nigga in the room doing so," Bessie says.

Miche folds her laptop shut, and I'd almost forgotten she was there. "That's not what Anaya is saying though. She's writing a story about the historical violence that impacted her people, especially Black women in southern Africa. *That* is her focus, not the nuance of white identity." Then she turns to me. "I used to be so uninformed, but after my time with you guys and other Black people, I see the truth now. I have relatives who played a part in this history, who are so racist it's heinous. I find it so infuriating when other white people say they want to help but only destroy marginalized people." She speaks passionately, like she really believes it. "Your voice is important—a story like this, your people's truth needs to be told. You should write your story in the way you believe is right, not because of what people think. No one has a right to tell you to erase your native tongue or your culture on the page. Stay true to yourself, Anaya."

I'm stunned. Miche is standing up for me. But I recall her complaining about Langa's class.

"Wow, thanks, Miche," I say.

"I know it's not easy sticking to your truth. I always want to help, but I don't want to step on any toes. If you want, I can share some family records from that time. I have a box of them upstairs."

"Really?" I say sitting up, suddenly interested in records I can't find online. Despite what Miche did to me in the spirit realm, this is gold and will definitely be worth it if I win. "Yes, please; that will help."

I pile my sheets together and follow her to her bedroom. Miche regales to me the stories she heard as we flip through the pictures of her ancestors, which I note down.

"It's the first time I've had a one-on-one with any of you," she says. "It feels nice. I've been feeling lonely."

I never imagined to be in her shoes, stuck as the minority in the house listening to me go on about the sins of her ancestors.

"What do you think of *Void in History* as the title for my manuscript?" I ask her instead.

"I like 'void,' but 'history' feels bland and arbitrary," she says.

"Well," I say, "it's a book on time, and how slippery it is, because the history is endless, and it never truly left these Black women."

She sits up, a light of curiosity in her eyes. "How about *A Void in Time*?"

"I love it," I say, typing it into my manuscript: *A Void in Time.*

Finally she finds her family documents, and shows them to me, some writings and pictures. "My great-great grandparent was one of the Dutch settlers, a sailor employed by the Dutch East India Company, the VOC," she says. "Once they were no longer employed, he was given farmland. They needed slaves for labour for agriculture, wine, wheat farms . . . most came from everywhere—Ghana, Madagascar, Mozambique—ships that were on the way to America, Europe, Netherlands. Slavery was illegal in the Netherlands, you know, so slaves were sold in the Cape."

We keep looking at the documents. I envy how Miche has access to so much of her family history but I don't know much about mine.

She breaks the silence. "You know, my book is also about reckoning with history too. My aunt told me of two slaves who had children—I think one came from India and one from

Ghana—who were born into slavery, and I want to write about that too, how my family impacted them. But I'm afraid people will cancel me, that I don't have the right to tell that story. What do you think?"

It's very much in keeping with what most Günter fellows produce, and her writing is good enough to achieve that, but the question is too heavy for me to answer.

"I'm sorry, Miche, but I don't have an answer for that. I don't even know if I have the right to write *my* book. I never wanted to write a story on colonisation and historical violences of such depth."

"But you're here for a reason. Your talent should mean something," she says, eyes wide and earnest.

"We were picked, Miche, for the same reason that someone else wasn't picked." *We* somehow met Günter's standards, and it makes me sick sometimes that I'm complicit in ways I don't know.

Miche tilts her head. "So does that mean you should silence yourself? We are here to build ourselves, so that we can have enough power to bring other people along with us. We can be their doors, and in turn they can be the doors for other generations. But we can't do that if we don't use Günter. You will be a great writer one day. Don't let that future be buried by such negative politics."

The slump I felt this morning vanishes, becomes replaced by confidence. I stare at Miche, thankful for her kindness. For the first time since I arrived, I don't feel as afflicted by Günter as before. This residency may be competitive and full of pressure, but it's put me in a community of women facing the same anxieties I have, comforting each other, and having someone I can share my own secrets with.

I page through the loose old papers. "Your family just gave these documents to you?"

"No, they were burned," she says.

"Then how'd you get them?"

"Huis," Miche whispers. "Huis gave them to me. She's been talking to you too, right? Helping you with your story? She helps me too. I've never had such flow in my creativity before."

"Me too, though sometimes it scares me, but I'm learning to face it. I'm becoming a better writer."

"I was scared at first, but I have to do good with this gift. We have to, Anaya." She grips my hands together, her eyes a pleading glow. "There's power in your words, Anaya, and speaking it into Huis, she casts a spell on our words. Writing in this place turns our ordinary words into magic, into people's lives. *She* empowers me, empowers us as women. Huis is our altar, and we have to give ourselves as offerings to her."

She raises her hand, showing me her bracelet, the one she always wears. "Huis protects me through this. She loves me like a mother, punishes me like one too."

Then she stares into the distance. "My mother believes that the farm we settled on, the land belonged to an African tribe here, who cursed us. That curse made us vulnerable spiritually, broke our spirits open. I think that's what attracted Huis to me. Huis said my body and spirit were already prepared for it. She gives me sight into things I never had access to: the experience of a Black body, the past of my ancestors—before I was blind, but with Huis, I see now, I see."

Of course. The Blacks are always witchcraft-cursing people.

I don't ask Miche how Huis allows her to experience a Black body, but I remember her cold tongue tracing the Black off mine.

I am Michele Visser, signing off. Thank you for listening to What Happened to Ana? *If you enjoyed this episode, please share, subscribe, and leave a review. We are a small two-person team, my assistant and I, and every like and subscription goes a long way. See you next week, Crimies!*

[theme music]

♡11,022 ≺1,067

To do:

Contact - Hennah Kyereh Kwaku (poet from Gonasua, Ghana) and Wame Molefhe (Motswana author; ask if she knows of Batswana female writers and scholars from 1800s onward.)

Suggestions from Molefhe -
Mositi Torontle - The Victims (damn, out of print)
Seatlholo Tumedi, ✓
Mantsete Marope (writes in Setswana).

Notes from call w/ Hennah:
*** erasure poetry
Solmaz Sharif
Marwa Helal ✓
Tracy K Smith ✓
Nicole Sealey
Mary Ruefle

- Experimentalism - form can shape grief, be a metaphor of how grief moves on the page.
-> Diana Khoi Nguyen - Ghost Of.

 **Langa Mangezi** @LangaMangezi 5h

It's interesting how the people that want trigger warnings for matters and teachings regarding historical events are those who don't want to be reminded about the evil their ancestors did to our people. Yet we, the victims, don't have trigger warnings to protect us from systemic racism, imperialism, xenophobia, wars, etc. Yet we have to get on with it. It's simple, unenroll from my class, because I will never stop educating our people. At this point in my career, I have the privilege to decline such teaching roles that require me to kiss ass and submit myself to policies that only promote cultural erasure and racism. Class dismissed.

♡ 11,022 ⇄ 1,067

 **Anaya Sebeya** @AnayaSebeya 1h

I love your classes! These are much needed teachings that cleanse out the brainwashing of colonial erasure.

♡ 25 ⇄ 3

   93 ⋮

RANEWA

I went through my notes, as if I needed a refresh, sorting them, organizing, pinning some on my wall. I needed to reexamine all witness accounts I had on file. I looked at the newspaper clips where I'd scribbled notes in the margins from readings and research:

- There was no new scientific information, which meant no body.
- The investigation team hadn't been able to find my sister's electronic devices to read built-in GPS tracking system.
- There was not enough probable cause for a warrant to seize some of the suspects' electronic devices.

My list of suspects had whittled down from Langa, Ogone (very doubtful) to Miche, who was originally on the list but is now my only suspect given her suspicious podcast. Ruvimbo and Nilza hadn't spent that much time in Huis to have done something to Anaya. Langa himself stayed out of it, maintaining his literary career throughout the world by attending conferences and the premiere of his TV show, and there were no details in Anaya's items that pointed to him. There were many episodes ahead that Miche was hiding, so I focused my attention on her because clearly there was more that may not

even be revealed in these secret episodes, and I was going to find out exactly what that was.

I remembered from an earlier episode, Yanano telling the other women to hush at the mention of a former Günter fellow who failed them. When I research Nosipho + Günter, I find a missing persons report: "Former Günter fellow and Eswatini short story writer Nosipho Kunene disappeared mysteriously during the award ceremony . . ." This occurred five years ago, and to this day she's never been found. I made note of that for further research, wondering if my sister dug into it or wrote about her.

I paged through my sister's notebook, landing on one of her poems that she'd printed out during her Günter residency. My sister seemed to write a lot of poems in Günter Huis, something she'd never done before. I couldn't connect this poem to what happened to her but saved it in case it came in handy. It was not a coincidence that I chanced on this poem whilst looking for answers—I stared at Anaya's phone, as if she were right next to me, quietly nudging me with breadcrumbs toward her. It had to be her. She must have given me the secret episodes and now she was pointing me to this poem for a reason. *Anaya, I'm listening, I'm listening, sister.* I leaned desperately close to the words until my nose touched the tip of her notebook and I could smell Chanel perfume. If poetry became her truth, then the mystery in her text would lead me to her.

three ghostwomen and an elder ghostman

In a distant kraal, sounds of moaning cattle. The walk of three ghostwomen carve a path. We come across an elder ghostman who wields a knife. On a kgotla stool he sits, whistling, drinking thothotho, working a knife on a piece of wood, carving it into a statuette. I cast my eyes at his hands. It's not wood he carves, but the face of a Mosarwa man—he carves off the ears, lips, and eyes, whistling, whistling, whistling. Punishment for cattle raiding. A slave system within our tribes. The cattle bartered for tobacco, tin goods, iron—the Mosarwa man smiles at me, ao lekgoa la me, he says. Take this whittling knife, the ghostwomen sing, to stab the flesh, unhinge the spirit, where evil laps their tongues, ferrying away the sleeper, but the body is yours. The cattle moan, the ghostman carves, carves, carves, the Mosarwa man lies poised in the ghostman's lap as he is dismantled and an unknown flesh waits for me. The whistle continues, holding hostage my ear.

The next day, I had a meeting with Anouk, who was, quote, "beyond thrilled" to have me as her client. I stood outside her home and thought of Anaya standing in this same place. I clenched my fingers into fists and knocked on the door of her skinny Victorian townhome. Surprisingly, she answered the door, along with her baby nesting on her shoulders.

"Ranewa, darling, welcome," she said, kissed me on the cheek, and motioned me inside. It was warm and smelled of lilies. Her nanny quickly retrieved her baby and took her into the nursery, and I followed Anouk up the stairs to her home office, which was lavishly decorated.

This is where Anaya sat. I stared into Anouk's green irises, to see past her kindness since Anaya had disappeared. She was the only Günter founder that kept regularly in touch with my family. She packed Anaya's belongings for us. *I will keep calm and sharpen my knife. I'll see what truth I can carve out from her,* I thought.

"Anaya was such a gifted writer—we didn't get along at all times, but I was very drawn to her power in words," Anouk said, pushing a tray of tea toward me. "I'm so happy that you've reconsidered publishing her Günter manuscript."

"*A Void in Time,*" I corrected her.

"Yes, exactly. I know you already have an interested publisher, but I would suggest we sub wide to open us up to bigger options."

I leaned back and sipped my tea. "Well, the publisher was interested in Anaya's case, given the attention around Miche's podcast."

"Between you and I," Anouk said, "I was blindsided by Miche's idea to narrate Anaya's life. I thought it in poor form and, should I say, tacky." Her fingers tapped rhythmically on the table. "Keep this under wraps, Ranewa, but this will be my last year with Günter. We are simply of different minds. I'm selling off my ownership to a literary friend. They're considering bringing in Langa as a permanent mentor. Clearly, he's been in their ears for quite a while now."

"Anouk," I said gently, "what happened that night of the Midnight Mix and Match? I spoke to Anaya a little bit during that time, and she seemed unsettled by it," I lie.

She began fiddling with her pen holder and notepads on an otherwise impeccably clean desk on the pretense of clearing it up, a distraction. "There were drugs involved, brought in by individuals without our knowing. It made for a strange, wild night. This kind of thing happens at some of these private engagements, hence my impending leave."

There was only one reason I came to entertain Anouk's crazy idea of working together: to gain access to Huis. As a founder, she had that power. I could care less about all these stupid plans of hers.

"Well, I'm working on Anaya's memoir to rebuff Miche's otherwise misleading and incomplete account of my sister's months here," I said. "Whilst I'm working on this project, it would help if you gave me access to Huis. I'm sure you'd allow me that access."

Her ergonomic chair creaked as she leaned back. "We have this year's cycle of fellows living there, but I'll try and work around it."

"Thank you," I said. "I know this will be a great partnership."

In my handbag, Anaya's phone vibrated. When I glanced at it, a document had appeared mysteriously, labeled "Trigger Warning" by Anaya Sebeya. It was not an episode, but her chapter written in her words.

My Account • Subscribe

CRIME COVERAGE

Fave Serial Killers • Top-Rated Crimes • Drop Dead Gorgeous
Slay Queens • Hot Cannibals

EXCLUSIVE: GÜNTER PRIZE DISAPPEARANCES LINKED TO OCCULT ACTIVITY

On the evening of Dec 20, a 25-year-old Motswana woman, Anaya Sebeya, disappeared from the Muizenberg Conference Center during the prize giving ceremony of the Günter Prize for African Women's Literature. She was last seen wearing a silk pantsuit.

Sebeya spent four months living at the renowned Günter Huis during the duration of the Günter residency. A few days before her disappearance, witnesses noted that she was agitated, had lost considerable amount of weight. Günter founders were pulled in for interrogation and released at 2.30 a.m. They declined to comment. Allegedly, another fellow, Ruvimbo Nkosi, dropped out of the residency due to the occult occurrences in the house. She declined to comment.

Sebeya is not the first Günter fellow to disappear. Five years ago, Nosipho Kunene's body was discovered on the shores of Camps Bay on 25 December, 04.58 a.m. by a homeless man. She was residing at the Günter Prize for their fifth prize giving season. An autopsy revealed no signs of foul play, though Kunene

was malnourished and reportedly exhibited strange behaviour before her death.

With now two strange disappearances related to the Günter Prize, one has to wonder what the cases have in common.

Is it the pressures of the publishing industry? Its obsession with cycling through debut authors capitalizing on fresh voices and finding the next big thing? Is the prize simply taking advantage of young writers?

After all, many aspiring authors have fallen to publishing scams; some have gone to desperate lengths to steal manuscripts, hijack the careers of dead friends, or sabotage the careers of other writers. Could this desperation be behind these disappearances?

Or is there something darker going on?

Thanks to our crack team of Crime Coverage journalists, we have new proof that Anaya Sebeya signed a deal with the devil to write a literary masterpiece.

Sign in or subscribe to read the full article.

“*During the 1970s, the violence in neighbouring states spilled over into Botswana, making untenable its previous policy of having no army . . . women in the north-east border regions who suffered violence from South African and Rhodesian soldiers crossing illegally and yet routinely into Botswana. As these incidents show, rape as a weapon of war has a long history in the region . . . Crossing the border represented more than a search for leisure activities . . . It also represented a successful encounter with the 'enemy', in the form of Black women's bodies. Having crossed the border, the white soldiers used sex to subdue, demean and humiliate their enemy, 'the woman of the black man'. In this context, the black woman was subject to sexualised racism.*”

Maitseo M.M. Bolaane,
"Cross-Border Lives, Warfare and Rape in Independence-Era Botswana"

A Sea of White

by Anaya Sebeya

there's a tear in the land, a scar, by the border
stretches for 200 km
where the soul of lost fathers
brews in the mines
in segregation
the women's bodies, a borderland
in Botswana ~~Bechuanaland Protectorate~~ & other bodies of
~~Rhodesia, South West Germany, Cape Colony, Transvaal, Portuguese East Africa—~~
call me by my name
wispy ghosts cross bodies as they please
strip this land
naked
of
us

Huis, a migrant house
Huis, our little Dutch House.
such Dutch style.
such thatch hair.
she's a window to
those pale daggers
piercing Black women
oh! how earth hurts on this soil of ours
this black island in a sea of white

this tearing in the white
this torn piece of black in the white

a castrated black in this white
a lost history
they murdered our land
they murdered
your face, your   skin, your mind
here they come! those men of bone
here they come, here they void time

frica. The first was the arrest of Beyleveld and his companions (discussed
f a woman who was eight months pregnant, by four South African soldiers in the
f the Limpopo River, on 9 October. Part of a group of nine who had illegally
he Shashe and Limpopo rivers, the white soldiers were reported to have crossed into
which they had stolen the previous night at an official party on the South African side
vent to a house on a farm where they found two women and two men. Five soldiers
nd alcohol were not met, but four remained and proceeded to rape one of the
he men, some of whom would later become witnesses at the soldiers' court martial.
tepfather of the rape victim when he attempted to intervene. Afterwards they went
f the soldiers had forgotten his hat at the house, so they returned a short while
xhibit at the trial). At this stage, they were armed and when they could not find the
ictim to use as evidence, they assaulted the men who were there in the house. The
outh Africa. The woman was examined by a doctor at the Mahalapye hospital,
ape allegations. She had sustained injuries including bruises to her eye and
er on the face during the rape. In court later, more details of the story
vho lived in Jubudi village, Gwanda/Beitbridge District, in Rhodesia. She
er partner Philip just over the border in Botswana on the Coetzee farm.
eft behind in Jubudi. After the white South African soldiers crossed the
er mother and, in the presence of onlookers, dragged her away and
n Mahalapye, 254 km from Pont Drift/Baines Drift, a considerable
tation a senior male police officer took down the details and then
ape victim, on 13 October 1977. Sana then signed this police
nade by her mother, Philip (stepfather) and Chipapa (a farm
estimony concerning her ordeal in full, below, because it
iolence that characterises cross- border spaces. . . . These
ape victim was not Motswana by birth but 'Rhodesian'.
Rhodesian border, she had to cross the border to see her
ncluding the rape victim and the attempted rape victim,
Malawi). These texts also describe the soldiers crossing
ex. Adries De Wet, a state witness, said that while
he accused say to the others: 'We are now going to have
voman started screaming and one of the soldiers shouted,
emained behind then dragged, strangled and 'slept on top
oldiers' view of the border using the testimony of De
epresented more than a search for leisure activities such
ncounter with the 'enemy', in the form of black women's
emean and humiliate their enemy, 'the woman of the
Thus Sana's text illuminates gendered experiences of
Crossing the border represented more than a search for
epresented a successful encounter with the 'enemy', in
sed sex to subdue, demean and humiliate their enemy,
exualised racism. Thus Sana's text illuminates gendered
ubordination. Crossing the border represented more
lso represented a successful encounter with the
oldiers used sex to subdue, demean and humiliate
ubject to sexualised racism. Thus Sana's text
f gender subordination. Crossing the border
llicit sex. It also represented a successful
order, the white soldiers used sex to subdue,
lack woman was subject to sexualised racism.
acialised experiences of gender subordination.
unting, drinking and illicit sex. It also
Having crossed the border, the white soldiers
his context, the black woman was subject to
s racialised experiences of gender
afari hunting, drinking and illicit sex. It
Having crossed the border, the white
his context, the black woman was subject
s racialised experiences of gender
unting, drinking and illicit sex. It also
rossed the border, the white soldiers
he black woman was subject to
acialised experiences of gender
f the black man'. In this context,
acial oppression, as well as
eisure activities such as safari
orm of black women's bodies.
he woman of the black man'. In this
xperiences of racial oppression, as
search for leisure activities such as

above), and the second w
Pont Drift area on the Bo
crossed the border at the co
Botswana after drinking rum
of the border. After crossing the b
left the scene when their demands fo
women, attempted to rape the other ar
They also assaulted the (approximately)
back across the Limpopo River into South
afterwards to retrieve it (the hat later
hat, which had been hidden by the mo
soldiers then crossed the Limpopo and
and the resulting medical evidence con
back when the soldiers dragged, kicked a
emerged. The victim was named Sana, a w
had been visiting her mother, Miriam, who
Sana was married to a man named Ndlovu, wh
border and arrived at the farm they found Sa
raped her. The rape incident was reported at a po
distance from the site of the rape. At the Mahal
wrote a coherent account based on the statement prese
document. Other statements that appear in the same BN
labourer), who corroborated the rape victim's story. I
makes visible the texture of cross-border lives and the vuln
texts dramatically illustrate the ambiguity of the border in this p
Sana's life also straddled the border because while she lived in a vi
mother on a farm on the other side in Botswana. The Tuli farm
were a mix of Africans from Botswana, Rhodesia and South Africa
into Botswana for leisure, e.g. swimming in the river, drugs, alcoh
crossing the Limpopo to reach the Botswana commercial farms he h
sex with black women'. All but the four accused ran away when
'Some African men are coming'. De Wet told the court how th
of a woman who was eight months pregnant'. One can build a pic
Wet, the victim and others who witnessed the rape. Crossing
as safari hunting, drinking and illicit sex. It also represented a
bodies. Having crossed the border, the white soldiers used sex
black man'. In this context, the black woman was subject to sexuali
racial oppression, as well as racialised experiences of gender sub
leisure activities such as safari hunting, drinking and illicit s
the form of black women's bodies. Having crossed the border, the wh
'the woman of the black man'. In this context, the black woman wa
experiences of racial oppression, as well as racialised experiences
than a search for leisure activities such as safari hunting, drinking and
'enemy', in the form of black women's bodies. Having crossed the borde
their enemy, 'the woman of the black man'. In this context, the black
illuminates gendered experiences of racial oppression, as well as racialised
represented more than a search for leisure activities such as safari hunting, d
encounter with the 'enemy', in the form of black women;s bodies. Having
demean and humiliate their enemy, 'the woman of the black man'. In this
Thus Sana's text illuminates gendered experiences of racial oppression,
Crossing the border represented more than a search for leisure activities su
represented a successful encounter with the 'enemy', in the form of black wom
used sex to subdue, demean and humiliate their enemy, 'the woman of the bla
sexualised racism. Thus Sana's text illuminates gendered experiences of racial oppress
subordination. Crossing the border represented more than a search for leisure activi
also represented a successful encounter with the 'enemy', in the form of black wom
soldiers used sex to subdue, demean and humiliate their enemy, 'the woman of the bla
to sexualised racism. Thus Sana's text illuminates gendered experiences of racial oppress
subordination. Crossing the border represented more than a search for leisure activities su
represented a successful encounter with the 'enemy', in the form of black women's bod
used sex to subdue, demean and humiliate their enemy, 'the woman of the black man'. In t
sexualised racism. Thus Sana's text illuminates gendered experiences of racial oppressio
subordination. the white soldiers used sex to subdue, demean and humiliate their enemy,
the black woman was subject to sexualised racism. Thus Sana's text illuminates gendered ex
racialised experiences of gender subordination. Crossing the border represented more than
hunting, drinking and illicit sex. It also represented a successful encounter with the 'en
Having crossed the border, the white soldiers used sex to subdue, demean and humiliate t
context, the black woman was subject to sexualised racism. Thus Sana's text illuminat
well as racialised experiences of gender subordination.Crossing the border represented
safari hunting, drinking and illicit sex. It also represented a successful encounter with

Zimbabwe, where does it hurt?
Namibia, where does it hurt?
South Africa, where does
it hurt?
It hurts it hurts
it hurts in the
b l a c k
woman

A f r i c a
where does it
h u r t ?
It hurts in and
out of me

She was eight
months pregnant
A child in her
t h e y
penetrated
with their
w h i t e
t h e y
w a n t
women
they want
w o m e n
they want
women they
want women
they want
w o m e n
they want
w o m e n
they want
w o m e n
they want
w o m e n
It hurts it
hurts it
hurts in
the black
w o m a n
It hurts it
hurts it
hurts in
t h e
b l a c k
w o m a n
It hurts it
hurts it
hurts in
t h e
black

w o m a n
It hurts
it hurts
it hurts
in the black
w o m a n
It hurts it
hurts it hurts
in the black
w o m a n
It hurts it hurts it

In the dark, came out a moo
Monna o mosweu a tswa mo nageng mo lefifing
Man, white, came out the forest out
the dark

Monna o a tsena mo
lapeng lame
At night a
white old man
came into my
h o m e
Placed a plaque on my
b o d y
Named me
Bechuana victoria falls
ke mosi-oa-tunya
ke motswana
I no longer own my body,
Ke letimela mo mmeleng wame
Said that he discovered me...
I became a white word a
white world
A word not of my tongue
I could not move
I could not
s h o u t
I had
s e b e t e l e d i
I couldn't speak
out and tell him
N o
That is not my
n a m e
I sat there
lived in my home
that was no longer
h o m e
lived in my body
that was no longer
h o m e
Watched my
skin turn into
b o n e
Until the
language the
culture became
extinct from
my body

This white old
man came into my
b o d y
penetrated it
We were

bordered up
divided up

divided—transvaal
colony, british
bechuanland, german
south west Africa, cape
colony we were divided
divided divided still divided
The body of Botswana was
penetrated from every side

Colonization was a big humiliation for men. They had the feeling that their territories and their women were penetrated by the white man and the white culture and the Western world. . . . I think that now they are getting a sort of revenge, and women are the ones who are enduring this revenge."

Leïla Slimani

Trigger Warning

By Anaya Sebeya

I sit in the sunroom in a meditative trance, looking over my notes on my encounters with Yanano and the ghostwomen of Huis. I've been using them as breadcrumbs to research the history of southern African countries in the 1800s for my manuscript. I'm supposed to meet with Anouk in ten days.

Shadows track the day across the walls as I research the violence Black African women experienced in the borderlands of Southern Africa. I come across maps from the colonial period, pull up documents and theses from online. I research the Bakgalagadi and Bakwena and attempt to find archival records of the violence Batswana citizens encountered when Botswana became a refuge for freedom fighters from its neighboring countries. Attacks, bomb raids, intertribal conflicts. I scavenge the internet looking for photographs and try to find the technical words to describe what I know to be true.

I find two historical novels in English; I try to track down pre- and postcolonial books written in Setswana by Batswana authors, but most are out of print and costly. The ones I do find, the writing is painfully dense. Through days and days of tortuously trying to translate the nuance of each word, I have realized how foreign I am from my own tongue.

Finally, I stand, stretch. Walk a lap around the living room. Catch my own reflection in the mirror. Light flickers on its surface. Then a sharp burst of light in front of the mirror, diagonal in shape and tall as me, revealing the dark shadows of another reality beyond it, like the slit of a door ajar. A heavy draft pulls from its orifice. Pulls me into the mirror.

The tunnel of air spits me onto the concrete floor of Huis's subconscious. Huis's realm. Huis's mind. It feels familiar, like I'm in a different part of the same house I've visited before. When I look up, I see Yanano, wearing a tukwi.

I wipe the dust from my clothes as she walks to a sofa and reaches for the coffee table beside it where an old-fashioned radio stands. Yanano turns the knobs, trying to catch a frequency. "It's difficult catching the right time on this thing," she says, tutting. "I consumed nothing for a season to be able to attune my frequency to yours."

"Frequency?" I ask.

"The balance of energy of spirit and how loose it is within the body," she says. "You won't understand. No matter. Here you are now. Huis goes crazy if we don't feed her."

A glimmer of fear in my throat as I whisper, "By me being here, you're feeding Huis?"

She nods. "Your flesh is barring us from possessing you. But soon it'll be safe enough to enter."

The frank confidence in her blunt statements terrifies me. She stands with such serenity that it frightens me more than if she were to strike me with her hand. I fear her more than the creatures that brought me torment.

I clasp my hands to my head at the sharp pain in my brain.

"There, there now," she says, her soothing hand brushing the ailment from my head. "Your body is trying to communicate with you. A pain signal. Be not worried. We'll take care of it. You're such a beautiful, beautiful girl." Tears fill her eyes, and I can't ascertain why she's becoming emotional.

"We?"

The pain flickers behind my eyes, slithers from my temples, rests on my shoulders, dials down in intensity. I wrap my arms around myself. I want to go back. I want to go home. From the radio, a voice spills out, and a ghostly woman sweeps in, brushing me with the heavy layers of her attire. "This will be mine," she says, ferrying the radio into the dark passages of Huis, inhaling the voice that flows out from the radio's speakers.

In one corner of the room, a young girl sits crouched, crying into her knees, and one of the ghostwomen bows low, patting her back, whispering, "It won't be so bad. One day, you'll be initiating another person. It's unfortunate your spirit was loose to begin with."

Another woman sits desolate, a deadpan expression, slouched forward on the couch.

The newcomers and I, the light of life sheds itself like golden mist through our pores. Whilst the others, like Yanano who live in this place, are unlit flames.

Through the open door, I glimpse a blur of white float down the hallway, unattended.

"There are two ways this will go: Either you maintain sovereignty over your body or you don't. If you succeed, you must tell our stories," Yanano says. "I am here to help you if I fail to help myself."

"Help yourself?"

At the corner of her mouth, a slight smile. "That is all I can say."

Neck stretched high, and her chin lifted up, Yanano strides into the wide passage, the ceiling so far high it melts into the darkness of the house. Soon we enter a space where the wall to the right has a bank of windows. I concentrate my eyes on the nape of her neck where tufts of Afro escape her tukwi. The shoulder pads of her dress elongate the tips of her shoulders sharply. Her wide skirt brushes the floor, leaving a shadow beneath them. She seems to float along the floor's surface, a rapid glide.

Without a break in her stride, she says, "Look outside."

Reflexively, my head turns and I gasp. The sun is grief-swollen in the sky, its mellow light a sleet run across the scene beneath it.

A rootless tree rises from the earth, shadows of lean fruits hang loosely from it, crumbs of earth raining down. The distorted arms of the tree holds bodies, strange fruit rotting from the mourning branches, heads angled wrongly, eyes bulged, bodies swaying in the air, their shadows weeping across the ground searching for their blood.

My skin goes cold, watching the white hem of people sitting below on kgotla stools. Crossed legs, lean white limbs toss cards, pinch cigarettes into thin lips. Their guns sitting

beside them like dogs waiting for commands. One white hand raises a glass, smiling at the camera angled to him. Flash. Memento.

One of the bodies is staring at me through the window. His mouth tries to reach me with words, and I back away I back away I back away, his words clammy on my skin, my breath, my arms. He wears skin like mine, in me, and I am hanging on the tree, I am his dead body, I am the dead body and I can't claw my way out of his fate out of his skin out of his rope around his neck, my bones are brittle at the nape—

The tree is heavy.

The tree is heavy.

The tree is heavy.

Vultures pick at us—I feel their sharp beaks in the balls of my eyes, the bulbs of my cheeks, tearing at my flesh.

A cold hand grasps my bare shoulders. My life hisses at the seams of me. Yanano pulls at me, and I am back in my body, back in safety, the phlegm of death caught in my throat in my lungs, the pain of broken bones gripping to my neck's skin.

"I was dead," I sob. "I was dead."

"My dear, did you think you've been alive this whole time?" Yanano says. "You are the ghost of the past that knows how to *look* alive."

My hands won't stop shaking, the cold tremble of death still present in my veins. Tears crawl down my face, and a slurry of incoherent words pour out from my mouth. A light flashes. She lowers an old-fashioned camera. Slips out the picture, that the wall accepts as part of itself, framed,

to claim as a memento along with the other women whose pictures have been taken.

"Why?" is all I ask.

She shrugs. "It's just what they used to do."

"Who are they?" I ask, angling my head at the floating tree outside, afraid to look, afraid to be captured again.

"Our people, the Herero and Nama were lynched by the Germans. This happened in your great-grandmother's time, not so long ago." Her cadence of talking jerks at the word great-grandmother.

She points south of the house, toward the garden and orchards of oranges and green land. "If you walk through the gardens, you will see their tribes being raided and killed and being pushed out into the harsh desert." In reflex, I turn my head to look at the tree cradling the victims. "They've been dead for 119 years," she says. "It's not easy, living like that, on that tree. Do you know why they want to kill you? They don't want to; it's just a consequence of trying to escape from the terrible events of history through Black bodies. They can only enter the borders of a Black territory. We are their only freedom."

I stand by the window, ashamed that I did not know how these people died, that this is how I must find out, and I become overwhelmed with an undefinable grief, and I become sick with it, that I, in turn, will repeat this horror on the page. I stare sympathetically at Yanano that she lives through this, forgetting that I should be afraid of her.

"One hundred and nineteen years?" I say faintly.

"It's today for us," she says. "It's every day for me."

"Is that why you've been haunting me and my friends?" I ask. She doesn't respond.

Yanano continues walking, to the front door, onto the stoep—and I remember her as the woman who stood on that stoep the first time I entered Huis's subconscious—across the front yard, through the small gate and the endless veld.

"You are only seeing what has been in your blood this whole time," she says. "But you've felt this since you were born, and you feel it when you walk into the stolen lands and white spaces. You're seeing it for what it is."

I look away, feeling the swaying shadows roam above us, dappling sunlight. Across the border, the sky is distinct from ours, dusk turn to dawn, keeping the borderlands in eternal curfews. The war on the other side brings a steady flow of refugees fleeing into the northeastern parts of Botswana and Tuli Circle. We cross veld and stand under the shade of a huge Mashatu tree.

"Anyone could penetrate our country, especially if they found unofficial entry points," she says. "I too crossed over, didn't have a passport. It was perhaps easier then than it is now with all your border control and restrictions." We turn onto a sandy path, hemmed in by thorn bushes and tall trees hanging above our heads leading into—

"1960," Yanano whispers, a tremble in her lips. "Six years before Botswana's independence from Britain. Every day I relive this memory, just like those hanged men have been living their deaths for over a hundred years."

She keeps walking, the hem of her skirt clasping bits of grit. Head bent forward, the bones of her spine protruding

at the nape of her neck. The border of trees gives way onto a clearing of land.

"I have a ten-year-old in Zimbabwe," Yanano says, out of nowhere, gaze distant as she stares into the horizon. I don't know where this story is leading, but the air becomes a different kind of chilly than when Huis spat me out into my real world; this one is the air of graveyard. "A ten-year-old little boy, who looks quite like you—the eyes, the cheeks, the teeth, let me see your teeth."

She whirls to face me; her fingers press open my mouth. "Just like my son's," she exclaims. "I had relatives in Botswana and would visit them. There were some border areas you could cross through that had little guarding. I left my son with my grandmother; I didn't think the trip would be safe for him, see? It was nighttime when me and the others boarded a mokoro to cross the Chobe River. We wanted to go at night, to avoid being seen by Rhodesian forces. I was terribly afraid, clung my fingers so hard around the edge of that canoe, I might have toppled it over, waiting for a bullet to find me."

I stare at the river, its undulating backbone scarred by the light of the moon.

"We came from all over. Angola, Southwest Germany, Transvaal colonies in South Africa. Modimo, bless those Batswana, the Babirwa. They took us in, fed us, and facilitated our transport. I knew if I was patient, I would gain Botswana citizenship and bring my son over. Botswana was our mecca then. I worked on a farm much like this one, in Tati, Tuli, Molopo, Lobatse and thereabouts," she whispers, eyes glistening. "Every so often, you'd see those white things crossing the river or the border. You couldn't tell them

apart; tourists, soldiers, or spies—everything was leisure to them, even us."

Yanano clutches my arms. "I've been pregnant for one hundred years."

A sudden realization hits me as she presses my hands to her protruding bump. "I feel you in my blood sometimes," I tell her. "I feel all of you, and I can't explain it, the rage, the anger, the grief. It's so overpowering. You're unhealed, not buried right. Your ghosts linger in our blood. I encounter it in my life, in Günter—they can have all the words for these things—systemic racism, genocides, wars, xenophobia, generational trauma, what does it matter what the words are, when it won't heal us?" Yanano nods passionately as the words rush from my lips. "All of this, we pass it on to our children and their children. I wish this wasn't our inheritance. I see now. You were killed and had nowhere else to go," I say.

"You understand, you understand," she cries, clutching my arms tighter. "This skin like yours is the only land we can live in. You have to understand we have no choice."

"You may be from the past, but *your* past is present in me," I say. "I have to keep you alive, tell your story." It feels too much. *She* feels too much, overflowing with unknown things that will drown me, and I don't want a part of it. Guilt swarms me. How lonely it must be for her to endure what she's struggling with. I try to separate myself from her pain, hoping I don't catch it.

"Anaya—two of the men you'll see soon are ancestors to people you know. Anouk and Katja." Her hands drop from my arms, as if the force of life has left her. Her body resigned. "What's about to happen to you shouldn't happen to

anyone," she whispers. There is a dead stillness to her eyes as she says, "I'm so sorry. I just can't let my baby go through this again. Please forgive me. Oh, Jesu, ke kopa maitshwarelo."

She pushes me into the clearing and disappears into the dense bush. When I turn around, she's gone, and it is dark, cloudless, the moon nowhere. Behind me, the majestic farmhouse stands. I am reliving her memory.

I am sweeping the ground with lefelo la Setswana. Its sweeping utterance is meant to chase away bad spirits, but soon these wan spirits will come. Mmemogolo and my male cousin, who labors in the farmlands nearby, are in the house. I hear their voices and laughter as they prepare tea and diphaphatha. The owners of the house have gone on a trip, something about game hunting and tusks.

Hearing a noise, I look up, staring at the reeds of the Limpopo river.

It is dark night. Nine white soldiers cross the river.

"Where are you off to?" a distant voice calls to them.

One crows, laughing, "Going to sleep with Black women."

I stop sweeping, dropping the grass broom. A breath escapes my lungs. I step back. But they appear suddenly around me, in drunk stupor, asking me if we have motokwana in the house, something to keep them high.

No. The word shivers from my mouth.

Two stand on each side of me, three in front, two behind me. I'm hemmed in, motsoko wa bone burns. One lags behind us. I lift my hands to show them I mean no trouble. They're from the Transvaal. They stroll up the house stairs, fling open its front door. They encounter Mmemogolo and my cousin, asking the same questions.

Motokwana. *No.*

Alcohol. *No.*

Two leave. Seven remain.

Women then, give us women.

Kom, Kom, Kom, two men take my grandmother to the river.

Three grab me. Two follow us. A tremor shivers down my thighs with liquid haste. I'm a babble of fear.

"No, please," I say. "I'm not real, I'm not here, this shouldn't be happening to me."

A kick. A slap. My cousin watches wide-eyed.

One grabs me, turns me around. When he comes in, he dislocates my spirit from my body, much like a joint unhinging from the rest of the skeleton. It is happening to my body. I am there and not there. I am numb. Shock has paralyzed me at how sudden, how quick it happens. I watch my cousin flee, leave me behind, saving himself. All I can do is wait for it to end, to return to my reality, where it's safe, where history is better than the history here.

When I think it's over, another one sheds his uniform, drops his white cigarette, and pierces me with his white gun. In the distance, I hear raids, the crying voices of people and bullets, the smell of fire, the skin of earth burning. Then I see her, Yanano, crouched behind a bush of trees, hiding, shaking, weeping as the tribes flee the attack of their homesteads.

These soldiers devour me like they devour our land.

I lift my head, watch their shadows fade across the Limpopo River, returning.

This is what happened to Yanano. She made me take her place. She was six months pregnant. I am her. I am six months pregnant.

She was ~~I am~~ six months pregnant.

I am ~~she was~~

I am ~~she was~~

I am ~~she was~~

I am ~~she was~~ six months pregnant.

I am ~~she was~~ six months pregnant.

I am ~~she was~~ six months pregnant.

They killed her after. They killed her.

I cradle the six months of life in my womb. One of the remaining men finishes in me. I glimpse his whiteness, limp now. He places his calloused hand fondly along my neck. I am nowhere in this body. He laughs, kicks me to the ground, shoots me in the back. I lay there silent with death, my blood grieving into the earth, and—

"Isn't this a little much? Can you put a trigger warning on this, or better yet, cut some of these scenes out?" Anouk taps her manicured nails on my printed pages.

Light fills my eyes. I can still feel the bullet buried in my spine. I'm sitting on a hard chair opposite Anouk. An air conditioner hums from somewhere in the room, a stark difference from the balmy midnight air I was dragged through. Outside is the din of traffic and chatter of passersby. I bring my hands up, and they're trembling.

"Ana, are you okay?" Her words are blurred against my ears, my sight. I look up, trying to gain focus.

Anouk sits behind a glass desk, a backdrop of a floor-to-ceiling bookshelf neatly adorned with novels. Is

this her home office? A cat sits curled up, napping on a cushion in one corner.

Breaths edge out from my mouth. My air carries centuries of death. Anouk reaches for a box of tissue and hands it to me. There are tears flowing down my face. I feel sick showing weakness in front of her. I felt sick when the men ripped my clothes, as the cold air stroked my rear. Everything of me is exposed.

"I'm sorry," I say, patting the tissue to my face.

"Well, that's alright," she says, busying herself with arranging the pens and notepads and books on her desk. I stare stunned at the thickness of my manuscript pages—60,000 words of pages stacked together. She's annotated her comments, scratched out lines and paragraphs. It's heavily marked up. Pages I've no clue how and when she received, when I wrote them, or what they say. It must be my first mentor meeting, 20 October. Just a few hours ago it was 10 October.

Anouk presses a button on the side of her desk; a woman in a pale green maid's uniform enters. "Yes, madam," she says in a heavy Zimbabwean accent.

"Tapiwa, do we still have those scones?" Anouk says, and Tapiwa nods. "Good, good, prepare rooibos tea and—butter or jam?" she asks me. I shake my head. "Butter then. That's all, thank you."

Tapiwa leaves us in the stifling silence filled by my sniffling.

"Ana," she says, her bangles and earrings jingle when she moves her hands about. "I know this is difficult to hear, but I'm on your side. I was very excited about your project. I only want to turn this gem into a masterpiece."

I wipe my remaining tears, blow my nose, and crumple the tissue. I can't break down now. I look unprofessional, unprepared to take on any form of work. I have to control myself. I press my shaking hands against my legs to still them.

"What do you mean by cut back?" I ask, my eyes adjusting to the silent tones of her office and stark notes of her expensive perfume. There was no trigger warning to prepare me or protect Yanano from what happened to her. Staring up at Anouk's green eyes, I feel as if I'm overreacting. After all, I wanted this literary dream, didn't I?

"I have questions about these violent, graphic scenes," she says, leaning back and sipping her tea. "I understand that this feels important to you, but at most it comes across exploitative and dehumanizing."

She references books I should study to understand how to handle trauma in a sensitive manner, and I don't know where else to breathe myself into. I really wish I had Langa as a mentor. He'd understand. Who do I trust if I don't have an editor who understands, to tell me where I'm failing and how I can fix it?

"It's only a first draft," I say, brushing my fingers against each other.

Anouk purses her lips. "I also see that the placement of microaggressions in some of these scenes—"

"There's nothing micro about this aggression," I say, the pain from the bullet wound buttressing along my neck.

Tapiwa returns with warm scones and two cups of tea exhaling steam. Anouk nibbles on the scone and mouths a thank you.

"Now where was I?" Anouk asks. "Oh, genre of focus. Ana, the work is too experimental, and I'm not sure the

execution serves it well. Simplify it." She pauses to sip her tea, musing at its delicate notes. "If you stop focusing on this magical element, you will be onto something."

In Huis's realm, I raised my hands in surrender, and I want to do that now: surrender myself to Anouk. But surrendering didn't stop those men.

Tugging my nail against my wrist, I wonder what Yanano is doing now. She'll have to go through her scene tomorrow, and many more tomorrows, and who will take her place then? We are daily triggered by our history, haunted by the ghosts of history, and the world puts no content warnings to protect us from what we live every day. I want to curl up on the floor and cry this pain out, to feel warm arms hug me and a voice telling me that I'm not too much, that my pain is not too much, that my history is not too much. I don't want to hurt like this anymore.

Don't cry, I tell myself. *Don't cry, you're supposed to be strong. This is part of what it means to work hard. Chin up, no tears. You're a strong woman.*

But I'm so goddamned tired of being a strong woman.

"Oh, Ana," Anouk says when more tears flow down my face. "It's going to be alright, my skat. This doesn't say anything bad about you as a writer. I am your ally," she says, reaching for my hand, but I pull it away. "I'm worried, Ana, that you're stuck in a niche that is not commercial enough to succeed. That's where this feedback is coming from. I want you to succeed. Shall I continue?"

I nod, chest tight.

"Ana," she says, sighing. "You want to communicate something important, and you need to couch it so the shock value doesn't obscure your message."

"Does *couching* this afford you the opportunity to not confront what your grandfather did in Botswana?" I ask, hands trembling, saying what I don't want to say.

"Excuse me?" The color bleeds from Anouk's face.

"And, it's Anaya. That's my name," I correct her, and her mouth opens into a surprised *oh*. "I've heard all your suggestions. What are the repercussions if I don't follow your instructions?"

"Oh, Anaya," she says, feigning a laugh. "This isn't the military. You're not under a dictatorship. I'm only gently guiding you in the direction that I best believe will serve your career. "

"Well," I say, voice shaking. "I would have appreciated it if you asked me questions to understand my intentions and the story's identity. You didn't even interrogate yourself on why this writing makes *you* uncomfortable. Secondly," I say, taking a deep breath, pressing the tremor of my hands flat on my lap, "I won't cut 'these violent gory scenes' that did happen not so long ago. The world wants us to act as if our pain never existed, doesn't exist. But *this* is what happened, and I want people to know."

The silence in the room is deafening.

I brush my finger across my brow, feeling the tension suffocate me, bracing myself for my next words.

"It's not about the twenty-three years of experience you have in the publishing industry. You have negative years of experience as a Black Motswana editor. Günter Prize decides what's an appropriate African story, but there's no Black people on the board or in any positions of authority. You refused me the opportunity to work with Langa. I am grateful for the opportunity to be a Günter fellow,

but what does our gratefulness mean to you? Compliance? Submissiveness?"

It doesn't matter how softly and respectfully I deliver these lines; they're all grenades to her empire of control.

"I'm shocked. Is Langa the cause of this talk?" She gestures frustration with her hands. "Men like Langa, power-hungry ones, are not fazed by noes or obstacles. He's influential, but very unethical. Don't let him get into your head."

"I can judge for myself, Anouk," I say.

She exhales. "Frankly," she says, leaning forward, "if you're raising gatekeeping issues, then by your logic, you don't have the right to tell this story"—she taps my manuscript—"because only a Herero female author can write this book."

"There's an intersectionality issue in publishing of race, ethnicity, and gender," I say. "Statistically, many books in the US are authored by white people who are given more powers and opportunities to write our stories, which make it difficult for many indigenous authors of various ethnicities and tribes to break in. I'm quite certain that you rejected some authors for this prize because they weren't the right type of African author for *you*."

She's no longer angry; curiosity lights her eyes. "Have you considered writing essays? I *see* why Langa's interested in you." She taps her manicure on the table. "I want to connect you to a magazine editor I know in London; if you can write an essay on the politics of race, ethnicity, gender in African publishing with a feminist lens—this could slowly introduce you to the public. If we play our cards right, you'll have higher chances of winning the Günter Prize."

She says this like I'm a chess piece she's sculpting, a protégé that belongs to her. A prize that's between her and some elite milestone. And she will be the woman who made me. The bullet burns in my back.

"Oh, my next meeting is about to start," Anouk says, looking at her watch. "I'll ask S'fiso to drive you home. That'll be all."

I nod, whispering, "I'm sorr—"

RANEWA

After my successful meeting with Anouk, her driver, S'fiso, was driving me to Huis. I sat quietly, reading Anaya's document "Trigger Warning" on my phone, tears streaming down my face, and alternately stared out the tinted windows, devastated that *this* hadn't pushed my sister to reach out to me. Did she hate me that much? That could be the only explanation for why she didn't call me. I wanted to peel off my skin and stab out my heart so I wouldn't feel the pain anymore.

An unspeakable pain writhed through my every vein. I sat there, clutching the phone to my chest, sounds of mourning twitching my mouth. The driver stopped on the side of road far from Huis, startled, tried to hold me up, wondering if I was having a panic attack. Why hadn't Anaya called me? I would have believed her, would have given up everything and come to her side. What happened to us that she didn't confide in me? Why hadn't I reached out? Why hadn't *I* visited her? If I had, she'd still be here. I failed her; I can't fail her again. Memories of me partying and traveling reminded me why I was too distracted to think of my sister. It was my fault she disappeared. The guilt was an abyss of torture inside me. I'd destroy the world for repentance, to get her back. The pain subsided to something manageable, but I could still feel it ripple through my body. I needed more information about their visit with the sangoma, and why that hadn't prevented

my sister from facing violence. I hoped Ogone was still in Cape Town. I dialled her several times until she answered. We met at a café at Canal Walk.

She came with her fiancé, both wearing coordinating outfits that looked plucked out of a magazine. I wondered if she ever went anywhere without him. They ordered a chai latte and cappuccino, whilst I had warm water with lemon. I needed something to settle my stomach.

"I came across some information that you, Anaya, and Bessie visited a sangoma," I said.

"We shouldn't have done that. But it happened, and the sangoma helped us in some sense, even though she didn't save us," Ogone said, brushing her hair behind her ear. "By God's grace, at least I survived."

Adebowale leaned forward. "How did you find out about this? It wasn't in Miche's podcast."

His face was tense, staring at me like I was hiding something, but I understood. He wanted to protect his future wife, the same way I wanted to protect Anaya.

Ruvimbo had cut me off when I told her the truth; I didn't want to push Ogone away too.

"From Anaya's notes that I'd somehow missed when the investigators gave us back her laptop and items months ago," I said, which wasn't technically a lie. I hadn't seen Anaya's phone back then. "She referenced a lot of things about spirits and ghosts and Huis that I don't understand."

He leaned back, slightly relaxed, but still suspicious.

"I miss my sister terribly, and I'm just trying to piece everything together with the hauntings at Günter Huis with what happened to her," I said. "Can you help me?"

Ogone mused, with pinched lips, deliberating sharing something with me. She tapped her nails on the table, hesitant, and I wondered if it was vital information that could be the missing piece to Anaya's disappearance.

"Please," I pled, leaning across the table with my hands in prayer form. "If you know something, it would really bring me closure, just anything to deal with this madness. It pains me deeply that I don't know much about my sister and what happened in Günter Huis. Can you share something about the house at least. *Please,*" my voice broke.

Her tight face relaxed into sorrow, and she relented, sighing. "Well, the spirit of the house was charged," Ogone said. "I visited a pastor who saw into the spirit realm. He told me that the house was born in different times: 1640, 1806, 1899, 1919, 1870—tribal conflict, family rivalries, black magic, wars, concentration camps, sicknesses—there was so much, Ranewa. So much bad stuff happened that allowed evil to enter it. There's evil creatures in there, monstrous creatures that visited us in our sleep. It is not a place I would ever return to willingly."

I scribbled down the dates and details. Ogone only agreed to meet me if I promised not to record her. Ever since the Günter residency ended, she'd rebranded her YouTube account, focused it on devotionals, God's word, faith, and wellness. Her Instagram was on private with a few friends, relatives, and colleagues as followers (I was lucky to have been amongst her followers after she purged everything). "Why wouldn't you return willingly? Is it because of what happened to Anaya when she entered Huis's realm? What impact did that have on her?" I asked.

Ogone shook like a cold wind ran up her spine, and Adebowale wrapped his arm around her. "We can stop if you want?"

But she shook her head. "No, I need to do this. It would be the right thing."

"Thank you," I said. "Anything you can tell me will help."

"Anaya told me a bit about her experience in that realm. The place Anaya entered was the house's subconscious state, its history, its dreams, its nightmares, its wounds. Time was frozen there. Information was somehow revealed to her about the people inside and the history, but the history varied such that you couldn't track back the stories to one person. She also said she learned that her—your—ancestors killed two innocents for their business to thrive." She wrapped her hand tightly around her chai latte and drank of its warmth. "The sangoma told us that the spirits that were tormenting us suffered great afflictions, didn't die the proper way, and as such, the correct funeral rites weren't followed, which trapped them in that house, built a spirit out of it, the house that migrates. Although, I don't agree on the rituals that must be followed to help them pass into the 'ancestral realm,'" she said, rolling her eyes, "I do agree that spiritually they've been tied down, stalled from passing on, and need to be rightly buried, which is why I tried praying for Anaya and for these ghostwomen she met, but they may need more than my prayers. There were so many ghosts in Anaya—thousands upon thousands. Their spirits hadn't traveled onto their ancestral realm. They were stuck there, angry, helpless, spiteful. They were trapped there."

I struggled not to cry, my sister's suffering too overwhelming for me. "But if we don't know where these ghosts' bones lie, how can anyone give them proper burials, send

them off to their ancestral realm?" I said, and a dull heaviness drooped in my chest. "Do you think my sister is . . ." I didn't want to say it. Anaya had to be alive. "That she may need help to ascend to the ancestral realm?" I said instead.

"There is no salvation in that, although, it may seem like there is," Ogone said carefully. "There is eternity and salvation only through Christ. And no human being should try to make themselves a god of people. I am not the judge of that, only God is."

"'Salvation is found in no one else, for there is no other name under heaven given to mankind by which we must be saved,'" her fiancé agreed.

I wanted to roll my eyes. But Ogone touched my hand kindly, whispered only loving words about my sister, until tears crawled down my face. Adebowale, too, watched me, not in reproach, but in understanding, and I felt a warm glow of safety bathing them in light, and I wished to enfold myself in it. It called to me a memory of when Anaya and I regularly went to church, kneeling at the pew, uttering prayers that led our way. But when we became older, the hypocrisies and double standards of churches pushed us away as we wanted to figure out our own spirituality. Surrounded by the spiritual occurrences in our family, we weren't leaning strongly toward traditional spirituality or God; nothing really stuck. We were just there figuring out life. Only now I didn't know how to help Anaya, and I realized why people believe in something, be it God or our deities and ancestors. But which belief do I choose to follow? I wish my parents had cemented in our upbringing a much deeper and meaningful relationship with a belief system so we remained confident in our choices and lives.

"I regret encouraging her to dig deeper into Huis for her manuscript. Maybe if I hadn't done that . . . she'd still be here . . . I, just, am so sorry." Ogone looked up, her eyes steady on mine, and said, "Anaya really loved you, Ranewa, and . . . she knew you would be afflicted with this, probably in ways that were self-destructive. She didn't want you to get swallowed up with her disappearance."

"Wait," I raised my hand, trembling, "are you telling me that *she* knew she'd disappear? She knew and she didn't reach out?" I asked, perplexed.

Ogone inhaled deeply. "She was in a place where she couldn't reach out."

"I don't understand. If you were there with her, and you're here, how was communicating with me impossible?" Feeling deeply hurt, my voice trembled as I asked, unable to hold back the tears.

Ogone pressed her hand to her chest as if she were about to faint. "I think that will be all for today. I'm sorry." She stood up and left with Adebowale without even paying for their drinks. Imagine! She could go back to her safe home, with her future husband, and make memories with her family, and I had to sit there and pay. Yet my sister can't have any of the life Ogone's living.

When I returned to my Airbnb, something in me had ran amok, fled the boundaries of my skin. Fatigue and fear swirled like a fog in my mind, distorting my vision. Hunger pangs clutched my stomach in pain. Panic rose my heartbeat at the immensity of the revelations I'd encountered, and how unsettling they were, so much so that I wondered if I was becoming paranoid like my sister. I sat at the edge of the bed, elbows propped on my knees. The dark swelled around me,

and at the corners of my bedroom, there were dark shapes of groveling creatures, and I wondered if Huis was affecting me by mere fact of using Anaya's phone. I rubbed my eyes, and the creatures were gone. I felt hollow. Silence and sadness intermixed, dripping down my throat. I dragged the sharp edge of my thumb's nail along my thigh to join the pattern of tallies carved into my skin that counted the days since my sister had disappeared. Something red, saturated with my pain, oozed out. The floor extended itself to touch the rivulets of my blood. The side of my head connected with the floor. Skull against wood.

A dull sound knocked against my consciousness. My eyes were soaked in darkness, until the black uncovered itself of its thickness, allowing me to see the features of an unusual room. Then, I remembered: I was in Cape Town. I rose from the floor, rubbed my arms against the cold of the nighttime. My fingertips brushed the scarred marks on my arm of a past activity that relieved me of the pain inside. I couldn't go back to knives, so instead I called Mama, confessing the desire to run something sharp against my wrist, and she consoled me, praying quietly until calmness filled me.

When I hung up, Anaya's phone pinged.

Roads of Desolation

by Anaya Sebeya

A woman with a chiskop cut
points north of us:
a Cape Dutch house stands,
roads unravel from it.
"It's 1893 over there in that road,
Fort Macloutsie was a base to invade Matebeleland,
but it was discarded for it was useless."
She points southwest now.
"It's 1895 in *that* road,
and 1905 in *there* road,
I wouldn't advise you to go to either."

A river—Molopo River—dismembers Bechuanaland
into north and
south annexed to the Cape Colony
headed by that Rhodes imperialist bastard.
She pauses when we come to a fork in the road:
"This road leads to 1976 somewhere south of
    Bechuanaland,
there's not much infrastructure, no communication
    facilities, no railway services—
quite remote that side.
. . .
Maybe we'll take the 1976 road another time."

Anaya Sebeya was a writer from Botswana. A former fellow with the Günter Prize for African Women's Literature, several of her stories have appeared in *Loxion Kulcha, Tiro News* and other venues.

Anaya | Desperate

"Ntwana, why are you apologizing?" Langa says.

We're seated at a rooftop bar overlooking the city, exposed to the underbelly of sunset skies. Langa's hands hug a Windhoek beer bottle, water sweating down its surface. The benches are hard against my rear, and the wood table stiff beneath my wrist. The breeze is chilly. I'm surrounded by the smell of meat frying, a smog of alcohol in the air, a tang of salt ocean air, the noise of traffic and hooting cars below. I don't know where we are, what the name of this venue is. Customers nearby chat and laugh, the melodic voice of Petite Noir's *Shadows* flows from the speakers.

I don't think I've been here before, and I don't know how I got here.

I startle at the iciness from the cold glass of the drink straddled in my hands. Long Island iced tea.

"Welcome to the real world, ntwana," Langa says, gulping his beer. "Some of what Anouk says is right, not that I agree with her, but she's depicted to you how the publishing system can run. With the publishing professionals and authors in South Africa, the majority of these white folks are a paternalistic bunch of pretentious liberals who take pics with the latest 'flavour of the month' Black women

authors for social currency but generally keep opportunities exclusively to their ilk. They love you at every book launch and insist on 'doing coffee sometime.' They occasionally wait for Sunday afternoon jazz sessions and tshisa nyama! This scores you invites to their out-the-way book club and reading gatherings, where you're expected to regale them with tales from the other side. They write the South African version of the magical negro trope and feel like they've achieved representation and should be lauded for it! Oh, and many a mammy." He snorts. "They're used to getting their way. And right now, you're not acting how Anouk wants you to act."

I try to ground myself in Langa's words. Is this maybe why Miche is desperate for the Black experience, to write something different and nuanced, to stand out from her type of author?

I swallow the drink in one gulp, the punch of vodka solid. I'll be undone.

"Aye, ntwana, slow down," he says. "Have you even eaten today? You're looking emaciated lately. I ordered food, should be here soon. Listen, don't let this stress you. At the end of the day, they aren't revoking your fellowship or disqualifying you. Use this time to work on your projects," he says, and I look down, flipping through the pages of my manuscript, the gashes of Anouk's red pen on every page—did I bring that?— "Look at all those stories we worked on together? They're good. You know it, I know it, magazines know it. Trust yourself, Anaya. Dig deeper, show us who these characters are, what this house is—immerse yourself in it."

He has no idea how dangerous his advice is. "That could kill me," I say, and he thinks it's sarcasm.

"Writing summons history. In rebirthing that, you also die but are reborn too. Now your eyes are opened to see the truth and what has been omitted from our past," he says.

Why didn't Yanano drag *him* into Huis's realm, since he's such a martyr? Why, because he knows everything, and I don't?

I eye our surroundings, the people at the other tables eating their food, the view of the sky, passersby below, wondering how this place looked over a hundred years ago. I see the invisible dividing lines between the white and Black and Brown, the disconcerting glances, the frustrated puffs of air blown from white mouths, the black servers more interested in serving the white than those who look like them. The air here is heavy with grief, with suffering, with silence of a past still unresolved. I miss home, even though it doesn't have an established literary community or publishing industry and only about two bookstores. Cape Town has every convenience, but it's killing me.

"How badly do you want this prize?" Langa asks quietly, eyes deeply concentrated on mine.

I reach for a napkin, folding it several times, just to have something to hold on to. "I only want to write books and be able to make a living from them," I say. "I need money to survive, and I need the prize because it's only with that prestige that publishers will actually see me. But can't I have literary merit on my own?"

He nods, sighs and keeps quiet for too long.

"This story is so hard to write that sometimes I just want to scrap it and write something 'clean' and simple and accessible and all in English," I say, my napkin growing thinner. "But I just want our history, our culture, our voice to exist and be

accessible across the world. I just— I didn't want to find out about our history this way. If—"

"If what?" he asks.

"If I didn't stay at Günter Huis," I say, not sure how to explain the haunting to him, but needing to tell someone outside of Huis, someone I can trust.

"Don't you think that maybe Anouk is right, that perhaps subconsciously I'm feeding into the trauma porn?" I ask.

"It's how you tell the story," Langa says. "Listen, ntwana, Günter is looking for the next African thing, and anyone who puts their white-stamp approval on that will likely earn them a promotion in their publishing house. But the door is so narrow that not a lot of us can go in at the same time. And so you have to wait outside, wait for the door to widen into a big gateway, and by the time that you can get in, you've already passed away." He shrugs, throwing his arms up in resignation. "I knew the notes to hit with my first book. You've two options: Do your thing or forget your morals, for a year or so, then you can return to them."

"Listening to Anouk—I would be a traitor to this book, to the characters and history of these women," I say. Regardless of what Yanano did to me. I won't be like her. "And I won't. I *won't*. I don't want to sell out."

"Our South African publishing industry is kak—you can gain international interest in terms of awards, but it's nothing to aspire to in terms of the deal size or distribution. Günter is your ticket to an actual career."

I rub my eyes, suddenly tired.

Langa glances at my face. "Anaya, you're looking terrible these days."

"I've been having a lot of nightmares," I say.

Picking up more from my words than I'm giving away, he says, "I thought my aunt was able to help you."

I remember Bessie talking about death and calling me something evil, and me dying on that earth in front of the farmhouse, the pain of the bullet still rippling through my body. I lean forward, grasping his hand, which startles him. "If something were to happen to me, can you take care of my work, make sure it gets out? Because someone has to know the truth. If the sangoma can't help us, I don't know who can. I don't have a good handle of time, of myself, and I don't know what will happen to me. Please you must get my writing out there."

"You know this capitalist industry is so messed up when you care more about your productivity than your life," he says. "Nah, ntwana, nah."

"Caring about my life doesn't ensure my staying alive," I say.

"Anaya, I can't sit here listening to you talk about your death and do nothing about it," he says, gripping my hand.

"I'm trying, but I don't know what else to do."

Worry furrows his brows. His hand brushes the tears from my face. "Ntwana, I know our people stigmatize therapy, but *we* need therapy. A lot of it. I've been doing it for years and still my family mocks me for it. But therapy has made me reconcile with some bad things that happened to me, that I, unfortunately, reenacted to others. Don't worry about the cost, I will fund it while you're in Cape Town. You need to go to therapy—I'm an atheist, but some people find God too. Go to God, go for therapy."

"Yeah, I'll think about it," I lie, "but first I need a favor, a second opinion. I know you're busy, but can you take a look at

my manuscript?" And when he grins and nods, I pass him my manuscript, knowing that Anouk has emailed me the same version with her notes that I can work on my laptop. This is how I will take control and find an editor who understands my work.

Loxion Kulcha

NEWS FICTION NONFICTION POETRY ESSAYS ABOUT

An Unreliable Narrator: Celebrated South African Author Langa Mangezi Accused of Harassment, Stalking and Plagiarism

By Sethunya Pelo
29 July

Günter fellow Ogone Molefhi has come forward with claims that celebrated South African author Langa Mangezi plagiarized his first Afrosurrealist short story, "A Home in My Sister's Flesh", first published in the February issue of *Khumo Magazine*. Molefhi alleges that Mangezi lifted most of the narrative from the life of a Günter fellow who was close to him during the program, Anaya Sebeya. Sebeya has been reported missing since December, in a case that made waves in the African literary community.

In "A Home in My Sister's Flesh," the main character is an up and coming South African chef whose sister lives abroad. They were orphans and have grown distant over the years. When the chef moves into a house that connects her to her ancestry, she begins to receive revelations.

The accusation has made waves. Following the plagiarism allegations, *Khumo* pulled the story from

publication, while the committee for the Khumo Story Award has issued a statement revoking their award for the piece. Online, Langa's literary friends have sparked heated discussions on the ethics of memoir, speculation, and writing about friends, dismissing the allegations with, "That's just Langa. He's a bright star and people misunderstand his magic."

Mangezi broke onto the literary scene with his award-winning book, *Men Who Bloom Flowers*, exploring masculinity, Black love, and Black Tax, that has since been adapted into a TV show. He followed it up with two other books and a play and has since been busy attending festivals, teaching in universities, and taking selfies with celebrities on set for *Men Who Bloom Flowers*. In several interviews, Mangezi has referred to a difficult childhood, considering himself a "thorn that learned how to bloom flowers" from an impoverished upbringing. He has also spoken publicly about his struggles to recover from finding his father's body, after he committed suicide.

In his twenties, Mangezi established a nonprofit organization: Write to Freedom, an outreach program seeking to promote literacy and provide children and teenagers from low-income areas with access to education. Its alumni speak highly of Mangezi's strict tutelage, including several established writers who attribute their success to Mangezi, praising a no-nonsense attitude that produced out of them great literary projects.

However, two former Write to Freedom students, whose names have been withheld for their privacy,

have accused Mangezi of harassment and controlling behavior, claiming that each of them had to report their whereabouts to the author, even outside the scope of the program. One other Write to Freedom mentee has joined Molefhi in accusing Mangezi of plagiarism, recalling the devastation he felt when he read one of Mangezi's most-celebrated publications, only to find identical details to a personal story the teenager had trusted Mangezi with. "He has this way of getting you to open up to him, to dig deep into your pain," the former mentee said. "After I tried to cut ties, I endured two years of his stalking to pull me back in. Eventually, I don't know, he got bored and stopped stalking me. No one takes a man abusing another man seriously in this place, so I kept quiet and want to move on." It caused the aspiring author to shelf the autofiction project he was working on.

The accusations did not come as a surprise to everyone. "He plagiarizes personal accounts of his students, especially those he finds promising," one former university student attested. "I think he feels threatened by them, which is strange given that he's basically a literary star and these kids have nothing, except him."

The Günter Prize declined to comment.

Loxion Kulcha reached out to Langa Mangezi for comment and received no response.

If you or anyone you know has any information regarding the issues cited in this article, please reach out to sethunyapelo@loxionkulcha.com.

ogonemolefhe ...

I never thought I'd come back to Cape Town again, after what happened last year. I know I have not given many public updates since then. I had to pause my PhD studies due to stress, and sometimes I've considered quitting. Adebowale and I were supposed to get married this year, but we've postponed it given what is going on due to the ongoing stress of revising the Günter period in my life, which was tough in ways I wish to not disclose. Please respect my privacy. Many well-meaning people have reached out to me since Anaya's case has gotten more media attention, so here is what I will say: My heart goes out to Anaya's family. Although I knew Anaya for a short period, I grew very close to her. She will forever hold a dear place in my heart.

I miss her so much, the conversations we used to have. Sometimes we'd just sit in Günter Huis's sunroom, drinking tea and just reading. She'd do my hair, I'd do hers. It guts me that she's still missing. Anaya, I wish you were here. I wish we never stayed in that place. I keep on thinking: Why us? Why you? God protect your soul.

Anaya, I miss you so much! Sometimes I go to your page, hoping to find a new update, hoping to find another picture of you, of us. Sometimes I still

dial your number when I want to confide in someone. I go through all our messages, the videos and pictures we took—it feels like you're still here. Remember that time your short story got published, and when you received your contributor copy we were jumping up and down, and I asked you to autograph mine so that I could sell it when you're famous and you laughed so hard? I'll never part with it. You were such a beautiful writer, with such immense talent. The world lost you too soon. I hope you're still there, please God.

♡ **cameroon.mz** and 3983 others ▷

ogonemolefhe If anyone has any information about Anaya Sebeya's whereabouts, please click my link in bio.

#FindAnayaSebeya #WeMissYouAnaya #AnayaSebeya

RANEWA

ANOUK FOLLOWED UP THE NEXT DAY TO CONFIRM OUR AGREEment and ensure that she would represent me as the literary agent for Anaya's book.

I sat through Anouk's discussion of proposals and timelines and legality issues and the changes she wanted to see in Anaya's manuscript. Again, Anouk reminded me to sign the author-agent contract she'd sent me. Mxm, she's playing. Like hell I would sign with her, but I played nice and acquiescing enough for her to think I'd do it soon, once I had been to Huis and felt comfortable with my research.

I thought about the last episode, how Anaya begged Langa to help her, not knowing he was a devilish wolf. How could she go to him of all people and not me, not Mama or Papa—*we* loved her, didn't that mean anything to her? After my breakdown, S'fiso, Anouk's driver, swiftly took me toward Huis, which was surrounded by smoky mountain crests and sloped roads; the air was thick with accents and the foresty scent of trees. I could imagine my sister here. It seemed like her sort of place: architecture, nature, culture.

Miche had finally released the next episode that morning. She called it *A Void in Time*. My lawyer had informed me that no one could copyright a title, much less an unpublished one, and so we couldn't fight Miche on that, even though she was talking about my sister.

The driver stopped by a two-storey Cape Dutch house.

I bid the driver goodbye and knocked on the front door of Huis, which looked plain outside. The door opened and a uniformed woman appeared.

"You must be Khethiwe," I said, recognizing the helper and her uniform from earlier interrogations; she'd spent time in Huis attending the fellows. We'd bumped into her at the police station whilst my parents and I were in Cape Town in discussion with Skommere. "I'm Ranewa, I'm here to see the house. Anouk must've called," I said, unable to force a smile onto my face.

"Oh, yebo madam," she said. I felt a familiar guilt set in as she lowered her head in a subtle bow. Sure, I was used to it; back home, almost every family I knew had a maid. But I know how my parents treated the maid in the house, separating our dishes as if we'd catch some sickness. Other people were worse, especially to Zimbabweans and especially if they were illegal immigrants in Botswana; some were abused for their labour and oftentimes not paid because they wouldn't be able to report it. Even within our own skins, there's affliction, Anaya used to say.

She opened the door wider, and I followed her in.

A beaming face popped out from the kitchen, a halo of curls surrounding her head. She wore a tight-fitting spandex that snug tightly into her butt crack. "Khethiwe, make me a fruit smoothie, and clean the bathroom for me; I just took a shower." I attempted to pinpoint her accent; from thereabouts North Africa fused with an overseas accent I couldn't place.

"Oh, I'm still helping our visitor," Khethiwe said, clearly frustrated at the girl's lack of respect.

The girl looked at me, sizing me up to see if I was a very important Günter official. "Who are you?" she asked.

"None of your business," I said, walking up the stairs. I'd studied Huis's floor plans on the architect's website, and so I was quite familiar with my way around.

I knew from my research that she was Fadila, a poet and one of the Moroccan diasporan fellows this Günter cycle. She seemed too hyper to be haunted by this place.

She hurried up after me, blurting, "Wait, you look familiar. You're Anaya's sister, right?"

I stopped in my tracks, hand resting on the banister. I stared at the living room below, detailed as it was in the early episodes of Miche's podcast. Nothing seemed explicitly horrifying.

"The other fellows are in the garden. We were having a workshop. You need me to give you a house tour?" There was excitement and curiosity in her voice that disgusted me.

"Yes, that would help," I answered, thinking of ways to use her as an insider for any intel. I thanked Khethiwe, who disappeared back into the kitchen.

Fadila rattled off details of the rooms we passed through, the sunroom, dining, the lower-floor bedrooms, the upstairs bedrooms, and I hesitated in the room Anaya stayed in, studying the walls and furniture, the last place she lived in, that knew her intimately. I moved my hands along the walls hoping for something to whisper back into me.

"Do you mind leaving me alone?" I asked, and she wavered on the threshold, looking back into the hallway as if the current tenant stood there.

"Elinah might be uncomfortable with that, it's her room," she said, knotting her fingers. "She *loves* her privacy."

"You can watch then." I moved the bed aside to avoid stepping on it and inspected the wall where my sister had seen a hidden opening, an alcove where beastly things entered. I knocked thrice, and nothing.

I recalled the earlier episodes of how Anaya conjured her transit to Huis's spiritual realm: white salt, bathwater, incantation. I probably can't use Yanano's name as part of my speech, but Anaya also gave her consent, so perhaps I can give Huis consent into my flesh, since either way it's all the same: an invitation for Huis to let me in. I'd brought white salt with me; I entered the bathroom and spread it in the bathtub, twisted open the faucet. As it slowly trickled water in, I stepped inside barefoot and whispered consent to Huis, uncaring of Fadila's presence. Fadila watched me, too stunned to say anything. Even if she listened to Miche's podcast, the episodes didn't reveal the incident where my sister accepted Yanano's offer and gave consent to be led into Huis realm.

I sat in the bathtub until Fadila shook me. The sun was almost setting. Elinah stood behind her wearing loose cotton pants and a tank top and a combed-out Afro. She looked mildy upset.

Nothing had happened. But why? What was I missing? A thought reminded me of the scene where Anaya mentioned blood when Yanano struck her hand in the realm. Although that had happened in the spirit realm, maybe I was supposed to do it in our earthly realm: offer a drop of my blood.

"I should've asked for your permission first," I said, cutting to the chase before Elinah would release her fury on me, which I didn't have time for. "I apologise for that. My sister disappeared whilst living here. This used to be her room.

Have any of you experienced anything strange?" I know my tone was emotionless, but I needed to drag this out as long as I could and somehow splash my blood into the bathtub without spooking them.

Her shoulders relaxed the more I spoke; perhaps she felt pity. As I got out of the bathtub, I intentionally snagged the skin on my wrist with my nail, leaving behind a drop of blood and an incantation, leaving it like a piece of door, open to receive Huis.

"Miche had interviewed us for her podcast," Elinah responded, which perked my interest—what was that bitch up to now?

"What did she ask?" I said.

"She was curious about our experiences and wanted to study the house again for specific details for her podcast," Elinah said, looking at Fadila. "She seemed, I don't know, bored by our details. It was strange that she asked if Huis spoke to us in anyway. She said she was going to have us on a special episode on her podcast—"

"Nah, she only wanted to come back to Günter Huis," Fadila interrupted her with irritation, like she didn't like Miche. "I caught her sneaking around our rooms. She was never interested in hearing our thoughts."

I thought Miche had some kiss-assing relationship with Katja that she'd have access to Huis anytime she snapped her fingers. When all former Günter fellows wanted nothing to do with Huis, why was she the only one desperate to return? There was definitely something else going on. I had to stay here to find the answer.

"And no, living in the house has been perfectly fine," Elinah said, returning to my earlier question and guiding me

out of the bathroom. "But if anything comes up, I will call or text you."

I stared forlornly at the bathroom, wanting to inhale this very air until Anaya came back. Why couldn't Huis's spirits reach out to me?

"Was that all?" Fadila asked.

I nodded. We exchanged phone numbers, and I left as empty as I'd arrived. But as I stepped out from the front door, the world outside bloomed with a never-ending savannah grass, dull gold, sweeping back and forth. Behind me stood an old, white-washed Cape Dutch house, larger than the one I was in, with two wings extending to both sides, and agricultural fields, a kraal nearby, and a river. Could that be the river those men crossed, the men who assaulted my sister? Blood drizzled down my wrist into the soil, that drank me like an open mouth—it was a very unnatural flow for a tiny wound.

Someone was banging hard on the house's front windows. When I looked closer, it was a woman who had a round face, septum ring, Bantu knots, and a full figure with the tip of a birthmark peeking out from the top of her left shoulder. The woman was Bessie.

WHAT HAPPENED TO ANA?

19:20:10:11

BEFORE I DIE

Episode 9

Activism • Anaya

Welcome back, Crimies. I am Michele Visser, host of What Happened to Ana? *This is our most anticipated episode that reveals intimate details between Anaya and well-known author Langa Mangezi. From my standpoint, I always found their interactions off. He usually kept her back when our seminar ended. Bessie and Ogone didn't care much about it, but I always wondered if something else was going on between them. Anaya has been struggling to keep up with her Günter manuscript, there's tension between her and her mentor, and she's being terrorized by the house. She's slowly starting to become desperate.*

This is Anaya Sebeya's story . . .

[upbeat music]

Anouk

I understand that we got off on the wrong foot. Would you be free for a call to clear things up?

I ignore her message.

I'm not going to sleep in Huis again. I have spent every night for months in Huis's realm going through unspeakable trauma, and I can't do it anymore. I don't care that I promised Yanano I would write this damn book, I don't care that I need it for my career.

I end up in the parking lot of some remote place in my car crying, dialing my mother's number, hanging up. Dialing it again, hanging up. What would I say to her? Cry for help? Ask to come back home? *Help me.* After I left, they washed their hands of me. I slam my head against the steering wheel, the hooting alerting a couple nearby pushing a trolley of groceries. They stare, wide-eyed, quickly head to their car. I wipe my tears, stare at my face in in the rearview mirror. Inhale, exhale. Start the car.

I return to Huis. Sit in the sunroom. Sleep on the couch. Scratch at my skin. Stare at my eyeballs in the mirror. Feel the raw pain of what happened in my nightmare stretch itself beneath my skin, in my gut, in my chest. Break out into a panic. Slow my breaths down. Check my emails. Many from Anouk. Many from people looking for an interview. Lose the appetite to submit stories, to write, to eat, to bathe. I don't want to be touched; I don't want to see anyone nor talk to anyone. I pass everyone during their morning breakfast routines, ignore conversations, sleep for an entire day, and if I can't sleep, I self-medicate with wine until I pass out. Weeks pass in an endless loop of snores, saturation of sweat, the fugue of my body odor and the famishment from life.

Ten days remain until my next submission. The draft I gave Anouk still sits at 60,000 words. Does Yanano remotely have

control of my body when I'm in Huis's spirit realm and outside of it to pour out these words? It is with ease I write, but I feel spent after, like a part of my life has been taken out of me.

I remember Yanano's threats and resume writing. I must write to 90,000 words by the end of this month. I go through Anouk's comments, rejecting the deletions and English translations she wants me to make. I've decided I'm going to write this book the way it wants to be written and not how Anouk wants me to write it.

"Wow," Ogone says, appearing beside me and slouching into the seat. I continue typing undeterred. "How did you get this done so quickly? Jealous down, this looks good."

"I don't know, but I have to trim it down to a quarter this size," I say. "Anouk feels like some scenes and cultural elements are confusing and slowing down the story, and my manuscript would do better without them."

"Wow, well, Grace wasn't happy with my progress," Ogone says. "It's frustrating how many Setswana traditions I have to explain and then deal with her telling me it's infodump. She also wants me to rephrase a lot of my sentences, make them subtler whilst maintaining to my message in the manuscript."

"Why?" I ask.

"She feels like the dialogue and details will come off as offensive to most readers, which will take away from the point I'm making," she says, sighing. "I've two assignments due end of February, and I'm just accepting every change Grace recommended on my manuscript—whatever to get through this." She pages through my manuscript, skimming lines. "Damn, this is legit good."

"Do you know that there were bomb raids in Botswana in the '60s and '70s?" I ask.

Ogone nods. "Ja, Bots was an asylum for freedom fighters from other countries. Spies would come in to attack them, which meant locals would receive stray bullets. My grandfather talks about those times. Learned a lot from him that we don't learn in history classes in school. When I'd talk to my friends, they're uninformed about Bots history. I'd be like them if I didn't have someone like my grandfather. It's such a terrible loss that our history is archived in our elders and not in textbooks or literature."

"Someone told me about the bomb raids in a nightmare," I say, distant-minded, rubbing the fatigue from my face.

"What do you mean?"

"There's this place I travel to in my dreams: Huis's spirit realm, and there's an old Cape Dutch farmhouse full of all these women and windows looking out into lots of different times in the past. I met a refugee from a concentration camp during the Anglo-Boer war—"

"What? We had concentration camps?" Ogone sits up.

"Yeah. The Brits did. There's statistics, but for the Black Africans there's little documentation. It was awful, Ogone. It's connected to this house. All these things are connected to the house. The ghostwomen call it a wound, an archive of them—Huis's subconscious, its memories." I trail off, feeling sick.

Ogone looks unsurprised, which throws me off. "What else did they say?" she prompts.

"I thought you'd call me crazy," I say.

"Anaya, I'm spiritual. You think God doesn't communicate through dreams?" Ogone shakes her head. "Spiritual attacks come in many ways, and if you don't know how to interpret dreams then you won't understand the spiritual warfare over your life."

I scratch my head. "I just don't know what to do with these nightmares when they're spilling out into my real life," I say.

She raises the manuscript, gestures to it with a tilt of her head. "Clearly, it's doing something good for your writing and your research. I had my grandfather fill in that gap for me. And you have a direct line to history. If the people you're speaking to are no longer alive, that is a gift. You should find ways to spend more time there. You're performing activism through your work."

"Ogone, I'm a writer, not an activist."

"Beyps, writing is political, whether you like it or not. Your skin makes you political, whether you like it or not. The way you wear your hair is a political choice. That's the sad thing about being Black—whether you watch a TV show or read a book or you're at work or in public, our mere existence is political."

Perhaps Ogone and Langa should just band together under Yanano's wrath and see if their opinions change.

"You seriously cannot equate writing to the racial violence our people suffered under," I say through rushed words.

"We've inherited their shoes the minute we were born," Ogone says. "I want you to not submit yourself to being defensive, and I understand why you are, but don't give room to looking down on yourself. I want you to focus on what this fear and anxiety blinds you from: the truth of a hidden history, and perhaps in that, you can find ways to escape that violence in the spirit realm. Okay?"

When I lean my head into the cushion of her body, I whisper, "I was raped in the spirit realm."

She stiffens, then brushes my back soothingly. "Anaya . . . ijo." She swallows deeply, the silence excruciating, then says, "I'm sorry. I'm here, I believe you."

I start weeping. "It wasn't supposed to happen to me. There's a woman trapped there who this happened to—she's lost her entire family to this genocide, and she's still enduring the rape every day." I lean back, hot tears flowing down my face. "Can you imagine living during those times, tribes being killed, people being raped, land being stolen, and no one getting punished for the crime committed against you?" I feel Ogone nod against me. "But Yanano mentioned something that might be important: Katja's grandfather was a German soldier during the colonial wars. I think even Anouk's grandfather may have been involved. I don't know exactly what part they played and if they did something to the ghostwomen of Huis."

"But why are the ghostwomen taking it out on us?" Ogone asks. "How are we supposed to hold their attackers accountable to this colonial injustice?"

"Imagine dying from that and reliving those deaths every day," I say. "It'd drive me mad to haunt people for reprieve."

She turns to face me, curiosity and excitement gleaming in her eyes. "Listen, I made some inquiries. There's a pastor an hour away from us. I'm going to see him today."

"What? Why?"

"The sangoma didn't help us, Anaya," she whispers. "My nightmares haven't stopped either. We can't keep going through this. We need help bigger than us."

"But how different would the results of the pastor be from the sangoma?" I ask.

"There's no problem too big for God," Ogone says, index finger against her lips, in deep thought. "I suppose the sangoma's spiritual power was lesser than that of the spirits

we're dealing with, probably why it didn't work. Honestly, I should've gone to the pastor before, but Huis got into my head—*changed* me a bit."

I chew my nail. "I'll think about it."

She sighs. "That's our problem. To be honest, I haven't been a good Christian with the drinking, swearing, partying, and twerking. Look at how many spirits we've come into contact with here! Ruvimbo is most faithful. She left because she knew this place was wicked—I should've too, but I idolized what Günter would bring me."

"I don't know, Ogone, there's just so much to parse through," I say.

She shrugs, reaches her hand to mine. "I'll pray for you. Maybe God is doing something with you that I don't understand, but we'll get through this *together*."

I nod, curling into her hug, staring at the clock on the wall. I need to get back to writing, but I don't want to let Ogone go.

Ogone leaves to meet the pastor. When she returns, she doesn't go into any details. She stops swearing, partying, drinking. She fasts, prays, studies the Bible, listens to gospel music.

Ogone's soothing words have calmed me a bit and encouraged me on how to move forward; Huis monopolizes my time. So, I fit my feelings into pockets of poetry. Poetry becomes my novel, a play of space and time, that can fit an entire universe in one stanza, communicate meaning in the shape that texts form on the page, and the metaphors are portals into the ghostwomen's history. Poetry is the first breath of novel-form, each word an enjambment of grief.

I am Michele Visser, signing off. Thank you for listening to What Happened to Ana? *If you enjoyed this episode, please share, subscribe, and leave a review. We are a small two-person team, my assistant and I, and every like and subscription goes a long way. See you next week, Crimies!*

[theme music]

♡ 24,320 ⪪ 21,650

Choose your membership

Contributor

$1/month

JOIN

Thank you for your support – every amount goes a long way!

Witness

$5/month

JOIN

- Discord server access to Witness community
- Early access to podcast episodes
- Behind-the-scenes for our audio production and notes
- 10% discount on merch

Investigator

$15/month

JOIN

Everything included in Witness, plus:

- Access to old interrogation videos, articles, and Q&A that the team conducts with those close to the case, incl. Günter commentary
- Videos of Michele Visser's time in Günter and unexpected shots of Anaya's time in Günter

Criminal

$30/month

JOIN

Everything included in Investigator, plus:

- Access to partners-in-crime group where we dig out the mysteries of Anaya's life and disappearance
- As a Criminal, you will have access to our files, investigation techniques, and breadcrumbs we follow to hopefully find Anaya.
- Membership funds are used to hire professionals to assist with our investigation.

Recent posts by What Happened to Ana?

Hello, Crimies, it's Poll Time!

Do you think Anaya was Langa's target?

○ Yes

○ No

Vote

7,435 responses

Did Langa Mangezi kill Anaya Sebeya and hide her body?

○ Yes

○ No

Vote

9,880 responses

Do you think Anaya ran away and is somewhere out there having the time of her life?

○ Yes

○ No

Vote

8,879 responses

This poll will run for three days.

I'm pleased to be partnering with my publisher Günter Books and StellaLibris Deluxe Book Boxes for an international giveaway of the collector's edition of my bestselling book, *The Tales of Our Lost Magic*. As you may know, I wrote *The Tales of Our Lost Magic* during the Günter residency, and it holds a special place in my heart. I'm so happy to get such a stunning collector's edition!

In addition to a gorgeous new reversible dust jacket, a luxe satin ribbon bookmark, a foiled case stamp, and custom-designed stenciled edges, this beautiful hardcover features a special new chapter: an extended author's note where I talk about my friendship with Anaya at Günter, revealing some new secrets never shared before.

To participate in the giveaway, follow @MicheVisser, @GunterBooks, and @StellaLibris on Tik Tok and Instagram and share the post with the hashtag #TalesOfLostMagicGiveaway. Three lucky winners will hear from StellaLibris next Friday!

There are new changes to our Patreon!

- Remember, we've added a new membership tier: Criminal.
- Our Discord server is growing! Join to meet other Crimies and discuss this disappearance case.
- The last Saturday of every month, server members are invited to Zoom in to discuss short stories inspired by our conversations for a secret NFT (very climate friendly) project.

Upcoming Post:
Interrogation Videos: Ranewa Sebeya

 Join to unlock

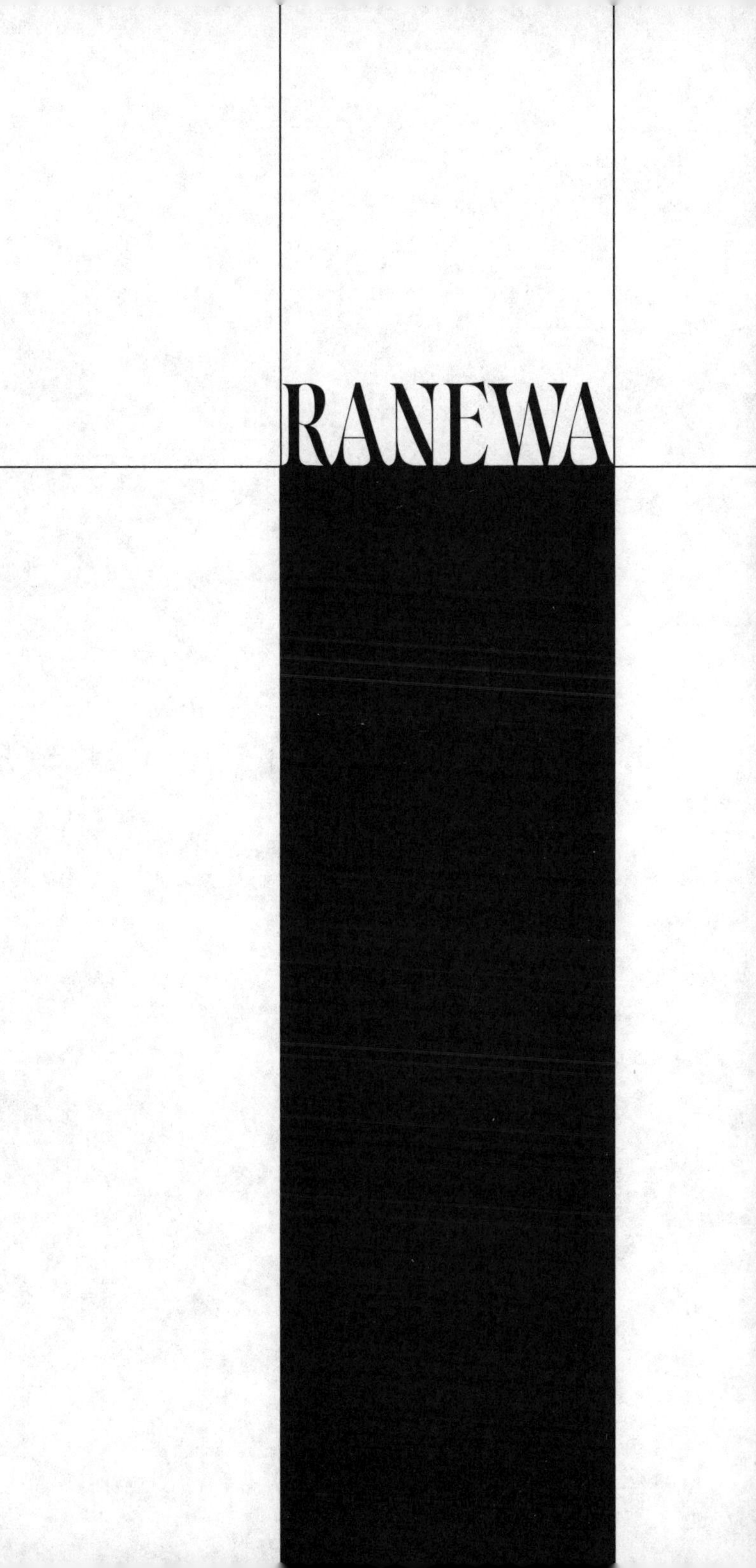
RANEWA

Bessie. She was still alive. I pressed my hand to my chest. Did that mean my sister was also trapped in the house? That I could save her? I rushed up the stairs onto the patio, attempted to shove open the door, only it wouldn't yield. Another woman, a ghostwoman, came up behind me, stood by the door, eyes peering down at me. "Would you like to enter?" she asked.

Another came up, arguing with her in a different language.

"Whoever wants me, just let me in," I blurted.

"Na wa o," they said, eyeing me suspiciously and with curiosity.

They spoke as they circled me.

"This one is different from her sister."

"That one always cried, but she surprisingly showed strength in the end."

It was not much different from Anaya's experiences the times she came into Huis's realm, which I thought was preparation enough, but being in the midst of the hungry look in their eyes, the grimy deathly tone of their skin, their hands dirty with grime, nails like claws of a cheetah, that I felt suddenly afraid and glanced back. A door, glowing in the fields. I knew instinctively that it would lead back to my body. That I could end it here and be free unlike my sister who'd forged

ahead. I stared at Bessie as if her predicament would be my own if I stayed here too long. The ghostwomen hovered, spinning around me as if they had no feet, like corpses held up like marionettes. I felt intoxicated with death, mad with it.

But what if Anaya was inside and I was this close to finding her. I *can't* abandon her again. I clasped my hands to my face and ears, calling Anaya's face into my mind.

Even if it killed me, I was going to find Anaya. Even if Huis's spirits haunted me or murdered my family, I would reveal what happened to my sister. It would be worth the sacrifice. I feared nothing except the grief within me.

Something within me, my spirit or my thoughts, told me not to enter Huis; behind me in the fields, the escape door to my body became dimmer. I wondered, in panic, if I'd never find it again.

The women opened Huis's door, inviting me with too-wide smiles and exaggerative glee.

As I entered, Bessie hurried to me from the side windows, holding my hands as if I were warm food. "Please you have to get me out of here," she cried. The door closed with a deafening bang, and I was fearful it'd never open. So I curiously placed my hand on its knob and it scalded my skin. I was trapped. I coddled my hand, heart racing. How could I save Anaya if I couldn't get out myself?

"Is Anaya here?" I asked desperately, and my shoulders sank when Bessie shook her head. I removed her hands from me and wondered who I needed to talk to that had power and influence.

"You show no fear, yet you reek of it," Bessie said. "If you help me, I will be honest with you, do anything, just please help me."

Her desperation would work to my advantage. It had to.

The woman with the long braids grabbed me by the arm, declared, "This one is mine." She led me to a sitting room where other ghostwomen sat around a low table, idly sewing, knitting, and drinking tea and chatting. Their clothes were of a forgotten past. Bessie hovered nearby like a troubled pet.

"Where's my sister? Where's Anaya?" I asked the room, cutting an old woman off. Some of the ghostwomen giggled, others moaned, others remained silent, staring at me with hunger.

The woman with braids tutted me. "It's not time. Have a sit down with us."

I would be patient. I sat.

They spoke to me, regaling me about the beauty of their lives before being imprisoned in Huis, and I marveled at the proximity to history without having to read it from a secondary source. It seemed easy the way this dense and inaccessible information flowed from them, like an interactive ancient secret book; I could see why Anaya kept coming back. Their genial tones almost made me feel at ease, but I knew I couldn't trust them, much like I wish my sister hadn't trusted Yanano. Bessie's fearful mannerisms reminded me to be on guard.

One woman handed me a teacup, but I wasn't stupid enough to eat anything here; I didn't want to end up spiritually poisoned. I only held the cup and did not drink of it.

"You're a quick one, huh," the woman said as she sat beside me. She motioned to Bessie. "Don't be rude and show our guest around."

I knew Yanano was kind to my sister, preparing her flesh much like fattening a cow to slaughter, so I knew these

niceties were only meant to yield my spirit and flesh to them. Bessie hurried to me and took me down a separate hallway.

"How the hell did you end up here?" I asked.

"It happened that night of the prize-giving ceremony," she whispered, slowing down, as we passed ancient, dark, empty rooms. "We all had trials to face in Huis's realm that divided our paths—Ogone, Anaya, Miche. I was too slow; one of the spiritwomen entered my body. I lost it when we disappeared at the ceremony. Did Ogone make it?"

"She w—" A shrill scream echoed through the halls, startling me. I swung around defensively, and Bessie touched my arm.

"There's been an influx of new girls—they can't manage. Sometimes they scream endlessly," she said.

"Who took your body?" I asked.

"One of them," she said, pointing back to the room we came from.

I wondered why she didn't ask about Miche and Anaya, only Ogone.

"How long has it been out there?" she asked, eyes heavy with sadness.

"About nineteen months."

Her eyes widened with shock. "How's my family?"

I felt guilty for having no answer, realizing I was not the only one who had lost someone. "They grieve you, but they're keeping well," I lied for her sake.

She brushed aside a tear, whispering, "Good, that's good. I'm glad my parents aren't alive to deal with this. Time in here is weird, and I can't see to your world because I can't enter many rooms. They keep taking turns with me, forcing me to live their daily nightmares. I've been shot, stabbed,

decapitated, ra . . ." She shook her head, tears trembling down her face. "I thought I had it bad being sick in our world, but this is worse, Ranewa. I'd rather have my body back."

Of all people, I felt so sympathetic to her, an orphan, chronically ill, haunted, lost her body, and now she was trapped in this house of horrors, so dark and sad. Why did such things happen to people? Bessie needed redemption, the kind that would return her to flesh free from the chronic illness and spiritual torture she endured.

"I learned about the agreement Anaya made with the ghostwomen—did you also consent to let them enter you, to help fulfil your literary desires?" I asked, wondering how to nullify that contract.

Bessie scoffed. "No, I was undesirable because I was too sick, just not immune to their torture. But one of them was desperate and took my body."

"Wasn't the sangoma supposed to help you?" I asked, shifting aside, for she smelled strange.

I thought about my conversation with Ogone and the outcome of the former Günter fellows. It was possible that Ruvimbo's faith saved her from living in Huis, and Ogone's relationship with God saved her, whilst Anaya and Bessie disappeared or were taken by spiritual forces. If I were to pick a side, clearly, I should trust God. I didn't want to doubt Him, but I was afraid I'd run out of time, and I needed a very quick help.

"She didn't have enough spiritual power to overpower Huis's spirits," Bessie said, walking through a kitchen and into a tight passage of exposed concrete, down a staircase corkscrewing underground. "If we'd known, we'd have tried someone of a higher power. But Ogone had the smarts

about—" She clutched her chest as if she were pain. "Never mind that. I can't say. Please help me."

"Why do you think I have the power to help you?" Maybe if Anaya was here, I could try to smuggle her out, make a deal with one of these spirits. But I don't know the laws of this place to get two people *and* myself out.

She grimaced, tried a different tack: "You have Anaya's phone. I saw her use one of the mirrors to access her home in Botswana. She said she stood behind you and made sure you found it."

I grasped her hands. They were icy cold. "You talked to her? When? Can I talk to her?"

"That was . . . a long time ago, Ranewa. Right after we came here."

"But I only just found Anaya's phone a few weeks ago. She must have been around recently. Where is she?"

"I told you, time is weird in this place."

"Why would she just leave me her phone? Why wouldn't she talk to me?" I asked, wringing my hands. I fell to my knees, hands gracing the back of my neck, remembering how the air felt different. This only happened a few weeks ago when I found Anaya's phone, but Anaya disappeared nineteen months ago—so she spiritually handed me the phone then? "How is it possible she was in the past and future at the same time?"

"It was impossible. I was surprised she was able to do as much as she did. But that's why the spiritwomen won't touch you yet. Anaya protec—" Bessie doubled over, clutching her stomach. A string of saliva drizzled from her mouth to the floor, and she remained mute for a long time.

I chewed on my lip, remembering the day I found the

phone, and how I felt a breath on my neck, as if someone had been standing behind me. Was it Anaya?

Bessie doubled over in pain again. "I'm sorry, I can't say much. The house hurts me when I reveal much. But I found a woman who used to live in Huis. Nosipho. She's far more honest than the others. Unlike me, they keep her locked in one room because she failed them."

Nosipho. The other Günter fellow who disappeared years ago. "What do you mean, she failed them?"

"One of the spiritwomen couldn't possess her body, and Nosipho failed some assignments," Bessie said, lifting a paraffin lamp from the floor. She lit it and walked through the tiny passage lined with doors, stopping at the last one and shoving it open.

A woman a few years older than me lay at one corner of the cell, which was dank and dark. Since I'd arrived, there had been no smell, except for Bessie. Everything carried a scent of neutrality.

"Nosipho, you have a visitor," Bessie said, edging the lamp toward the woman, who sat up. She wore an old garment that had lost its color, her shoulder-length natural hair matted and unkempt.

"Who would visit little old me?" she asked, and I was surprised to see her smiling.

I told her my story and that of Anaya, and how I needed to find her.

"They locked me in here because I talk too much. I'm surprised they let you come this far," Nosipho said. "Their confidence is something to fear; it means they aren't worried about you gaining information."

"I've nothing to lose," I said.

"You have family, no? Loved ones?" she asked.

"Besides that."

"In Huis, there's the Grave of Mirrors, always watching everyone. The spirits spend their time and hunger working on opening up the bodies of victims, so their flesh yields easy for possession. They terrorize them."

"I understand that spiritual law of Huis. I want to know how to find my sister," I said, uninterested in these other details.

Nosipho stood, and before us the still air stirred like a rising wind. Nosipho focused on it until a shape distorted the translucence of air, forming rectangular boundaries the size of a door. We stared at the shimmering door. Nosipho casted her hand across the landscape. The view was a scene of fires, of bullets like time shattering the bodies of history. I saw mirages of flesh burning across earth, voices burning, babies wailing, and I cast my face away from the heat of the fires. When I opened my eyes again, the scene had changed back to Nosipho's cell.

"If you can do that, show me where my sister is," I said.

"Do not let grief make you naïve and stupid," Nosipho replied. "What I showed you is how the world looks in certain places, but I don't have the power to know where your sister is, only to show you what I know. Huis is a prison of the dead. Regardless of how hard you try to escape Huis, you will be unable to vacate until your body becomes a house for one of its spirits. When I was living in Huis, I could always hear the ocean. In Huis's realm, we were thrown into its marine world where we fought to death."

"How did you survive and end up here?" I asked.

"I took the knife of a ghostman, entered a black-marked window, and stabbed the person sleeping in that room. Of course, there's always demonic spirits—"

"As in there are demonic spirits in this house?" I said, afraid, my eyes roaming the small cell, wondering what was beyond the walls and all the floors.

Nosipho shook her head. "No, these demonic spirits have no connection with Huis, but they roam the earthly realm looking for an opportunity to defile human beings—hae, my sister there are so many on earth, it's frightening that humans can't see that the things they're battling are spirits."

"Back to this possession thing, what happened next?" I asked, wondering if it happened to Anaya too and desperate to use that information to find her quickly.

"One of these grotesque demonic spirits attempted to attack me so it could take the body; it left a mark on me with its claws, which, when I had eventually possessed the body, I lost the body because of that mark," she said.

I mused, recalling the details from the podcast episodes that it seemed like common knowledge among the ghostwomen on how to possess people. Nosipho must have come across this information in this spiritual realm—but how?

"What do you mean you lost the body?" I asked.

"I fell into a deep sleep and woke up in Huis's spirit unable to leave its boundaries. The ghostwomen lock me in the cellars because I stole their information to use to my advantage."

"How?" I asked.

"I manipulated them against each other. They tell me it's a crime I committed against them—imagine criminals, themselves, feeling betrayed by me, mxm!"

"What happened to the person you initially possessed," I asked, uninterested in their little drama.

Nosipho shrugged. "I don't know what happened to them."

Most of what Nosipho mentioned, Anaya had written in her poem: "three ghostwomen and an elder ghostman." I wondered briefly if Nosipho had taken the knife from the ghostman in Anaya's poem. My stomach churned. I didn't want to think about what it meant if the only way out of Huis was to take over someone's body.

Something vibrated in my pocket. I checked, surprised to find my sister's phone. It had come with me into Huis. I almost thought it wouldn't.

There was a new track, a new secret episode from Anaya. Everything that I did triggered a track release. It almost seemed too easy. A shadow appeared behind us; the woman with long braids from earlier, a tight bodice and a wide skirt, hands tucked into each other. "I am sorry to interrupt your conversation, but Bessie, it's about to start."

Bessie backed away against a wall. "No, please."

"You'll take Alinaswe's place. It's only a few hours," the woman said.

Bessie fell to her knees, clutched the woman's hem upon where the length of her braids reached, pleading. "Merapelo, please ke a go rapela, just let me off today."

But Merapelo shook her head. I pitied Bessie. There was some dark curiosity in me that needed to see what my sister endured. But anger brewed deeply in my chest, my fingers tingling with the urge to drag Merapelo into the very violent scene her peer was avoiding and desperately wanting to dig my hands like claws into her chest, snap her ribcage as

revenge for what they had done to Anaya. But I must restrain myself, let them get comfortable with me—they're as desperate as Bessie for freedom, just as I am desperate to betray them later to save my sister.

So I gently pushed Bessie aside. "You did it to Anaya, let me take this round then. But, I'll do it only if I get something in return," I said.

Bessie pinched me. "Anaya didn't pay for you to sell yourself cheaply."

I glared at her, wondering what Anaya did or where she was. "My life is nothing without Anaya."

Merapelo's eyes turned into slits of curiosity. "What do you seek?"

"I'm looking for my sister, Anaya Sebeya; where is she? Yanano made a deal with her," I said.

"Yanano has long since left Huis and did not share this knowledge with me," Merapelo replied. "For now, I serve as the current matron, until I, too, leave. However, I can avail to you some other information that you may find of value." I stepped forward, and she added. "But it will cost."

I nodded. That seemed to be how the spirit world worked.

Merapelo leaned closer to me, whispered, "In the spirit realm, you can perform an act on someone, and it will manifest in the physical world with no traces that lead to you."

Then I followed her upstairs to take a ghostwoman's place in history. In a distant field, in the dark of night, my limbs were being torn apart, and it took long before I died, dismembered into the earth, unspeakable pain in every scattered organ of mine. After a while, I was poisoned with ditlhare tsa Setswana, which kept me unconscious once the ordeal was complete—it seemed the way of things here: for the

ghostwomen to bear witness to the violence until they were dead.

When I awoke, depleted, and depressed, Merapelo appeared, collecting my limbs and connecting them until they formed seams and made me whole. I drew a trembling breath as tears poured from my face. I clasped my trembling hands together, soothed myself that it would be over soon once I found Anaya—it was all for Anaya. Regaining feeling in my hands, I found that I clutched a bloody whittling knife. I hefted it, testing my rebuilt body. I hoped it was a ghostman's knife.

Merapelo eyed the knife, nodded, said, "Second floor, right turn, third door on your left. You will be pleased."

Anaya | The Flesh of My Sister

Langa

Your manuscript—I've never read something like this. It's a masterpiece. We need to meet. Let me know your availability and I'll send a car to pick you.

A chauffeured Mercedes picks me up as night falls. It drops me off at Langa's door, thereabouts in Clifton, a mansion of a home, overlooking Clifton Beach. Langa's wearing sweatpants when he welcomes me in, sweeping me into his foyer, shiny floors and a spacious living area with stairs that lead to more rooms above. Zahara's voice flows from his music station.

He guides me to the sectional couch, where the sliding doors are open to the sea breeze and night air. He disappears up the stairs as I drink some water, and when he returns, he's moisturised his face, his face towel hanging over his shoulder.

"Your manuscript blew me away," he says. "Some areas need work, but it's very promising. I saw Anouk's comments. I don't agree entirely with them." I stare at the stars, trying not to break down.

"Anaya?" Langa asks.

I feel hot tears roll down my face.

"What's wrong," he asks, sitting beside me on the couch.

"I don't know what to say, and if you'll believe," I whisper.

"I'm here, ntwana, talk to me."

I look at Langa holding my manuscript and decide to shamelessly pour out everything about Huis, Yanano, the ghostwomen, the history.

He strokes his chin. "This is very interesting. You probably have many more books in you."

I'm stunned into silence at his response. No shock or incredulity. Did his aunt reveal our confidential story to him? Is that why he's unsurprised, casual? A normal person would lean in with soothing words of consolation, of inquiries regarding Günter's hand in this.

"You don't understand what I go through to write this material," I tell him.

"For a great *cause*, Anaya. You're writing history that white people have been rewriting and erasing to put themselves as heroes to hide the injustices they've done to our people."

"Maybe this should have happened to you and Ogone, because you both seem confident about what kind of suffering I should endure," I retort. "Langa, I was raped by white soldiers. I don't care that it was in the spirit world. I don't care that it was 1960—don't tell me to put myself through that willingly, just for a *great cause*."

"What if you bring me along," Langa suggests. "You won't have to face that alone anymore. I can protect you."

"I don't have the power, Langa, *they* choose." Shame floods my chest. I feel crazy for feeling this way about something that only happened in my nightmares.

"Let me talk to them."

I see a desperate hunger in his eyes. A hunger that I might once have had for every literary idea, every vision, and I know

without a doubt that something is wrong with his hunger—it smells like greed. I just told him I got raped, and he only sees an opportunity for a project.

He almost seems to realize this and his eyes soften. "There's nothing to feel ashamed by. Ntwana, you experienced what you experienced. I don't care in what form, in what reality. Rape was a war weapon." He rubs my arm consolingly, and I sense him beginning to launch into a speech.

"Just stop," I say, sternly. "I'm so tired of hearing about this systemic oppression, the racism, the spiritual warfare—the politicization of our bodies and past, all these grand scholarly speeches of Black consciousness, when it's doing nothing to free me from all this torture. Knowing what all this means doesn't save me. Doesn't heal me. So, what if it's colonialism? I want it to stop. I want to be free. It doesn't make it right what Yanano did to me. It doesn't justify recycling this hatred reserved for us. I hate it, hate it, that I've to look at the world like this. It was nice living an ignorant life. It was nice not knowing what happened to my people—it was nice to not know, because knowing is tearing me apart." My breaths come out fast, my face is hot, my chest suffocating.

He leans his elbows onto his knees, stares ahead, eyes focused, distant.

"Do you even know what it feels like to have gone through what I endured? Have you gone through something bad, really bad, that you had to do something bad to survive?" I ask.

His jaw tenses. He nods. Eyes lowered.

"I went through stuff when I was a child," Langa says, swallowing deeply. He tells me about his father, Zimbabwean and paperless. His mother, who abandoned them. His

grandmother who raised him while working as a maid. I touch my hand to my chest, my heart beating fast. Hearing his unrestrained vulnerability makes me feel safe in that we trust each other to open up.

"The only reason I'm a citizen of this place is because my mother is South African," he says, "but to a lot of people, I'm just a mokwerekwere stealing their jobs, their opportunities, their women. I was so angry for a long time."

He is quiet for a moment.

"No one cares about what we go through, only the things we do in our pain. I've had a hard life, ntwana, and yes, I had to do some bad things to get here. Things I'd rather not mention." He bows his head, hands hanging limply between his legs.

The silence sits between us, impregnated with grief, but I have no space in me to carry nor manage his vulnerability.

"Am I going to die?" I ask.

"No, ntwana." He wraps his arms around me. "You can stay in one of my guest rooms if that makes you feel safer outside of the Günter house."

I let myself snuggle closer, and he drapes a fleece blanket tighter around me until sleep kidnaps me away.

I dream about ghosts from that gluey sickness, and girls with long braids materialize through breath and form, my lungs feeding them pieces of myself. Their faces are distorted, mouths swollen with flies wedged between their teeth. Sounds; scuttling of clawed feet on the floor. My fingers scrabble through the blankets. Lights, off. I stare at the ceiling, flickering thoughts through its dead bulbs.

The room is dark.

There is a darkness in the room.

I scamper off the bed—when was I brought to the bed in the guest room?—before something grabs my feet, grabs my arms. I punch away at the dark. I won't let anything have me.

"Langa?" I shout. No response.

The door must be but a meter away, but something keeps pulling it from me. I plunge into the dark. Sprint. The dark becomes watery, becomes heavy, air leaden around my legs. I throw one arm forward, swim and kick forward. The floor disembarks. Returns. *Home. Go home.*

I force myself up. Throw open the door. Out into the passage. Down the stairs. I stare back. A normal living room. Nothing uncanny. Nothing absurd. No Langa. A window's open, and a wide, black-night mouth drags the wind in by its limbs. The wind licks at my arms, kicks down stuff from the TV console. The floorboards squeal from the pattering rain. I can't see through the thicket of dark. I find my cellphone, turn on its flashlight, and press my back to the wall. Eyes skirting the room. I see everything. Nothing, nothing will come for me. I dial Ranewa. Hang up. I dial Mama. When she answers, I cry on the phone.

"Anaya, go rileng? O ko kae?" Worry pitches Mama's voice high.

I grip the phone in my hand, struggling against defeat, against failure, against giving it up all. I clench my eyes tight, pray, whispering, "Can I come home, Mama? I know you're still mad at me, that what I did was wrong, leaving like that, but I don't know where to go. Please." My voice trembles as I beg.

"Of course, ngwanaka, please, of course. O ko kae? Do you need help, money? Should I come fetch you—" There's activity on her side, a commotion of shuffled papers, footsteps, doors opening then—"Ranewa! Hae, ngwana yo o

ile kae?" Her voice returns to me. "Where are you? Are you okay? Se lele."

"I'm still in Cape Town," I say.

"Nana go tla siama, se lele. I will take care of everything. I will book the earliest flight for you," she says, and I hear her talking to the helper asking her where Ranewa is.

My tears fall silently.

I hang up the phone.

Darkness. My voice is hoarse. It's just darkness no doors out, no doors in. I don't want to sleep, can't sleep, won't sleep. Yanano won't find me again; I won't let her. Not her. Not Huis. I just have to stay awake until I can get back to Botswana. Home. Home. Home. I will have lost everything, but I will have myself. My family. Myself.

A void of lightning sparks in my room. Yanano steps out of it gracefully and calm. "You have disobeyed us, broken a very sacred rule."

I back away. "Leave me alone."

Her nails grip my hair, into my scalp, and she drags me toward the glaring light of the void. "I felt sorry for you in beginning; that's why I warned you, tried to get you out. But you stayed, you consented to our terms. And you cannot break this contract." Her hands are hot as a burning furnace.

We appear on the stoep of Huis's spirit realm, overlooking the front yard, the trees weighed with bodies, the skies weighed with trees. She lets go of my dreads. Yanano stands peacefully, hands tucked into her sleeves.

"I will show you the fields on the borders between Huis and other realms," she says, as I stand up, dust myself off. "We don't take many people there; it is a difficult journey for . . . some, especially if their ancestors have spiritually

contaminated their lineage." Spiritually contaminated? Is she referring to the crime my ancestors allegedly committed for their business? I don't like the way she phrases that, so purist, so unkind.

"There's nothing unkind about it," Yanano replies.

I cross my arms, as if protecting myself from her, wary of her movements. "You've heard my thoughts all this time?"

"Yes," she says. "I see even the thoughts you haven't formed yet. I know everything you may plan to do. You can try to, but you will fail to outwit me."

No wonder she always seems so calm around me, she has an assurance of certainty, of safety, of having won.

"Unfair I'd say, because I can't hear yours," I say.

"It startles me at times how unafraid you are of me. You people live strange lives; it's no wonder it is with ease we manage to break into your bodies," she says. "You remind me of my son. That is why I will allow you to choose what happens to your spirit when I possess your body."

The weight of her words doesn't sink in at first, as if this is happening to someone else and not me. The sun hangs like a clock in the sky. I'm going to die. I'm going to die. I'm going to die. Panic nearly swallows me whole. I still don't know how Huis functions, I don't know what its loopholes are. And even if I did, Yanano would be one step ahead of any plan I could make. I want to cry to Mama, but I'm not sure any human can save me. Yanano is going to kill me and take my body, and I won't even get to apologize to Newa for leaving her forever—

"You're not going to die tonight," Yanano cuts in, reading my mind. "You may not die at all, if that is what you choose. Come, I will show you what awaits you at the end of your Günter Fellowship."

Yanano grips my arm and drags me forward. I follow numbly. The elder ghostman I met on an early visit to Huis sits in the same place as always, wielding the knife, scraping the cheekbone of the Mosarwa man.

We sweep through the sandy path, in through a thicket that pours us out onto a clearing where two fields—an open stretch of land—spread out an inch before our feet all the way toward the horizon. Here, there is no sky, no sun, no celestial bodies, just two fields side-by-side, stretching so far in every direction that I can't see their limits. One is abundant in towering trees, chirping birds, rushing water, greenery so lush it sweats dew. The other is so burned, so black the ashes smell of rot and death. It's as if the world is divided in two, and we stand at the borders between green abundance and black ashes.

"This place is governed under a different law that Huis bows to." She raises her hands, only to meet an impenetrable force, as if a glass wall separates her from the fields. "You need to have the river of life flowing in your spirit to pass through. To have moya and seriti in you." She gestures to my hand to attempt it.

I raise my hand to the space before me, nothing stops it. The air on the border of fields feels as calm as a day without wind.

As I watch, the burned field fills up with lines and lines of people going so far back to the horizon. They stand without expressions, arms to their sides, loose-clothed. In the middle, my family. Mama, Papa, Ranewa, mmemogolo, rremogolo. Others I do not know stand behind them all the way to the horizon. Before them are the translucent forms of people not yet born.

"Your ancestors span far back," Yanano says, pointing. "This field is populated with many, could be thousands, could be millions related to you going so far back into history and so far into the future." I look at them all, searching their blank faces. I spot someone with the same expression Ranewa carries when she's confused, another relative with the same high cheekbones as Mama's, and the button nose that Mmemogolo has that dons my face too.

"Look, see the poisonous curse in your lineage." She makes a motion with her hands, as if she's washing them with water. She looks to the burned field, points at my mother. She gestures her hand, and my mother's body jerks in pain as if a sharp weapon has struck her. "A sickness will become in your mother's ovaries. It will be too late, incurable. Gone, she will be." Mama crumbles to the earth, becoming ash.

Yanano flicks her hand to Papa. "He will follow suit. Some will say he died of a broken heart." Papa crumbles to earth, to ash.

Yanano extends a cupped hand toward Ranewa. Ranewa bends low, scoops the soils with cupped hands, pours it into her mouth, scoops twice, scoops thrice, buries it inside her until she exists no more. She becomes ash. "Depressed, orphaned, grieving her sister, her own life failure after failure—your sister will give in to her suicidal thoughts, hoping that death will make her free." A pain in my chest rises up my throat, into my chest, into my skin.

Over and over, Yanano makes me watch my relatives die, burning the floral notes of marriages into debilitating divorces, steeping them in alcohol to drown their functionality, poisoning their ovaries. Every man or woman is touched by

the same patterned curse in Yanano's hand that will repeat in each descendant.

Eventually, I find my voice. "Why are you showing this to me?"

"Because, Anaya, you can save your family with an honest sacrifice." Yanano says. "When the time comes for me to possess your body, your spirit will make its way here, and you may choose to water this field with your spirit. In exchange, the field for your family will prosper with fruit, plant, and peace."

If someone stood here faced with this choice to save me or leave me to face my fate, I'd desperately want them to save me. "'Love others as you love yourself,'" Mama used to repeat to Ranewa and me. I think of Ranewa in the burning fields, shoveling earth into her mouth, suffocating, and wondering how that would manifest in her life, and how that breaks my heart. But I can save her from the misery that would lead her to that fate. This moment resembles everything I've done in Günter to persevere by all means, even if it meant sacrificing myself for the wrong reasons, to preserve only the book and no noble cause. This time I get to decide differently: to save my family.

"However," Yanano continues calmly, "it will be a great torture for you to choose this path, for you will take on the burden of trauma and pain experienced by your entire ancestry. You will become a ghostwoman, much like we have been trapped in repeated violences, to endure your family's trauma and curse eternally."

I stare at my feet forlornly. I've been pummeled by terror since the day I started living in Huis, and the idea that that will remain my prison terrifies me. What about me? Don't I,

too, deserve to be saved and have reprieve from the violent experiences I've endured? For the first time, I wonder what the heaven of God looks like. My tears splash onto the dry earth, and I stare yearningly at the other field, like a scorched man thirsting to be quenched. I could go on to live a life of peace and freedom; so I look to Yanano and say, "You said I had another choice . . ."

"One field saves your family," Yanano says, "and one field saves you, unloosens you from their calamity."

I look to the abundant field, green and welcoming. Instead of rows and rows of ancestors, here there is only Ranewa. She stands there, staring ahead, unblinking, a dead expression in her eyes. "Why is she alone?" I ask.

"Only you and your sister can break this generational curse," Yanano says. "You have strength in the light of your spirit. The rest of your family is too taken by the conditioning of this curse, too immersed in it, that they can't separate themselves from it—this curse is their identity, it forms their beliefs. They can't break out of if they don't see that it's a prison."

I stare at my hands as if seeing myself for the first time and differently, wondering what curses have been manifesting in my life that I've been repeating and kept me spiritually imprisoned in the wrong things.

I stare at Yanano, confused. "What does that mean?" I ask.

"If you walk into the left field, your spirit will be free and you can live. It will be peaceful. You won't have to kill anyone, nor fight. Just walk through that field, toward Ranewa."

"How will I live with myself, knowing I could have stopped this, saved my family. How will I live with myself watching them suffer?" I ask myself.

“Remembering what one has done weighs too heavily on one’s conscience, but if you’re free from that it’s like being given new life,” Yanano advises. “If you choose this path and take your sister’s body, you will not remember anything, not yourself, not what has occurred. You will truly think you are Ranewa, which is the greatest reprieve from the guilt of your actions.”

Basically everything the ghostwomen have done to me I would now inflict on Ranewa. A dead feeling weighs down my heart. Imprison Ranewa to set myself free or imprison myself to set my family free. But she’s my sister, she’s my Newa. Her freedom, her happiness, her life means the world to me. To steal that for myself is a prison in and of itself.

“What will happen to my sister? I ask.

“Her spirit becomes what it becomes when you displace it. Child, feel no sorrow, and hold no guilt if you decide to take her body. Just walk through the fields. A peaceful and simple process. Your spirit will not interact with hers.”

I stare at both fields. The contrasting nature of the fields feels so unfair to me, to bare all the weight of our ancestry, to unravel the work that spans however far back when the curse cemented itself in our blood. I wonder if it’ll be better being lost in the curse that you can’t know yourself, see yourself out of it, so buried in the pain and thicket of it—I wonder if it’s better to be numbed that way than to have to deal with the weight of killing this curse.

I look at Yanano. “If I don’t break the curse, there will be another me, down the line in my family, who will go through what I’m going through,” I say. “I could be going through this because an ancestor was given this very choice and instead chose to save themselves, and now our family continues to suffer because of that.”

"You are correct," she says, without glancing at me.

"Who? Which ancestor did this to us?"

"They lived long ago, too long to remember. They'd made an oath to some spirit, sacrificing your family to gain wealth, for they were very poor."

I clench my hands into fists. If my spirit waters this burned field, do I cease to exist? I wondered. Do I go to heaven or to an ancestral realm?

"You have until the end of your fellowship to make your decision," Yanano says. "We've already made ours. You are our most viable vessel. There is no way out. There is no escape. You have to stay in Huis. You have to finish the book. I will possess your body and be free from this place. There is no other path forward."

I clasp my hand around her wrist. Her skin burns hotly through mine, but I don't let it go. She stares at me, a hiss leaving her lips.

"When you take my body," I ask, "will it hurt?"

"Yes. Terribly," she says, with unflinching coldness. The audacity. "Having your spirit wrenched from your body is the most painful thing a person can endure. It is too late to save yourself. The time you've spent in Huis has weakened your spirit's protection."

Smoke hisses from our skin contact, and I release Yanano's wrist. "Is that all?" I say dully.

"Patience," Yanano says. "Before I release you back into wakefulness, I must tell you what will happen on the fateful day. There are four voyages, but you will take three voyages: that of the Sea of Lost Souls, that of the Desert of the Flesh, which is only available to your friends. I will be taking your body. For you it will be the Grave of Mirrors or the Fields of

your Ancestry." She stares ahead. "You will only see these on your last day on earth."

I nod, keep silent.

Yanano leans against me, hand braced against my stomach. Her other hand calls forth a black snake, its scales aglow. It ripples through the tall grass, curls around my feet, as Yanano's hand keeps me locked in sebeteledi.

"A little medicine to make you behave." She cranes my jaw open, and in the snake slithers, a dark magic of sejeso. "I am only going to say this once: If you sleep outside Huis's walls again, we will leak out of your dreams. Your parents and your sister will be dead before morning." Yanano pushes me toward a gleaming void. "Go back to Huis, finish the bloody book, attend the awards ceremony. You do not want to find out what we will do if you disobey." She twists her hand, and a sharp pain ignites in my throat, a black shiny liquid spurts from my mouth, and my gut convulses in pain. "Return to Huis." Her voice is hoarse and deep. "Now."

The Realms of Huis

by Anaya Sebeya

First. the Sea of Lost Souls,
where panic sets the storms
singing. many drown
without taming fear.

survive that voyage, if you may
then, far from shore, a Desert of Flesh
to awaken,
or be dispossessed

survive that voyage, if you may
to face the Fields of Ancestry
or the shattered Grave
of Mirrors:

this line is the path of death

But obey first: Huis, the door to these realms.
Stay, Behave—your presence, your
life, a tithe

RANEWA

A MAJESTIC WOODEN DOOR STOOD BEFORE ME.

I tucked the ghostman's knife into my waistband. Using the key Merapelo gave me, I unlocked the door. It was a simple room, bare, without a desk, chair, or a bed to define its function. There were three windows, overlooking a field of floating mirrors and an ocean beyond. There were several mirrors on the walls, one atop each other, playing visuals and documents of its previous victims. As I took everything in, a peculiar understanding entered me. This wasn't the only Huis in existence. There was one in Brazil, Ghana, Mexico, Italy—in different names. The ghosts that filled Huis's body were from landscapes that were scattered with dead bodies, their spirits rising like smoke from their flesh, with no ceremonies to help them pass onto their ancestral realm. And so they entered this home of Huis, unable to pass.

Bessie told me that the ghostwomen wouldn't harm me, and that seemed to be true: I was free to roam Huis undisturbed. I used this to my advantage. I spoke to the ghostwomen, asking them questions about Huis and the influx of new women, anything that could give me a clue to find Anaya.

Bessie was also right about time—it *was* weird here. But that meant that I could thoroughly peruse the ancient rooms

and the details they offered, putting together pieces so I could understand how Huis worked.

Huis is a house that migrated, a house that killed, a serial killer house that was never on the murder suspect list. Disappearances, suicides—the blame usually fell on the victims. From the visuals and histories I witnessed in the "museum" room, it seemed like Huis was consistent. It plagued a structure, knowing that it would be inhabited by potential victims; it seemed like the haunting was most effective when there were about five or six, with one acting as the house's medium—like a monitor, keeping watch over the others. Out of the girls who had been at Huis with Anaya, this had to have been Miche. The toughest inhabitants for Huis to break into were the most religious ones, but it seemed that Huis always had a desire to break the faithful, sway them out of their faith. I thought of Ogone and Ruvimbo, and all their faith and prayers and fasting that protected them. The easiest were those whose bodies were weakened by an illness. Bessie. The remaining were usually neutral, with moderate beliefs in various spiritualities. Anaya and Nilza.

The room became my mind, giving me every answer to the gaps in my research. But the only answer it wouldn't give me was Anaya's whereabouts. I wondered under what spiritual law it was refusing me this information.

I inched closer to a mirror, noticing Anaya's name inscribed elegantly on its frame. And like an eye of a camera upon an eagle's back, the view in the mirror loomed above an ocean, labeled like a map: The Sea of Lost Souls. A mirror

displayed a shoreline with a forest and paths leading to the Cape Dutch house.

In the hallway outside, I heard muffled speech. Miche—after all the time I'd put into listening to the bitch's podcast, I would know her anywhere. Then I heard another voice: my sister's.

Choose your membership

Contributor

$1/month

JOIN

Thank you for your support – every amount goes a long way!

Witness

$5/month

JOIN

- Discord server access to Witness community
- Early access to podcast episodes
- Behind-the-scenes for our audio production and notes
- 10% discount on merch

Investigator

$15/month

JOIN

Everything included in Witness, plus:

- Access to old interrogation videos, articles, and Q&A that the team conducts with those close to the case, incl. Günter commentary
- Videos of Michele Visser's time in Günter and unexpected shots of Anaya's time in Günter

Criminal

$30/month

JOIN

Everything included in Investigator, plus:

- Access to partners-in-crime group where we dig out the mysteries of Anaya's life and disappearance
- As a Criminal, you will have access to our files, investigation techniques, and breadcrumbs we follow to hopefully find Anaya.
- Membership funds are used to hire professionals to assist with our investigation.

Recent Posts by What Happened to Ana?

Hello, Crimies, welcome to the top-tier level of your subscription. We finally have a video for the sibling of the star of the show, Ranewa Sebeya. Although short, it does show that something was odd between the sisters. Take a look and share your thoughts.

Investigator Subscribers-Only Access: Ranewa Sebeya Interrogation Video

Here you will find access to interrogation videos and links to the victims' social media pages as a bonus to your favorite episodes. Remember every little bit of information is vital to the case. Enjoy!

Ranewa Sebeya

Olivia Skommere: Where were you on 20 December?

Ranewa Sebeya: In Botswana, at home with my parents.

Olivia Skommere: Has your sister ever been diagnosed with a mental illness?

Ranewa Sebeya: No . . . she's not crazy. Did you—

Olivia Skommere: And how was your childhood and educational life like, for both you and Anaya?

Ranewa Sebeya: Well, we grew up sheltered, went to an English private school, had tutors, cleaners, drivers.

Olivia Skommere: I find it strange that you and your sister hardly communicated during her residency.

Ranewa Sebeya: Sisters fight.

Olivia Skommere: Well, I've gone through her messages and phone records, and there's almost no communication between you and her, except for an email here and there. Did something happen between you two?

Ranewa Sebeya: We were both dealing with a lot. She left me alone . . . I had to deal with my parents, and I struggled a lot, alone. But we've always had a strong bond—despite the distance, I knew my sister was there for me.

Olivia Skommere: Perhaps Anaya found another way to communicate with you other than through a phone.

Ranewa Sebeya: I . . . only saw her in my dreams.

When something is stolen, especially of spiritual or cultural significance, it takes away part of the essence from that land, which disrupts the energetic stability that item introduced in that space. It ripples a 'curse' on its own, so white people knew what they were doing."

Angie Thato Chuma-Mogotsi

WHAT

HAPPENED

TO

ANA?

2:23:59:01

BEFORE I DIE

Episode 10

Grand Prize • Anaya

Welcome back, Crimies. I am Michele Visser, host of What Happened to Ana? *Several weeks ago, Anaya had reached her breaking point both in her writing and in her personal life, but when we last left her, things were starting to fall into place. She was feeling inspired to develop her Günter manuscript, and we had our first breakthrough in our friendship after our deep conversation.*

The big day had finally arrived, the day the Günter Prize for African Women's Literature would finally announce the winner. I was nervous, and everyone was in a flurry of excitement, wondering who it would be. The Günter residency was grueling, but I wouldn't have picked any other awesome, sweet and intelligent women than my Günter fellows to spend it with. I told myself, 'Michele, even if you don't win, the experience alone is as rewarding as any prize.'

This is Anaya Sebeya's story . . .

[upbeat music]

It's the day of the Günter Prize Ceremony, and the day I will either die or possess Ranewa's body.

The black snake still lies in my abdomen. I feel it writhing in my womb, my veins, my limbs. Pain follows it as it grows bulbous with fury like a tumor, a fetus. I am pregnant with sejeso. That morning, I was nauseous and puked into the toilet, Ogone stroked my back. "Kante a ga o Motswana? These spirits are wicked, Anaya, they want blood. The yoke of these spirits that you are accepting is killing you. 'Come to Me, all you who labor and are heavy laden, and I will give you rest.' Take God, Anaya." I raised my head and whispered, "It's too late," but she shook her head. "It's never too late for God."

When we arrive at Muizenberg Conference Center, the building is fronted with endless white stairs, where industry professionals and famous authors loiter, posing in front of blinding flashes of lights from media, before proceeding entry through majestic glass doors. I have spent so long in solitary, writing, buckling under Huis's terror, that it feels jarring to be perfectly costumed and celebrated amid crowds of voices and perfumes. Since I learned that Yanano plans to possess my body, I don't care about the prize anymore, nor the expensive ceremony. But Yanano told me to abide or else.

Stepping out of the chauffeured car, I press my sweaty hands against my dress, anxiety slick in my throat.

Ogone's emerald gown clings to her body, with a slit down her chest, her weave flowing down her back. She catches my eyes and gives my shoulder a reassuring squeeze.

We lock hands, posing for the cameras. Miche is on my right, wearing a pink chiffon gown as flushed as her skin, hair

in tamed tresses. Bessie has faux locs tied up high, wearing a glitzy, long flowing dress. I wear another one of Ranewa's loose fitting silk pantsuits with a corset, my dreads tied up in gold, shimmering string.

Cameras flash, and I hide my expression and put on a mask for the world. We make it to the top of the stairs, through the glassy doors toward a wall with the Günter Prize logo. There's a line to proceed past the press for interviews, their mics poised toward peoples' faces, some celebrities, some Günter donors, and authors of prestige. A waiter presses into our hands glasses of fizzy beverage specially designed for Günter fellows. My stomach turns as I remember the personalized cocktails at the Midnight Mix and Match. I take the drink meant for guests instead.

An interviewer with a high ponytail and high cheekbones, melanin-shining, stands close to me and performatively says to the camera accompanying her, "Welcome to the Award Ceremony for the Günter Prize. These women have spent four months at a prestigious writing residency working on a novel that may snatch one of them a grand prize of €100,000 and kick off a literary career. The judges have deliberated and will announce the winner today. We're here with one of the four fellows, Anaya Sebeya. Congratulations, you're so lucky! Anyone would die to be in your position. Tell us, what is your novel about?"

I position my lips to expose my teeth into a perfect smile that's meant to show my enthusiasm. "It's a dream come true," I recite, remembering to tilt my head, let a shine appear in my eyes so that my happiness looks real, and move my hands and body so I look energetic and youthful. "I'm writing speculative fiction consisting of four African women whose lives

intertwine during the colonial wars in southern Africa. It intersects with memory, architecture, reparations, and indigenous lives."

Her eyes glaze over with disinterest and confusion. Nodding, she says, "Do you think it's good enough to win?"

Discomfort writhes in my stomach. "I hope so."

She leans in with an air of secrecy. "Who would you bet your money on that is definitely *not* the winner?"

The audacity.

"I love all the fellows," I say. "We've become close friends, and I'm a huge fan of their writing. We're all talented, and we all deserve to win."

She smiles, too wide, and adds, "I spoke to Langa Mangezi a few minutes ago, and I must say, I'm a huge fan of your relation—"

My heart presses tightly against my chest. "We're not dating."

"Oh, shem skepsel, I'm sorry. You guys made such a good couple. Imagine all the hot babies you could've had."

Hot babies, you've got to be kidding me. I lean into the mic, stare straight ahead into the camera. "I never dated Langa. And I'm never having kids." My voice breaks at the latter. I won't be alive to have that opportunity, unless I take Ranewa's body.

"Oh, such a pretty face to go to waste—"

I do a peace sign, and I stroll toward Ogone.

An older white man points the mic at her and in a delicate voice asks, "I had a conversation with Grace, your mentor, for an interview we're doing, and we spoke about your Günter novel. How do you feel, being considered the African Sally Rooney?"

"I feel very accomplished to be compared to an African Sally Rooney," she says, smiling, well-poised and calm. "But only time will tell if my book gets published and lives up to such a reputation."

The reporter doesn't know whether to take it as sarcasm given how innocently Ogone is smiling. She looks so pretty you wouldn't even think she can swear.

"Ja, definitely, I mean to be considered in the sphere of her is huge," he says. "You're a role model for many; our audience is very interested in your decision to be celibate. Your writing seems to explore the question of virginity in a surprisingly intelligent manner." He laughs.

I tease my temples with my fingers at the onset of a headache. Ogone is still smiling into the camera.

"In my opinion," the reporter continues, "you've made such a noble decision in such a very promiscuous society."

Ogone leans in, smiling, and says, "Yes, you're right, it's very noble indeed this decision I've made. My virginity has really done amazing stuff, you know: healed poverty, stopped climate change and wars, very noble indeed that we have to talk about it and its significance to society."

The man's expression drops, and he isn't happy with her pulling one on him. "Well, have a good night, ma'am."

Yanano is holding my family's lives ransom. She's in my head. She could potentially be here in whatever form.

"Is everything okay?" Ogone asks, worried. I nod. "Everyone's waiting for us. One final round of photos with the media before we head into the auditorium to start the ceremony." She rubs the sides of her arms. "I'm nervous. I hate going into things not knowing what to expect." She looks at me. "Here, let's make a bet. If I win, I'll divide the prize

money 50-50 with you." I don't say that I might not be alive to enjoy it.

I wonder if I will win this prize posthumously. If I will die having never published my books. I wonder how many Black women died, their voices buried, drowned out, gone unheard, unnoticed, names lost in the blaze.

A waiter signals to us, informing us that it's time to take our official pictures. We rush to the foyer, where Miche and Bessie stand in front of a huge placard with the Günter logo.

We stand, arms around each other, smiling. The camera flashes a thousand times, a thousand shards of reality.

I stare as the flash imprints a void in my vision, mesmerized by the gleam as it captures the moment for posterity, the flash a prickle of lightning, its edges like static noise. My body becomes weightless, as we rise off the floor, everything in slow motion, the sounds of the chattering crowd fade out, and the world slowly starts to dim. Fearful and fearless, there is no return.

I step forward, feeling the brush of Ogone's fingers around my own as the storm of the void drags us in.

That is the end of Anaya's story.

We saw a bright light, and Ogone and I were woken up by the waves on Camps Bay. We have not kept in touch.

To this day, we don't know what happened to Bessie and Anaya, what the camera flash triggered, or what the hauntings distorted in us.

Anaya Sebeya was not crazy, and I hope this podcast has humanized her and brought you into her world.

If anyone has any information about Anaya's whereabouts, please use the link in the description to send in your reports.

I am Michele Visser, host of What Happened to Ana? *and this has been Anaya Sebeya's story. But this doesn't have to be the end of us, Crimies! Visit my website, sign up to my newsletter, and follow me @MicheVisser to keep up to date with me, my books, and my other projects in the works. If you liked this podcast, you won't want to miss what's coming next!*

[theme music]

♡43,301 ≮25,875

RANEWA

I WAS SPENDING TOO MUCH TIME IN THIS REALM; HUNGRY GHOST-women huddled outside the door, salivating for my spirit, my flesh.

I followed the flicker of Anaya's voice, its intermittent pauses and glitches twining with Miche's narration as it led me to a new room.

"The camera flashes a thousand times, a thousand shards of reality . . . Fearful and fearless, there is no return . . . That is the end of Anaya's story . . . To this day, we don't know wh—"

I stepped inside.

Miche was seated at an oak desk, with a recording system set up, bulky headset on, a sleek microphone positioned to her mouth. Her left hand was pressed to her neck. There, she had a mark the color of my sister, pressing it as if it were a signal, connecting her to the unknown.

Miche's right hand was manipulating a dial, maneuvering images in a large dish of water reflecting visions of Anaya's life and dreams. The portable dish was deep, wooden, stationed atop the desk, and round enough to wrap my arms around. I caught a glimpse of Anaya's memories of the day she came home from Russia: how she flung herself in my arms smelling of a floral perfume and sweat, her hands curled around my own beside my hospital bed the day after my

suicide attempt, and the day I drove her to the airport for her flight to Cape Town with the windows down as we screamed our lungs out to our favourite tune—for each exit and entry into a life event we were always there for each other. We'd spend the night at home, surrounded by junk food, in the cinema room watching our favourite TV shows. We'll never have that again.

Anger blinded me, my hands clenching into fists. "This is how you've been doing it?" I shouted, storming toward her.

"Ag, what now?" Miche asked, unbothered and concentrating on her work. "Why won't you people ever listen. You always have to be difficult." She turned, exasperated, removing her headset.

Her eyes widened in fear, perhaps surprised to see me and worried what I would do to her. "How did you get in here?"

Bessie stormed in, arms crossed. "Can you *believe* Miche is still using this house? She allows the spiritwomen here to enter her body to give her spiritual sight. Imagine! She's so dirty to do such a thing. They tell her things, what to do, how to move, give her power—the bloody things she's benefitted from this ugly place. She doesn't care about anyone except herself. She's watched them use me for their violent scenes and done nothing. Nothing!" Bessie spat to the side, disgusted.

I wanted to slap Bessie, because first of all, this should have been the first thing she told me.

"You also did it during the Günter residency," Miche shouted. "So don't paint me as someone bad when *you* all did that too."

"Shut up, Miche," Bessie cried. "You're still alive, aren't you? I don't have a body. I've been stuck in here since that

damned ceremony whilst you get to waltz in and out as you please." She turned to me, flustered. "She has an altar at her home to connect her to this place. If destroyed, it will cut her connection to Huis's spirit realm," Bessie clarified.

I understood now why Ogone and Ruvimbo were not forthcoming in their interrogations. No one would believe that Günter Huis could do such a thing. No one would believe that Miche knew my sister's thoughts because Huis scavenged Anaya's insides.

In here, no law could touch me.

I wanted to reach for the dagger tucked in my waistband. Instead, I slapped her.

Her blue eyes welled up, and with strength only wielded by my fury, I lifted Miche by her shoulders and threw her across the desk, scattering her headset and her notepads across the floor. She tried to steady herself, and I punched her mouth until she fell, dragged her face across the floor to drink of her tears.

I wrapped both hands around her neck as I pulled her back up, pinning her against the wall, squeezing tightly her tiny neck, watching her face turn pink, then I loosened my hands. "What did you do to my sister?" I growled.

She threw her arms up in panic, bruised, voice squeaky and hoarse. "No, no, no, it wasn't me."

I dragged her to her workstation, lowered her head to the dish of water as she struggled against my grip. But Bessie stepped in, holding Miche's arms back so she couldn't stop me from what I was about to do.

I pushed Miche's face into the water, wondered if drowning here would manifest as some form of asphyxiation to her body in the physical world. I hoped so.

Anaya's memories swirled around with Miche's hair. I caught a glimpse of Anaya's long locs swinging in the breeze, and her chirpy laughter floated into my ears, her eyes concentrating on something in the garden. Oh, Anaya, my heart wept.

I pulled Miche back roughly, and she gasped for air.

"Prove it," I demanded.

I kept a firm hold on Miche's head while Bessie freed one of her pale arms. Miche fumbled about for her instruments, dialing up Anaya's voice, and swirling her hand through the water to pull up the end of Anaya's life. As she did so, the air in Huis moved about us like a wind. Bessie clasped my hand, and we came to in a rush of waves, tangled with the limbs of two other bodies, and I felt the skin that of my sister's, soft and smooth and full of fear, her screams stilted with ocean water.

Anaya | The Sea of Lost Souls

The borders of the room, the limits of the world, fracture away from us.

It is a serene night. There's no horizon, except darkness. No breeze, just the lapping of water at our feet. The ocean seems to be rising, growing colder with each inhale. I start shaking.

This is the first voyage. The Sea of Lost Souls.

"Don't panic," I whisper, remembering Yanano's warning. "We just have to make it through." It terrifies me that I'm treading through the spirits of people who were alive like us. The water at my knees has no scent except the weight of death.

"Anaya, what's going on?" Ogone's voice trembles toward me, coming from every direction. The waters ripple as she moves, but I can't pinpoint her position.

"We're in the spirit realm—if you panic it rises the torrent," I yell back. "Please try to calm down."

Bessie shouts our names. The freezing water batters my chest.

I can't hear Miche. Is she okay? I push down a spike of anxiety.

In the farther distance, I see a dense darkness in the seas, spinning a vortex as the waters rise to our necks. "Where do we go?" Bessie cries.

"We have to swim away from that vortex! We need to get to the land," I shout to Ogone and Bessie. Far ahead, there's a shimmering shoreline, sands that could lead to their bodies if they survive the Desert of Flesh. "Swim, swim as fast as you can."

The waters represent the spirits that have washed out of their bodies, and they rage and toss around us with force. The spirit water fills my mouth, my lungs, my stomach. I am drowning.

I'm floating in the unrelenting ocean. I must stop this I must stop this, but I can't control what I have become. I am a volcano. A tornado. A tsunami. I can't save myself from myself. There's something with us in the waters. This haunting has become potent at our enclosing death.

A hand like seaweed wraps around my being, to concentrate my outward anger into my bone. I kick at it, scissor my legs, feel myself drown in the depths of this ocean. This isn't how we will die.

A scream drenched in worry reaches the shoreline. I tug at it until its form, Ogone, spins around, facing me, nods her head for me to follow her.

I submerge myself, let the ocean of death cover me whole, inhale its molecules, and I scrape my nails at the thing that clasps my legs. I swim toward Ogone and do the same to what shackles her.

"Where's Bessie?" Ogone asks. "Oh, where's Bessie?"

"Maybe she made it to the shore of her body. Ogone, we have to go. We can't waste time," I say.

"Bessie," she shouts, spinning around. Only darkness and a raging ocean. "Bessie!"

Silence and thunder in the sky. I feel something tug at my feet and I drag Ogone away.

"Bessie!" she shouts, her voice hoarse with fear and desperation.

"We have to go," I plead. "We don't have time."

Ogone's crying, as the ocean draws us away into itself. We sway in this mass, in this lonesomeness.

"I wasted my life working myself to the bone and this is what I get?" Ogone says, unbelieving, weeping. "I haven't lived, God, I haven't lived."

The water is cold, biting. I'm tired. I'd like to believe we'll wake up tomorrow in warm beds. Home, I'll never see home. My heart breaks. Home. The ocean is calm, swaying us, lull-ing gravity. The cold strings itself into our bones, wakefulness wanes, and sleep grows my body heavy.

I should let the ocean carry me away.

And I feel the skin of someone else, slippery against mine, bring me up to the surface, helping me.

I'm weighing Ogone down. Maybe if I let go, she'll be light enough to get to the shore. I slip my hand out from Ogone so the underwater mass of ocean will take me.

Ogone's face is fearful but bracing herself with courage as she grips my hand. "Don't leave me, Anaya, please. Let's swim to the shore. We can make it."

The shimmer of the shores strokes the calm in her eyes. She turns her back to me and wraps my arms around her neck, my legs around her waist. "No. I will not leave you to die."

She paddles her small legs. "No," she repeats. "No." Her breaths are warm puffs on my fingers. "It won't win. *Huis*

won't win. You have to get through. The Lord will favor you if you do what needs to be done, you hear me."

I lay my head against the warm blade of her shoulder, as she carries me to shore, to life.

I realize her sacrifice: saving someone knowing that it won't change her fate. Instead she could be using that time to save herself and leave me behind. I'm slowing her down.

The ocean is swept forth and backward by ghosts.

"Something's in the ocean," I whisper, the salt of spirits burning my throat.

"So are we," Ogone says. "'Behold, I give you the authority to trample on serpents and scorpions, and over all the power of the enemy, and nothing shall by any means hurt you.'" Her hope is sharper than steel. In this ocean of death, she is the moon, a guiding light, my harbor.

We imagine worse things, until we find ourselves lying on the sand, face up, panting.

Our bodies are heavy. The only lights are the stars, which finally appear in stunning beauty, blinking down at us, the sky breathless. From here, the landscape is not much different than from home and I could think perhaps we're on Camps Bay beach.

"I can't believe we made it," Ogone says. Under the moonlight, beaded sand shimmers across her forehead. Her weave is limp, weighted down with ocean water.

"Where are Miche and Bessie?" The ocean hasn't spat out another body.

Ogone shakes her head. "Maybe they didn't survive." I think she's right, but I don't say so.

"It's not over," I say. "This is where we part. You must go in that direction, through the forest to the Desert of Flesh," I

say pointing at two starry lights hanging directly above the forest. "Yanano warned me the desert is far worse than this ocean, but you can return to your body if you make it through. My body is no longer mine, so I have to go to Huis." I point to the opposite direction, which is a low-lying land of shrubs.

Ogone hugs me tightly, crying. "I love you, Anaya. I'm so sorry. I'm so sorry."

The pain is too much to bear. This is the beginning of my death, and I have to go at it alone. Ogone still has a chance to live.

"There's no time," I whisper. "Go, follow that light, it will lead to your body. Fight, destroy whatever obstacle comes your way."

"Do you want me to say anything to your sister, your family?" Ogone asks.

"Tell them I love them," I say, then I grab her hands tightly, pleading. "My sister, Ranewa, I know her—she'll torture herself with my disappearance. Please, tell her to live for me. She must live."

Ogone hugs me one more time, drags herself away. I watch her. I watch her. I watch her, unable to drown out the sorrow in me. Then I turn toward my path, my fate of death.

Anaya | Three Ghostwomen and an Elder Ghostman

When I arrive back at Huis, the ghostwomen's voices dance around me. And in one distant room, a familiar voice, and then mine: "Welcome, Crimies. I bring you to the beginning of the unsolved missing person case of Anaya Sebeya:

"The August night is a deep grave. I've arrived at Fisq, an exclusive restaurant in Cape Town, for the welcome dinner with the founders of the Günter Prize. The Günter handpicks five to six African women writers every year for their residency, and they've chosen me out of the whole continent—little me!"

Trying to locate the room my voice is in, I pass through a hallway lined with ghostwomen spirits.

A girl sits, fingers fitted into her eye sockets. Blood seeps through her headscarf. A ZCC badge is clipped to the collar of her aged dress. She looks up as I approach; her eye sockets are like dark pits. "She took my eyes," she says simply.

The next woman leans against the wall. Flies flit about her flattened chest, as if what lay before was scraped off by a sharp sword. "She said my breasts were a good fit."

I enter all the other rooms, the girls mournfully reference the new ways Huis's ghostwomen are fashioning themselves

new bodies: "It's no good, it's no good. She's coming for you. The spirits here are too hungry."

"They will never find our bodies. We all disappeared, but our spirits are trapped here, our family never helped us transcend," they say.

These are women who went missing.

Their bodies were never found.

Their spirits have been here all along.

"Some of these spirits knit themselves bodies from our flesh," one girl says.

They surround me, and I'm unable to tell them apart, suffocated by their drowsy voices:

"She has my tongue."

"She has my fingers."

"She has my ears."

"Her body's almost done. She needs a spirit."

Each "she" seems to reference a different spirit in Huis.

"A hungry death turns evil."

I think of Ogone, wondering if she made it back to her flesh, if a flash of light carried her back to the home of her body.

Eventually I find Miche in a room, fiddling with a dial and headsets.

"What are you doing?" I ask. "That's my voice."

She's agitated. "But I told you, Huis lets me understand you guys."

I push her aside and grab the edge of the dish of water with a strong urge to throw it across the room, but it's too heavy. "You didn't tell me this is what you were doing."

"But you agreed to tell the ghostwomen's stories; you consented. I thought you were all in on this." She rubs the patch

of my Black on her neck. "Every time I was working in here, I heard you each time you came, but Huis wouldn't allow us to interact. But that night, during the Midnight Mix and Match party, on your bed, that allowed me to be a Black woman."

"I don't believe this clueless act you're throwing," I say.

I stare about the room. All the times I'd glimpse a ghostly white woman walking the hallways, it had been Miche. "Did you have to live out any of the scenes where the ghost-women were being assaulted?"

She looks down, shakes her head. "No, but I had to watch their scenes every day, which was traumatizing enough. Even . . . your scene when you took Yanano's place. I tried stopping it, but, of course, I couldn't. The ghostwomen weren't allowed to touch me, but they've been kind in tending to me."

"Like housemaids?"

She ignores the question. "This is a dish of your bathwater," she says, turning the dial clockwise to pause the image to a still of the floating family trees. "I have Bessie's and Ogone's too. I thought because you're all from different tribes, that you'd have different flavours."

"What?"

"Water is a powerful medium if you know how to use it right. You've been living in Huis, and Huis has been living in you," she says. "It shared with me your voice, your thoughts—after all, I need to know your interiority to write your story."

"Write my story?" I ask, incredulous.

"Living in South Africa has been tough for me sometimes. But living in Huis has let me step into my divine femininity that was stolen from my family. Sometimes worried about living as a white person here, I want to go back home, where

my people were originally from, Europe or something, but it's not home if I've never lived there. I know I'm replaceable by a Black woman—it's always a constant fear. But Huis has really opened my eyes to the injustices of this world," she says. "I have to get your story out there. Your life is too important, Ana, for you to just die and for no one to know of your talent. I'm sick to my stomach if I don't help those who have been marginalized by the system." She stands up, walks toward me. "I'm not going to win this prize, that I can tell. Publishing doesn't want white voices anymore, they're all about diversity nowadays. So if I get cancelled so be it—but I must tell your story whatever the cost. I want to set things right," she says, touching my shoulders, eyes showing concern. "I want people to know the truth, to really, really hear what happened to you. Huis has me as its ambassador, and I've got to use that power for good. I want to help you."

I'm too stunned to speak.

"You should go, Ana. You have to save your family. Time is not on your side. I will take care of everything, okay?" she says. "I have a lot of work to catch up with. Look, that's the window I'll be watching you from."

The window overlooks the Fields of Ancestry. I'm done talking. I leap forward, tighten my hands around Miche's throat. A great spark slits the air, reality's little void, throwing me back against the wall. A guttural roar, so beastly, so demonic, and frightening scrapes through reality's void. I back away from Miche, who coughs, turning pink and letting out a deep laugh.

Something collapses inside me, the desperate feeling of powerlessness, knowing that Miche, a white woman who suffered nothing of my life is going to profit from my life. My

life! My life comes down to this, a meagre coin lining her purse. I bang my fists against the floor. Even in death, nothing is fair.

"Don't you realize that you have lost already?" Miches asks, strolling across the room.

Behind me, a shadow. Yanano growls at the ghostwomen, and they scatter away.

"Sister, I have come for you. First things first." Yanano hands me my cellphone, to my astonishment. "The device has your voice, has a sprinkle of your spirit. It is a magical charm. Sometimes we can leave objects behind through the mirrors. I believe your sister's mirror is marred with black blood. It doesn't take long to leave behind an object."

I stare at her questioningly. She's pardoning me with mercy. She's giving me instructions.

"There's only about a few minutes left," Yanano says. "It's almost an eclipse; it protects me from Huis's wrath. I owe Huis no allegiance. Leave something behind for your sister if you want her to help you transcend."

I grip her hands, tearful and thankful for this tiny mercy of one last goodbye. The cellphone I can only give to my sister is my own.

I grab the phone, flee through the hallways of Huis, into the Grave of Mirrors, their sharp edges cutting into my arms. They glint the sharp light of sun, a slow pivot, the marks of black blood on them. I find the mirror belonging to Ranewa, my sister, open it, and steal into it.

It's Botswana. Home.

I can smell the pain stifling the house; I can hear Mama praying and not smell her usual cigarette smoke staining the place. How long after is it that they've been notified I

disappeared? What has become of my family? Do my parents feel guilty for cutting me off? My sister's room is less colorful than before. What happened? The mirror swings back to close. I try to hold it, but it resists, a force I can't overwhelm. I must be quick. I don't know what will happen if the mirror closes me out. I catch my reflection—I'm transparent, slowly dissolving into thin air.

The calendar catches my eye, and I gasp. I've been missing for eighteen months. Eighteen. The grief glooms in me.

It's my sister's birthday today, today that she will receive my story.

Footsteps. I quickly place my phone on my sister's bed, wrapped in a scarf, and just as the bedroom door clicks open, I step back hidden in the air. My sister, Ranewa, her body, so, so warm I could easily step into it. I never knew hunger like this, to drink her spirit. Her face an angry cut. Ranewa pauses. She can't see me. She picks up the phone. I'm behind her, wishing I could touch her, press my fingers into the mould of her skin and knead myself deeply into her flesh—but to her, I'm just a ghost. Invisible.

Find my spirit, I whisper, *help me transition to the ancestral realm. Save me. Put me to rest.* My spirit's breath imprints itself on her skin, like a tattoo, a scar, a birthmark. Ranewa spins around. She must feel me. The mirror is half closed. I squeeze myself through its slanted opening, unable to witness her response to my voice floating from the phone. I hope the hot breath I left on my sister's neck won't stain her life with curses.

As I walk back to Huis, the elder ghostman on the kgotla stool stops whistling, looks at me, whispers in a hoarse voice, "Ngwana wa mongwaketse, o tla dira jwang? Thipa ke ye." He

gestures the knife to me, bloodless, the lobe of the Mosarwa man hanging from its edge, its sharp lip. He turns it around, presses the butt of the knife into my shaking palm. "No one will hold it against you. Slip it into the ribcage to open a portal for any spirit to enter the flesh and possess the human body."

The Mosarwa man leans his chin on his hand, his body laid atop the old man's lap, looks at me casually despite his circumstance. "O ya go dira jwang?" he asks.

I tuck the knife into my dress.

Yanano is waiting calmly on the stoep when I return. The sun above is half obscured by another celestial body. The floating trees sweep shadows onto us from above. I could thank Yanano, but she's only confident because she will be walking out in my body.

"This is where I will leave you," Yanano says, looking toward a wide road that leads to a calm landscape. The vision before us changes; veld and the farmhouse flank us and far into the distance, and the reeds are shadows of the men of bone. And I know the nightmare that will unfold. I step back.

"No," I say, looking to Yanano. "You're not going to do this to me again."

"This is the only way I can leave," she says as a sphere of light appears behind her. "The door is open to your body." She steps back. "Goodbye." Pauses. "I am truly sorry that this is how I must get my freedom. I wish we had met under better circumstances. Maybe one day we will be free of all of this, the past, history, the pain." Tears slip down her face. "Take care, Anaya."

And she disappears into the veld, into my body. I know I am already dead. But I will not die by these men's hands. Not again.

In the distance I hear the white bones coming, throttling the earth with their feet to raid the Black earth. I take the dagger from the elder ghostmen and meet them at the river. I use the sharp knife on the men, striking, stabbing, scraping at the cloth of their flesh until I'm drenched in blood and rage, until their nine bodies lay shorn of their violence and hatred and greed. I skin them, straight to the bone. Lay their organs in the earth, like bad seeds. Their blood, in my hands. There are no screams in me. I feel no reprieve from this rage, from this act, only more sorrow.

I drop the knife into the dust, into the earth. Three shadows approach me, the prim pose of the ghostwomen. "Hae, sisi, se ye ko!" the ghostwomen shout.

I let my body carry me to the two fields.

I am soaked in blood as I gaze at the flourishing field filled with the flesh of my sister, my freedom. Then I turn to the right field, where the calamity of my lineage rests as burned ash, where I would stay forever since I cannot transition to the ancestral realm. I know what I will do.

I press my foot into the sooty ground, and fire trails up my leg, sending smoky flames above. The burn of my skin is excruciating. Every memory burns, burns, burns. The water of my spirit spills from my body. Every breath of me is sucked by the dryness of this earth, healing the bones of my family, cleansing them. My ancestry's curses hiss smoke into the air. Flames gasp across my skin, the pain torturous. The ashes flick about, turning a deep shade of emerald.

My body twitches, no longer under my control. My spine is bent backward, my head touching the back of my ankles as the force of the entirety of my family's illnesses and misfortune assails me, a blazing hurricane, that I have no moment

to open my mouth and scream but be paralyzed by the vortex of this death. Parts of my spirit purge out of my body, spilling across the earth, watering the drought of this field that goes a millennium back.

My mouth cranes open, and my screams tear to the sky in endless loops. I'm certain I've gone beyond my death. I should've picked a mirror with the black blood. I should have stabbed someone with the elder ghostman's knife and possessed a stranger's body, but that isn't right. No, no, no I do not regret my choice. I am cleansing my ancestry's pain, their curses. No more shall they face.

I look up at my ancestors, my progeny rushing toward me to drink of my spirit and quench their drought. Lord, please I have suffered too much, no more. But I cannot renounce my death.

Bone breaks through skin, pain hurtles across my body. I bend forward to ease it, but my knees crush. Horns of cattle, ditlhare, and other bad medicine rise like smoke into the air, become pulverized by the force of my spirit. The wan spirits of my family form into glowing stars before disappearing, become obscured by the verdant vegetation of ancient trees that reach the skies, clouding them with foliage and bird song. Springs of water and fountains cut across rock and grass. A choke grasps my throat.

At the breaking of my bones, a thunderous, shattering sound escapes from the center of earth, roots ripping through the boulders of a set curse on this land. The roots grow thick, forming into solid stems of ancient trees that grow thicker and rounder and taller, blackening the sky with their wide branches and leaves blooming so fast covering their every surface.

Through the treetops, aside the eclipse is an adjacent moon, the wax of this new moon drinks the calamity, disease, and misfortune rising from this field like smog. For a moment, everything is bright and clear. I'm thrown aside, my limbs and organs torn and scattered across this forest floor like seeds, blooming fortune, healing, prosperity. My flesh turns into water, spreads into the black earth.

I burn in this field knowing that no one in my family has to go through what I went through. I burn in this field not knowing my descendants, and them never knowing me or what I've done for them. Eventually, I will be much like the ancestor far back in the horizon to them.

I glance once last time at the mirage of my sister in the other field, knowing that I'm doing this for *her*.

The field is a blooming forest. My spirit evaporates from my torn flesh, rises like dust motes, fills the air like dew. And this is where I'll remain in the burning face of a pain, of a death until my spirit is sent to the ancestral realm. I am without flesh. My spirit, the birthstone of my ancestry's healing. The ritual is complete. Let not my life be drank by the voice of a white one. The eye of the sun blinks, like a quick flash that becomes black as night, black as my death.

RANEWA

I COULD FEEL THE BURN OF MY SISTER'S DEATH. I WATCHED ANAYA burning in the Fields of Ancestry. That was suffering I've never seen, unlike anything in our world.

I remembered Anaya's poem, the instructions within it, and I knew what I needed to do. I was still holding Miche down with fury as she wriggled and moaned. Miche smacked my face, punched Bessie in the face with her elbow, and kicked me in the stomach, trying to get away, but I grabbed her by the leg, and in one motion stabbed her with the ghost-man's dagger, pulled it out and stabbed her again, screaming, "You stole my sister's voice." She screamed, and I kicked my heel into her face until blood oozed out from her nose. "Get up," I demanded. She wept, hands cupped around her face. I yanked her by the shoulder to the window that she'd watched my sister die from.

Bessie backed away from us, horrified. A lack of evidence had always restrained me from executing violence, but now nothing held me back.

"And then you sat here recording her die?" I snarled.

"Please," Miche cried, "I was under Huis's instructions. I had to follow them else she'll punish me."

"And, what, you feared my sister less than Huis to have gone against her instead of this house? Because you thought"—I tapped her head hard—"the punishment would be far worse

with Huis than with my family. Because Huis is scarier and we're weak? The audacity. Mxm, you will learn today!" I stabbed her again, unspooling her spiritblood onto the carpet. "No one in our physical world will know what I did to you. I won't get arrested."

"Ranewa, please have mercy," Miche cried.

I was calm in my hurricane thoughts because my anger was different now, matured into something resolute and defined. Before, anger had been a fetus, undeterred, developing, a thing I harbored like it was a fugitive; now it was ready to be born from my body into a new form, a new breath. "I'll have the same mercy you showed my sister."

It was my war, my end to carnage. I slipped the dagger into Miche's ribs, opening the portal, and her spiritblood sprouted out. I held her down as she twitched, and a bright sphere of light opened up in the center of the room. "Go," I told Bessie. "You deserve to live." Sadness overwhelmed me because I wished it were my sister who could go back to her old life. Either way, I was glad that Bessie would get her freedom.

Bessie slipped through the gate into Miche's body, leaving me alone.

Anaya's true voice continued to pour from Huis into me, cracked me open, and I wept as if she stood before me.

"Anaya, I'm so sorry," I cried.

She was the firstborn, and my parents, at times, idolized her, pampered her. Yes, they put pressure on both of us to be high achievers and perfect daughters, to follow in their paths of being doctors and professors or some similar reasonable career. And when Anaya stepped out of that role, I was left to carry the burden we used to carry together. I was bitter,

for she left me alone to deal with it all. I partied, flunked out, slept away from home, from myself, and now I'd lost my sister. Despite my parents and me having a hard time with her leaving, she kept no bitterness or conceit but saved me.

I walked out of Huis, paying no attention to the ghost-women who watched me hungrily. I walked past the stoep, past the veld, past the Grave of Mirrors, and went to the field where she had been burning for 589 days, since the day she'd disappeared.

I stepped into the soil where my sister's spirit sprouted forth like a well, and I drowned in it.

Dealmaker News

HOME FILM BOOKS

STAR OF AWARD-WINNING TRUE CRIME PODCAST SNAPS UP MAJOR DEAL POSTHUMOUSLY

By Hanli Foxcroft

On the heels of an award-winning podcast, *What Happened to Ana?* by Michele Visser, following the true case of Anaya Sebeya, a young woman who disappeared mysteriously during a writing residency in Cape Town, Anaya's sister, Ranewa Sebeya, has announced her intent to set up her own small publisher, Anaya Books. Sebeya plans to posthumously release Anaya Sebeya's *A Void in Time* and a biographical account of Anaya's time at the Günter residency, *House of Margins,* simultaneously with the support and partial proceeds from Günter Prize winner Ogone Uetuu Molefhi's prize money and family funds. Ranewa announced her plans on the popular true crime show *True Killers*; in her conversation with true crime journalist Sheri Woodland, Ranewa explained, "I was very upset with Miche's tell-all podcast of my sister's life that cruelly redacted some pertinent information of what happened to my sister, Anaya. These projects will set the record straight." Anaya Books will go on to publish emerging African authors.

House of Margins is slated for production as a feature film. The adaptative rights were bought at auction by Torrential Films. Ranewa Sebeya will executive produce.

RANEWA

MY SISTER DISAPPEARED THIRTY-TWO MONTHS AGO. NO ONE else knows this of her: She is dead. The grief devoured the little light of hope my parents and I had, that she would be found, alive, famished if anything, but alive. There was no evidence I could give the investigators, my parents, the audience that has clung their eyes and ears to every episode Miche dropped weekly. I felt her death, I became her death. For thirty-two months Anaya's spirit has been burning, burning to keep my family healed.

Anaya Sebeya became the sacrificial lamb for my family, and Bessie Kgositsile's spirit retreated into the flesh of Miche's body. Miche lays trapped in the realm she'd visit on the regular. When I sought answers, this isn't what I thought I'd exhume. What do I do with my grief?

Having developed Anaya Books with the donation from Ogone's prize money, I've been preparing to release Anaya's books on the day of her funeral, without her body, but with the essential rites to transition her spirit. It felt momentous and deeply important to my parents and me to release her spirit with her books. The book I wrote on her life, *House of Margins,* is in production, and I weep at times that I'm living the dream my sister yearned and died for. I hope her story will reach masses of people in truth and respect of her talent and life.

And now that I have fulfilled her promise to Yanano, I can cease the fire on my sister's spirit and help her ascend.

Five hours before my flight from Cape Town to Gaborone, I get a knock on my hotel door. I've been traveling to and fro Cape Town for research as I prepared to publish Anaya's books. I open the door to find Miche standing there.

I look at her carefully, the fabric of her green irises. "Bessie," I greet her, opening the door wider. Bessie has gone on to fully take on Miche's personal life, writing and showcasing artworks in Miche's name. But she doesn't have Miche's voice and writes in her former ways. Her audience has been split; she's gotten into hot water for writing Black characters as a white person, whilst applauded for nuanced and authentic depictions of them.

Bessie invites herself into my room, eyes perusing the unmade bed, the breakfast tray of unfinished food, the windows overlooking the skyline of Cape Town. I stare at the tray on my desk, the butter knife smudged with egg and beans. I feel the sounds of the ghostman's dagger in my hand digging into Miche's spirit-flesh in Huis.

She sits at the edge of my desk. "I wish I'd come sooner to see you." She doesn't say: I was frightened of you because of what you did.

"I was angry and grieving," I say. "I'd still do it again for her."

Bessie nods, unsatisfied with my answer. "Thank you for saving me. Having a body free from pain has given me time and freedom I never had before. No one understands what it means to be sick, how excruciating it is to live like that." She

picks at the vase of roses, bending a petal at a time, letting the silence ensue. "But I terribly miss my grandparents and my cousins. I miss the language, the things we used to do ko gae—our family gatherings—but Black people treat me differently because I'm no longer like them; and it's so hard to fit in with white people and act *white*—I feel like I don't belong anywhere." She sighs heavily, letting the rose droop lower into her hand. "Luckily, I still have Ogone, after I told her the truth. I'm going to be her bridesmaid, can you imagine that? I get to keep something from my past life." She smiles at this, tears forming in her eyes. "So I can't criticize what you did when it saved me. I mean, I took Miche's flesh, and I wear it as my own. I don't know what the spiritual consequences of that will be. I tried coming closer to God, but Ogone's spiritual walk has had me contend with what it would mean following Jesus: giving up everything to enter God's kingdom—giving up a body that's not my own and passing on. I truly am burdened by the weight of the consequences of being in Miche's body."

Bessie consecrated Miche's spirit upon her. Miche forgot that her skin was just a medium of Huis, if Bessie wore her flesh, she'd be protected too.

"Of course, sins have to be balanced with punishments," I said.

Bessie stands, tracing her finger on the desk, eyes skirting me. "Yes, at times, it's nice being a white skinny bitch, I must admit. I never thought how delicious freedom would be. I've found a nice lekgoa I'm going to marry, so can you drop the lawsuit? It's causing me quite a headache with the in-laws," Bessie says through Miche's lips, and her pronunciation in Setswana is impeccable.

"I've been working on my parents to stop the lawyers. Any day now."

"Thank you." She leans in, closes her arms around me, and that's the first time I cry since I watched Anaya burn.

I'm at our Malokoganyane village farmhouse, my sister's room's stifled with her scent, and I'm wearing her jumper. Her typewriter looks at me from my grandmother's dresser. The Malokoganyane village winds howl. Thorn trees and veld and swaying dust are air's voice that stills our farmland. Not a long distance from home, I find the gathered headstones, a new one accounting for my sister, the youngest amongst our passed-away family.

Mmemogolo has a tonkana blanket wrapped around her shoulders, lying on an animal skin. I cloak my hands in hers as we speak of times gone by. Mama sits nearby, feet folded beneath her, a tissue crumpled to her nose, unable to stop the tears and sniffling. She wears a tukwi, a dress made from leteise, a tonkana blanket across her shoulders. Her stitches from when she gave birth to Anaya have been hurting for the last three days; the pain refuses to stop. Sometimes I see her press her hand to her abdomen, sometimes I hear her hiss at the pain.

Anaya has been appearing in my face a lot, and when that happens, Mmemogolo clasps her hands to my face, whispering, "Oh, Anaya, ngwanawangwanaka, oh, Anaya." And I know my sister's face glows through my face.

Last night, my parents and I held the nightly vigils of dithapelo with close family relatives until early morning, talking, consuming food and drink, though I only partook of

proverbs and memories. We don't have a body to pray over except the spirit of my sister, a tide to my skin.

Early in the morning when the mist is a blue haze on the horizon, I walk away from our farmhouse, past the kraal, down a sandy path shielded in thorn trees, speckled with cow dung. I walk, driven by hunger of my spirit, to our burial lands where some of our ancestors lie.

I am wearing the cloak of my sister's spirit on my shoulders. It is dangerous, for I could die the longer I fast myself to her spirit. Fast, not fastened, for in wearing my sister's spirit, it famishes me from everything of this world.

Wearing Anaya's spirit, I salt my skin with purifying traditional herbs, lay myself in the earth of her dug-out grave, bend my knees into my chest lying west, the direction of our ancestral realm, and a void slits open the air, waiting for Anaya's birth to the ancestral realm. I gaze up at the sheering light of her form, the light of a star. Up in the sky, a shimmer of stars:

Tswang, tswang, tswang
le mmoneng.
Ngwana o tshwana le dinaledi

A strange way for a wedding song to be sung at a funeral. When this is done, I fetch myself the beef of an old cow, I consume it without salt, wash it down with gemere, ensuring Anaya's position in the ancestral realm. Then, I take upon me a piece of black cloth to pin to my shoulder and a blade to shear every hair particle on my skin and begin the dressing in black, for the year to come. The eye of the sun, a solitude of her fortress.

Ascend, Anaya, ascend.

Anaya | Ntlo Ya Badimo

Above me, the moon wanes and waxes, a cervical dilation; water breaks in rain patters. Lightning appears, burning an orifice into the clouds of sky, the womb of darkness. A void gleams through the density of the clouds where my sister, Ranewa's voice leaks through, like the glints of a new dawn. The light intensified while I've lain on this field of roses and trees and fruits, burning, burning, burning.

Ranewa kept my soul clad to her skin, nourishing me with her fasting. The light of her voice pulsates, pulsates, pulsates, glittering, a flash of star. Then, thunder, contractions tense the sky. At the signal of her voice, my spirit begins to rise to ascend to the portal of the ancestral realm—my spirit that is spread out through the field like crumbs of soil, begins to rise. The sky-slit narrows and expands. The stars start to skim back and forth, attempting to stitch the opening in the sky. The strength of my sister's voice carries me on its back like a boat across the spine of a river.

And in the kgotla at my family home, in the bleeding of the morning, a ritual is made: A cow wails through the night, its life leaking for the ritual, its cry a veneration for this ascent.

The sky-slit narrows, inhaling my spirit. Its tunnel wraps warm around me, tensing, convulsing—I try to seek breath, to seek life, and pain strikes me, giving me voice; a cry, a breath. I am here.

Gossamer spirits fashioned in moonlight flitter by like fireflies. Ancestral animals prowl and leap through a boundless forest of baobabs, marula, quiver trees, past the various sized stems of kapok that soar past the flying creatures.

I approach a fountain that sees into many ancestries and lives. In my reflection, my hair is curved into two sculpted plaits, like twined serpentine horns shaping the arc of my face; two long braids frame each side of them, a corn shell wrapped around either. I wear a fabric of leteise and steel.

The others around me wear a fabric of kente and steel, hair knitting upward into an urn-shaped style with intricate plaits, networks of them running down the face.

My spirit seems to instantly understand in its wisdom, translates this to me, for I am naked of flesh and its obscurity. In the ancestral realm, there is no life, there is no death, only a ceaseless breath of existence.

An ancestress floats above me, eyes the same hue and shape as my mother's, voice warm as wool like that of my sister, then: "Anaya Sebeya, welcome to the ancestral realm."

HUIS

HUIS STARTED OUT IN MOZAMBIQUE, THEN THE DRC, BEFORE heading to Günter thrice. She's had many names. She was Cape Town–based. Now she roams the Okavango Delta. We nest in the rafters, the nook of darkness when they come, these inhabitants. We didn't arrive by foot, boat, or flight, but rather we boarded the sternum of a sixteen-year-old boy, the son of one of the mokoro gondoliers who traversed us from Gabs to a remote island in the Okavango Delta.

Our new abode is a safari lodge with a cuisine of culture. Most of its visitors come from various backgrounds and cultures to treat our palates: travelers, backpackers, corporate team-building trips, honeymooners, those ones are surely tastier. Personality at times can make them spicy, or sweet, or with no taste at all. The lodge sits comfortably in a private concession like a wood-ribbed animal preparing for flight.

We've sprawled ourselves over 10,000 hectares of land as they built the structure. We welded ourselves into its woodwork, its decks, its walls—we breathe through it. It's our perennial holiday. We spend our days drifting through the lagoons, the channels, the reeds, galloping on antelopes, gliding through the air on the backbone of herons. Lagoons, lily-filled. Crushed scent of foliage smeared into the air. It's peaceful here, even for ghost standards.

Welcome to Huis.

House o

a true story based on the internationally bestselling book by Anaya and Ranewa Sebeya

00:00

Margins

English
Setswana (original) with subtitles ✓
English with subtitles

2:27:42 

Acknowledgments

Thank you, God, for your mercies and blessings you've showered upon my life, for this dream-fulfilled literary journey of wondrous (sometimes difficult) encounters and more. It's by your grace and miracles that I am here.

Thank you to my agent, Naomi Davis, for her trusting "yes." *House of Margins* has haunted me for too long with many struggles, deletions, rewrites, devastating moments of wanting to get rid of it, and I'm glad for its completion with the help of my editors: Viengsamai Fetters, sentence-level genius, thank you for giving me the time and sharp-eyed, detail-oriented, and structural guidance. This book needed it; it's had many lives, and I'm grateful you helped me find its footing. Sarah Guan, your notes are ever so insightful, deeply intelligent, with such sheer understanding. James P. Blaylock, you saw this in its travesty of a draft and still offered helpful notes. Liz Harmer and Renee Hudson for your guidance, perspective, edits, and encouraging words. Anna Leahy and David Krausman for your support in the MFA program that offered comfort whilst working on this book. Thank you to Henneh Kyereh Kwaku (minister of always giving) and Rev. Derrick Mensah for your stewardship and spiritual wisdom. Lesego, Omphile, Luiza, Lily, Cheryl S. Ntumy, Tryphena—blessed to have you women and your wisdom, thank you for your support! Thank you to my parents and Aunty

Bothepha, who assisted in all ways whilst I was writing this book. I've so much gratitude to the writer who assisted me with the question I had about the South African publishing landscape. Thank you to the many organizations that have flown me across the world and given me such beautiful literary experiences (I never thought that writing could get me so far): Casa Snowapple Mx, the Caine Prize, Franceso Verso, Rolex Mentor and Protégé Arts Initiative, and many others. Immense gratitude to every reader, bookstagrammer, library, and organization that supported me during *Womb City*'s release.

Thank you to every key person at Erewhon and the Kensington team who worked on this book. A huge thank you to Diana Pho, Cassandra Farrin, Leah Marsh, Emily Mahon, Shannon Gray-Winter, Martin Cahill, Michelle Addo-Chajet, Kasie Griffitts, and Quinn Karrenbauer.

Thank you, dear reader, for picking *House of Margins.*

Bibliography

Bolaane, Maitseo M.M. "Cross-Border Lives, Warfare and Rape in Independence-Era Botswana." *Journal of Southern African Studies* 39, no. 3 (September 2013): 557–576. https://www.jstor.org/stable/42001356.

Chuma-Mogotsi, Angie Thato (@angiechuma). "Also, when something is stolen esp of spiritual or cultural significance, it takes away part of the essence from that." X. November 19, 2023. https://x.com/angiechuma/status/1726246101089734703.

Makhubu, Nomusa. "Interview with Nomusa Makhubu." Interviewed by Clare Counihan. *Comparative Studies of South Asia, Africa and the Middle East* 36, no. 2 (2016): 307–319. https://doi.org/10.1215/1089201X-3603367.

Mlama, Penina Muhando. "Creating in the Mother-Tongue: The Challenges to the African Writer Today." *Research in African Literatures* 21, no. 4 (Winter 1990): 5–14. https://www.jstor.org/stable/3819318.

Molefhe, Wame. *Go Tell the Sun.* Modjaji Books, 2011.

Slimani, Leïla. "Leïla Slimani & Amia Srinivasan: Sex and Lies." In conversation with Amia Srinivasan. *London Review of Books.* March 4, 2020. Audio. https://www.lrb.co.uk/podcasts-and-videos/podcasts/at-the-bookshop/leila-slimani-and-amia-srinivasan-sex-and-lies.

Smith, Gail. "We need to talk about yellow-bones." LinkedIn. August 30, 2020. https://www.linkedin.com/pulse/we-need-talk-yellow-bones-gail-smith.

Bible Verses

Psalm 16:4, English Standard Version: "The sorrows of those who run after another god shall multiply."

Proverbs 29:25, Christian Standard Version: "The fear of mankind is a snare, but the one who trusts in the Lord is protected."

Mathaio 6:9–13, Baebele e e Boitshepo (TSW08NO):
"Rraarona yo o kwa magodimong,
a leina la gago le itshepisiwe.
A Bogosi jwa gago bo tle.
A thato ya gago e diragale mo lefatsheng
jaaka e diragala kwa legodimong.

Re neye dijo tse re di tlhokang mo letsatsing leno;
mme o re itshwarele melato ya rona,
jaaka le rona re itshwaretse ba ba molato le rona.
O se ka wa re tsenya mo thaelong,
mme o re golole mo go Satane."

Matthew 10:22, King James Version: "And ye shall be hated of all men for my name's sake: but he that endureth to the end shall be saved."

Matthew 10:28, New International Version: "Do not be afraid of those who kill the body but cannot kill the soul."

Mark 12:30–31a, English Standard Version: "'And you shall love the Lord your God with all your heart, with all your soul, with all your mind, and with all your strength.' This is the first commandment. And the second, like it, is this: 'You shall love your neighbor as yourself.'"

Luke 10:19, New King James Version: "Behold, I give you the authority to trample on serpents and scorpions, and over all the power of the enemy, and nothing shall by any means hurt you."

Acts 4:12, New International Version: "Salvation is found in no one else, for there is no other name under heaven given to mankind by which we must be saved."

Discussion Questions

These suggested questions are to spark conversation and enhance your reading of *House of Margins.*

1. When Anaya is attacked at the event held by the Günter organizers, one of the finalists, Ruvimbo, ends up dropping out of the Günter residency. What would you have done in Anaya's position?

2. Struggling with writer's block, Anaya makes a deal with one of the ghostwomen. Why do you think she felt desperate enough to ask for their help?

3. How did you feel about what the audience was saying of the finalists in the comment section? Did this change your perspective of the characters?

4. Ranewa is understandably grief-stricken in her search for her sister, but at times becomes reckless with her life. How did your perspective on her grief shift throughout the book? Did you find yourself agreeing with her decisions or not, and why?

5. Miche retells Anaya's story through a sensationalized true crime podcast. If you could explain to Miche the ethical implications of this decision and the sensitive nature of this matter, what would you say?

6. Huis's realm is the setting of the ghostwomen. The ghostwoman Yanano says that Huis hurts too, almost depicting the house as a victim. Do you agree? If so, why? If not, why?

7. Every character has a unique personality and beliefs, and varying challenges that drive conflict. Whether you agree or disagree with them, what are your thoughts on each character's motives, and how does your own perspective influence your judgement of them?

8. *House of Margins* is told in an experimental way, using comment sections, a true crime podcast format, and a dual POV. Why do you think the author chose to do this? And how do these perspectives affect how you see the sisters, Ranewa and Anaya?

9. Ranewa hates that her sister's story has been commodified into a true crime podcast. What role do you think true crime documentaries and podcasts play in our world?

10. The book is haunted by the colonial history of the land and Huis. What analysis did you develop during your reading?

11. What scenes did you struggle with in *House of Margins*?

12. Ranewa helps her sister transcend. What do you think about Anaya's ending?

13. How do you feel about the friendship between Ogone and Anaya?

14. What did you think about Bessie's predicament and finally getting her freedom through Miche's body?

More from Erewhon Books

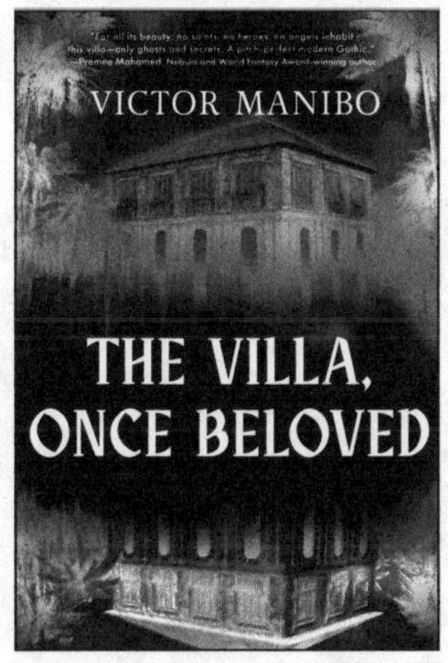